Harvest of the Heart

Laurel Ridge Series, Book #15

Tara Baisden

Sterling Ridge Press LLC

Printed in the United States of America

First Edition: October 2025

For permissions, contact: tara@tarabaisden.com or visit www.tarabaisden.comHarvest of the Heart © 2025 by Tara Baisden

Cover designed by Sterling Ridge Press LLC

Published by: Sterling Ridge Press, LLC www.sterlingridgepress.com

ISBN: 978-1-966093-33-6

Dedication

To every woman who has ever loved quietly from the sidelines, believing she wasn't enough to catch the golden boy's attention—you are seen, you are worthy, and your season of harvest is coming. And to the brokenhearted souls learning that winter doesn't last forever when God is writing your story.

Contents

Chapter 1

Amanda Baker stepped back from the front window display, tilting her head to study the arrangement of miniature pumpkins nestled among burgundy mums and twisted grapevine. The early September morning light streaming through the glass cast everything in gold, making the orange and amber glass candle holders sparkle like captured sunshine. She adjusted a small wooden sign reading "Grateful Hearts Gather Here" and smiled at how the burnt orange ribbon she'd woven through the display picked up the warm tones in the hand-painted autumn leaves scattered across the vintage wooden crate.

Perfect.

Well, almost perfect. Amanda reached for a small ceramic turkey, moving it two inches to the left, then back to the right. There. Now it was perfect.

The familiar satisfaction of a job well done settled over her as she surveyed Indulgences Gift Shop in its full autumn glory. Every corner of the store had been transformed over the past week—fall wreaths hung at carefully measured intervals along the exposed brick wall, while garlands of artificial maple leaves draped the wooden shelving units she'd had custom-built three years ago. The scent of cinnamon apple candles mingled with the vanilla honey soap display, creating the kind of welcoming atmosphere that made customers want to linger and explore.

She'd built this. From the polished hardwood floors to the carefully curated merchandise that ranged from locally made pottery to imported Italian kitchen towels, every detail reflected her vision of what a gift shop should be—a place where people could find something special, something that would bring joy to both the giver and receiver.

Amanda glanced at the antique clock above the counter. Nine-thirty. The store wouldn't open for another half hour, which gave her time to double-check yesterday's inventory order and review the weekend's special events schedule. She was reaching for her planning notebook when the sound of the back door opening made her look up.

"Morning, Amanda!" April's voice carried from the storage room, followed by the gentle thud of the swinging door as her assistant manager entered the main shop area. "Oh wow, you've been busy. The front window looks spectacular."

"Thanks. I got here early to finish it. I wanted everything ready for the weekend influx of customers."

April Martin had been with the shop for three years now, and Amanda couldn't imagine managing without her steady presence. At thirty-four, April possessed the kind of calm efficiency that made complicated tasks look effortless. Her chestnut brown hair was pulled back in its usual neat ponytail, and she wore the kind of practical yet stylish outfit that made her equally comfortable helping customers select the perfect hostess gift or unloading delivery trucks.

"The autumn transformation is my favorite time of year," April said, tying her apron around her waist. "Though I think Mrs. Tillman might cry when she sees you've packed away the summer beach theme. She was so attached to those seashell wind chimes."

Amanda laughed. "I saved her a set in the back. I'll probably end up gifting them to her for Christmas just to see that smile again."

The back door opened again, and Coral Dunmore's cheerful humming preceded her entrance into the shop. Where April embodied steady professionalism, Coral brought artistic flair and boundless enthusiasm to everything she touched. This morning, her curly hair was contained by a bright yellow headband that matched the sunflower pattern on her flowing skirt. Somehow, on Coral, the eclectic combination of colors and textures looked perfectly natural.

"Good morning, beautiful people!" Coral announced, spinning in a small circle to show off her outfit. "How are we doing this glorious Friday morning? I brought homemade blueberry muffins, and before you ask, yes, April, they're the kind with the crunchy sugar topping you love."

"You spoil us," April said.

"Of course!" Coral's hazel eyes sparkled with mischief before turning to Amanda with a more serious expression. "So, I heard through the grapevine that you volunteered for something big at last night's festival meeting. Details, please."

Amanda's stomach fluttered with a mixture of excitement and anxiety.

"I volunteered to chair the Decorations and Parade Committee for the Fall Festival."

April paused in the middle of straightening a display of autumn-scented hand creams. "Amanda, that's wonderful! You're the perfect person for a job like that."

"It's a huge responsibility," Coral added.

"I know." Amanda sank onto the wooden stool behind the counter, feeling the burden of what she'd committed to. "When they asked for volunteers, I just... my hand went up before my brain could talk me out of it. Margaret Thornton was saying how they needed someone with an eye for detail and organizational skills, and everyone was looking around the room like they were hoping someone else would step up."

"Your hand went up because you're exactly what they need, and because you have a good heart," April said firmly. "You've turned this shop into one of the most beautiful spaces on Main Street. You coordinate events and workshops here all the time. You know how to work with vendors and manage timelines."

"But this is different. This isn't just arranging merchandise or planning a workshop for twelve people. This is the whole town's celebration. What if I mess up? What if my ideas aren't good enough? What if—"

"What if you stop borrowing trouble from tomorrow and focus on the fact that you're talented, organized, and care about this community more than almost anyone I know?" Coral interrupted gently. "The festival committee wouldn't have accepted your volunteer offer if they hadn't believed you could handle it."

Amanda wanted to believe that. She really did. But the logical part of her brain kept cataloguing all the things that could go wrong, all the ways she might disappoint people who were counting on her.

"The practical side is what's really making me nervous," she admitted. "I was thinking about it this morning... there's so much coordination involved. We'll need decorations and supplies, and lots of them. Pumpkins, gourds, hay bales, cornstalks, and mums. And decorating the parade float... that's something I've never done before. Traditionally, the majority of the fall decorations come from..."

She trailed off, suddenly reluctant to voice the name that had been circling through her thoughts like an anxious refrain.

"Whitaker Farm," April finished. "Which means working with Brandon."

"Poor Brandon," Coral said, her expressive face clouding with sympathy. "What that man has been through this year! First Samantha left him like she did, right after the holidays, and then his daddy passed away so suddenly just a few weeks later. I can't imagine."

Amanda's chest tightened from a combination of sympathy and something else she didn't want to examine too closely. She hadn't seen Brandon in months—not since James Whitaker's funeral in January, where she'd sat in the back of the church and watched from a distance as Brandon stood beside his mother and sister, his shoulders rigid with grief.

"Rachel says he's barely left the farm since the funeral," Amanda added quietly. "She's worried about him."

Amanda and Rachel Whitaker had been inseparable since grade school, the kind of friendship that had only grown stronger through high school, then different colleges, career changes, and all the transitions life had brought. Rachel was the sister Amanda had never had, and their bond remained as solid as ever.

"Brandon used to be so different," Coral mused. "I remember in high school, he was always laughing, always in the middle of everything. Captain of the football team, homecoming king... he was always so fun to be around? He was just... golden. Like everything came easy to him."

Amanda's throat tightened. She remembered that version of Brandon too—remembered watching him from across the cafeteria or stealing glances during the few classes they'd shared, wondering what it would be like to be noticed by someone who seemed to move through the world with such easy confidence.

"People change," she said quietly, more to herself than to her employees. "Life has a way of... reshaping us."

April shot her a curious look, and Amanda busied herself with straightening an already-perfect display of harvest-themed kitchen towels, hoping her expression didn't betray the complicated tangle of emotions Brandon's name always stirred up.

The truth was, she'd harbored a massive crush on Brandon Whitaker throughout their senior year of high school. Not that he'd ever noticed her, of course. She had been the kind of student who earned good grades and stayed out of trouble, but she'd never been the kind of girl who caught the attention of golden boys like Brandon. She'd been average in every way that mattered—average height, average looks, average social standing. The kind of person people liked well enough but never really saw.

Even now, years later and with a successful business to her name, that eighteen-year-old girl lived somewhere deep inside her, whispering reminders that she still wasn't the kind of woman someone like Brandon Whitaker would notice.

Which is ridiculous, she told herself firmly.

"The thing is," she said aloud, forcing her voice to sound more confident than she felt, "the festival has to happen regardless of... personal circumstances, sad as they may be. The festival committee is counting on me to make sure we have everything we need, which means I need to speak with Brandon about the supplies that his farm usually donates every year and the parade float they store in one of their barns."

"That's the spirit," Coral said, brightening. "Besides, you'll probably be working mostly with Helen and Rachel anyway. Rachel mentioned that Brandon's been letting his mom handle more of the community-facing aspects of the farm business."

Before Amanda could respond, the bell above the front door chimed, and she glanced at the clock in surprise. Nine fifty-five. She'd been so absorbed in conversation that she'd nearly missed opening time.

"Morning, girls!" Martha Kincaid's familiar voice filled the shop as she stepped inside. At sixty-two, Martha moved with the purposeful energy of someone who'd been the unofficial mayor of Laurel Ridge for decades, even though she'd never held an actual political office. Her silver hair was styled in its usual neat bun, and she wore the kind of practical dress that could transition seamlessly from serving breakfast to attending a church committee meeting.

"Mornin' Martha," Amanda said, grateful for the distraction. "Your special order came in yesterday."

"Wonderful! That vanilla honey soap is the only thing that keeps my hands from cracking, and heaven knows it smells divine! It's one of those small luxuries we women need to indulge in now and then." Martha approached the counter with the kind of brisk efficiency that made her diner run like clockwork. "But soap isn't the reason I stopped by this morning, dear."

Amanda felt a flutter of anticipation mixed with anxiety. In a town the size of Laurel Ridge, news traveled fast, and Martha Kincaid was often the first to know everything and the fastest to share it.

"I heard through the grapevine that you've taken on quite the responsibility," Martha continued, her eyes twinkling. "Chair of the Decorations and Parade Committee, no less. I have to say, I'm pleased as a peach to hear this good news."

"Thank you," Amanda said, moving to retrieve Martha's soap from the special orders section under the checkout counter. "I'll be honest, I'm feeling a little overwhelmed by the scope of it all."

"Nonsense. You've been organizing and beautifying for years—first in your shop, then with those lovely seasonal displays you coordinate for the business association. This is just a larger canvas for your talents." Martha accepted the wrapped soap with a satisfied nod. "Besides, it's about time someone with fresh ideas took the lead. Not that Margaret didn't do a fine job all those years, but the festival could use some new energy and some fresh young blood... just being honest!"

"I hope I can live up to everyone's expectations," Amanda said, and meant it.

"You will. If you need any help, let me know. I volunteered for that position a few years back. Let's see... you'll need to coordinate closely with the Whitakers for supplies and the parade float. They've always been so good to this town," Martha's expression softened slightly. "Brandon... that poor boy has had such a difficult year. He sure does hold a special place in my heart. He's been in such a funk lately."

Amanda felt heat rise in her cheeks and hoped it wasn't visible. "I'm planning to drive out to the farm soon to speak with him."

"Good, good. His mama's been so worried about him... said he spends too much time wrapped up in that farm." Martha paused, studying Amanda with the kind of shrewd assessment that had made her a successful businesswoman for forty years. "You know, dear, sometimes the things we think will be challenging turn out to be exactly what we need. God has a way of arranging circumstances for our benefit, even when we can't see the bigger picture."

There was something in Martha's tone that suggested she was talking about more than just festival planning, but before Amanda could analyze it further, the older woman was heading toward the door.

"I'll let you girls get back to work. And Amanda? Don't overthink this... I know how you get sometimes. Trust your instincts. They've served you well so far."

The bell chimed again as Martha left, and Amanda stood for a moment in the sudden quiet, Martha's words echoing in her mind.

Trust your instincts. If only it were that simple. Her instincts where Brandon Whitaker was concerned had always been a confused mess of attraction, admiration, and the bone-deep certainty that she wasn't enough to hold his attention.

But this wasn't about attraction or attention. This was about community service and responsibility. She could do this. She had to do this.

Amanda walked toward her small office in the back of the shop, her mind already shifting into planning mode. She needed to create a list of everything the festival would require—decorations, supplies, a timeline, and volunteer coordination. She needed to research what had been done in previous years and identify areas where fresh approaches might be welcome.

And tomorrow, she decided as she settled at her desk and reached for a legal pad, would be the perfect day to drive out to Whitaker Farm.

It was time to have a conversation with Brandon Whitaker.

Chapter 2

Brandon Whitaker drove the last fence post into the ground with more force than necessary, the satisfying thunk of wood against earth echoing across the field. Sweat dampened his flannel shirt despite the cool September morning, and he paused to wipe his forehead with the back of his work glove. The fence repair had taken longer than expected, but there was something about physical labor that helped quiet the restless thoughts that seemed to follow him everywhere these days.

He straightened, rolling his shoulders to ease the tension that had become his constant companion, and surveyed his work. Four new posts, wire stretched tight and secure. Good for another twenty years, just like his father would have done it. James Whitaker had taught him that anything worth doing was worth doing right the first time—a lesson that applied to everything from fence posts to relationships to keeping your word.

Dad would have had this finished by eight this morning.

The thought surfaced before he could stop it, bringing with it the familiar ache that settled in his chest whenever his father's memory intruded. Eight months since the heart attack, and the grief still caught him at unexpected moments—when he heard a John Deere tractor in the distance, when he caught the scent of his mother's coffee drifting from the farmhouse kitchen, or when he found himself reaching for the phone to ask a question only, his father could answer.

The morning sun painted the farm in warm light, highlighting the produce that was grown here. Somewhere in the distance, he could hear the farm manager, Rusty Thompson's, voice calling to the other farmhands as they worked in the fields. Normal sounds of a working farm, the kind of sounds that used to bring him peace.

These days, peace felt like a luxury he couldn't afford.

He was loading the post-hole digger into the truck bed when the sound of tires on gravel made him look toward the long drive that wound from the county road as a blue sedan approached. He frowned as he watched the car slow near the barn before pulling to a stop in the gravel area where visitors usually parked.

The driver's door opened, and a woman stepped out, her blonde hair catching the morning light. Even from a distance, something about her struck him as familiar. She turned, and recognition hit him like a splash of cold water.

Amanda Baker.

It had been months since he'd seen her. Not since the funeral, where she'd sat quietly in the back of the church while what felt like the entire town filled the pews to say goodbye to his father. Brandon had been too lost in his grief that day to notice much of anything, but he remembered her being there, and remembered the sympathy in her blue eyes when she'd offered her condolences afterward.

Now she was walking toward him with purposeful steps and the energy of someone on a mission.

"Brandon." She stopped a few feet away, close enough that he caught the scent of her perfume, something light and floral that reminded him of spring mornings. "I hope I'm not interrupting anything important."

"Nothing that can't wait." He set down the toolbox he'd been holding and studied her face, looking for clues about what had brought her to his farm on a Saturday morning. "It's good to see you, Amanda. It's been a while."

"Too long," she agreed, and there was genuine warmth in her voice that made something twist unexpectedly in his chest. "I know I haven't stopped by as much as I used to... you know, work and all. I imagine the past few months have been..."

She trailed off, searching for words that wouldn't sound empty or inadequate. Brandon appreciated that she didn't try to fill the silence with platitudes about his father being in a better place or time healing all wounds. He'd heard enough of those to last a lifetime.

"We're managing just fine," he said, which was both true and completely inadequate. "Life goes on."

Amanda nodded, but he could see questions in her eyes that she was too polite to ask. Questions about why he looked like he'd aged five years in the span of eight months, why he'd stopped coming to church, and why he'd let his involvement in community activities dwindle to practically nothing.

She was quiet for a moment, then seemed to gather herself. "I should probably explain why I'm here," she said. "I volunteered to chair the Decorations and Parade Committee for this year's Fall Festival, and I know that traditionally, Whitaker Farms has been incredibly generous in providing most of the decorating supplies and barn space for volunteers to work on the parade float."

The Fall Festival.

Brandon had forgotten it was coming up—which said something about how disconnected he'd become from the rhythms of community life that had once seemed as natural as breathing. Every September, for as long as he could remember, the festival had been a highlight of the year, two days of celebration that brought the whole town together and drew visitors from across the state.

His father had loved the festival. Had insisted on providing the best pumpkins, the finest gourds, and the most beautiful fall decorations the farm could produce. He and his father had both spent hours in the barn, working alongside volunteers to construct elaborate parade floats that became the centerpiece for the town's annual fall parade.

"Of course I'll still provide supplies," Brandon said automatically. "Same as always. Pumpkins, gourds, hay bales, cornstalks, and mums. Whatever you need."

Relief flickered across Amanda's face, but it was quickly replaced by something that looked like nervous excitement. "That's wonderful. But actually, I was hoping we might be able to expand on tradition a little this year."

Here it comes. Brandon crossed his arms, waiting for the request he could already sense.

"I really want to make this year special," she said, her hands moving as she talked. "I'm thinking bigger displays and more elaborate decorations throughout the town. I really want to jazz things up this year. Maybe some themed areas in the town square or in the churchyard... things like photo opportunities with autumn backdrops, maybe a fun hay bale maze for the little kids to enjoy... you know, that kind of thing."

Brandon listened to her describe her vision, noting the way her whole face lit up when she talked about her plans. There was passion in her voice and the kind of genuine excitement he hadn't felt about anything in longer than he cared to admit.

"We can provide more supplies if you need them," he said carefully. "The harvest this year is looking good."

"How about the parade float? The barn space for the volunteers to work on decorating it? I was hoping we could start that process next week... maybe get more volunteers involved. I have some pretty big ideas for this year, and the more time we have... well, the better."

Brandon felt something cold settle in his stomach. The idea of people gathering here, of the farm becoming a hub of festival activity again like it had in the past, felt like more than he could handle.

"The barn space is fine," he said. "Same as always. The parade float is still stored in there. Keep me out of it, though. Talk to Rachel or Mom and work out the details."

He saw the flicker of disappointment in her eyes and felt like a major jerk for putting it there.

"I understand that you're probably busier now than you've ever been, Brandon. But I also remember how much you and your father both loved the festival. How much you both contributed over the years. You used to love working on the parade float. I thought maybe—"

"Dad's gone, Amanda."

The words came out sharper than he'd intended, cutting through her sentence like a blade. He saw her flinch and immediately regretted his tone, but the damage was done.

"I'm sorry," Amanda said quietly. "I didn't mean to—"

"Look, Amanda," Brandon ran a hand through his hair, suddenly exhausted by the effort of maintaining even this basic level of social interaction. "I'll provide whatever supplies you need. You can use the barn space. But as for the rest of it... I'm just not the same person anymore. I have no interest in the parade float."

He saw her studying his face, and for a moment, he had the uncomfortable feeling that she could see more than he wanted her to. Could see the grief he carried around like a brick in his chest, the loneliness that had become his constant companion since losing both his father and his wife, and the fear that if he let himself care about anything too deeply, it might be taken away from him too.

"Okay," she said finally. "I understand."

But even as she agreed, Brandon could see the determination in her expression that suggested this conversation wasn't over, just postponed.

"I should probably let you get back to work," she said, gesturing toward the tools scattered around the truck. "Thank you for agreeing to help with supplies and the barn space. It means a lot to me."

"Of course." Brandon walked with her toward her car, some vestige of the manners his parents had drilled into him kicking in despite his emotional fatigue.

They reached her car, and Amanda paused with her hand on the door handle. "Brandon? I know this year has been hard. If you ever need anything—help with farm stuff, someone to talk to, whatever—I hope you know you can call me."

The offer was made simply, without fanfare or the kind of dramatic sympathy that always made him want to run in the opposite direction. There was something about the straightforward kindness in her voice that made his throat tight.

"Thanks," he said, meaning it. "I'll remember that."

Amanda smiled, the first completely genuine smile he'd seen from her since she'd arrived. "Good. You know... your sister volunteered to help me. So don't be surprised when all you hear her talking about is the festival. She has a special way of getting people excited."

"That she does."

Amanda opened her car door. "Take care of yourself, Brandon. And tell your mom I said hello. I'll pray for you... I hope you know that."

"Appreciate it... I'll give Mom your message."

Brandon stood on the gravel drive and watched Amanda's blue sedan make its way back down the lane, raising a small cloud of dust that caught the morning sunlight. When her car finally disappeared around the bend that led to the county road, Brandon remained where he was, listening to the silence settle back over the farm. The morning was warming up, and somewhere in the distance, he could hear his mother moving around in the garden beside the farmhouse. Normal sounds, familiar rhythms that should have been comforting.

Instead, he felt unsettled. Amanda's enthusiasm for the festival and her obvious passion for making it special had been exhausting.

He turned and walked back toward his truck, telling himself that he'd done the right thing by limiting his involvement.

But as he gathered his tools and prepared to tackle the next item on his endless list of farm chores, Brandon couldn't shake the memory of Amanda's face when she'd talked about expanding the festival decorations. The way her eyes had lit up, the gesture of her hands as she'd described her vision—there had been something infectious about her excitement, something that had awakened echoes of the man he used to be.

And that, more than anything else, was what left him unsettled as he drove toward one of the back fields to see to the next task on his list, Amanda's unexpected visit echoing in his mind.

Chapter 3

Amanda's hands gripped the steering wheel a little too tightly as she drove down the winding lane away from Whitaker Farms, the dust cloud trailing behind her car visible in the rearview mirror. The morning sun had climbed higher, warming the September air, but she felt oddly chilled despite the bright light streaming through her windshield.

I'm just not the same person anymore.

Brandon's words echoed in her mind, along with the way his face had shuttered closed when she'd mentioned his father. She'd seen raw pain there before he'd hidden it behind careful politeness.

Instead of driving toward home when she reached the town limits, she drove toward Main Street, her thoughts too tangled to face the quiet of her house just yet. She needed to talk this through with someone who would understand, someone who knew both her and Brandon well enough to help her make sense of what had just happened.

She parked near her gift shop, then walked a few doors down Main Street to the Sugar Maple Sweet Shoppe. The familiar red and white striped awning came into view, along with the hand-painted sign featuring a cheerful maple leaf that Rachel had commissioned from a local artist three years ago. Even from the sidewalk, Amanda caught the scent of caramel and chocolate drifting from the open door—warm, sweet aromas that usually made her mouth water but today felt at odds with her unsettled mood.

The bell above the door chimed a cheerful welcome as Amanda stepped inside, and she was immediately enveloped by the sensory feast that was Rachel's domain. Glass jars lined the walls, filled with colorful hard candies, gummy bears, and chocolate-covered everything. A refrigerated case displayed rows of Rachel's famous fudge in flavors ranging from traditional chocolate to adventurous combinations like maple bacon and lavender honey. Near the window, a display of caramel apples gleamed under the warm lights, their surfaces decorated with chopped nuts, mini chocolate chips, and drizzled white chocolate.

The shop itself felt like stepping into a candy wonderland—bright yellow walls adorned with vintage candy advertisements, checkered floors that somehow looked both retro and timeless, and small round tables where customers could sit and enjoy their treats with cups of locally roasted coffee that she served free of charge.

"Amanda!"

The delighted voice came from behind the main counter, where Rachel Whitaker was arranging a fresh batch of chocolate-covered strawberries in the display case. At thirty, Rachel possessed the kind of natural beauty that had made her homecoming queen in high school, but it was her personality that truly made her shine. Her dark hair was pulled back in a ponytail, and she wore a cheerful yellow apron over jeans and a white t-shirt. Her face lit up with genuine pleasure at seeing her best friend, the kind of unguarded joy that had been Rachel's trademark for as long as Amanda could remember.

"Perfect timing," Rachel continued, wiping her hands on her apron and coming around the counter. "I just finished the Saturday special display, and my curiosity about your festival plans is about to get the best of me. Spill everything."

Despite her tangled emotions, Amanda smiled. This was exactly what she'd needed—Rachel's irrepressible enthusiasm and the kind of friendship that had weathered everything from high school drama to career changes to family crises.

"It's going good," she said, accepting the quick hug Rachel offered.

Rachel led Amanda toward one of the small tables near the front window. "I told Mom yesterday that if anyone could bring fresh energy to the festival, it would be you. I'm so proud of you! Want some coffee? I just made a fresh pot."

"Coffee sounds perfect." Amanda settled into the cheerful red chair, grateful for the familiar comfort of Rachel's attention. "How's your mom doing, by the way? I saw her briefly at church last Sunday, but we didn't get a chance to really talk."

"She's good. Keeping busy with her garden, the greenhouses on the farm, and the church ladies' auxiliary." Rachel poured coffee from the pot she kept on the side counter, adding cream to Amanda's cup. "She's been worried about Brandon. We both have, actually."

The mention of Brandon's name sent a flutter through Amanda's chest, and she wrapped her hands around the warm coffee mug to give herself something to focus on besides the way her pulse had quickened.

"That's sort of why I'm here. I went out to the farm this morning to talk to him about festival stuff."

Rachel's eyebrows rose with interest as she settled into the chair across from Amanda. "How did that go?"

"He agreed to provide supplies," Amanda said, then paused, searching for the right words to describe the encounter. "The same things your farm has always contributed—pumpkins, gourds, hay bales, that sort of thing. And he said we could use the barn space for decorating the float."

"But?" Rachel prompted, clearly hearing the hesitation in Amanda's voice.

"But when I started talking about the float and meeting next week to begin, he just... shut down. It was like talking to a stranger, Rachel. He was polite but distant. And when I mentioned how much he and your dad used to love working on the float..."

She trailed off, remembering the way Brandon's face had changed—the flash of pain before the careful mask had slipped into place.

"I felt like such an idiot, Rachel... and I barely recognized him. I mean, I know I haven't seen him since your dad's funeral, but gosh... he's just... changed," she continued. "He's so... guarded now. So careful with every word, like he's afraid of something. He made me feel like I was... I don't know the right word for it, maybe like I was annoying or bothering him," Amanda leaned back in her chair, exhausted by the morning's emotional ups and downs. "On the drive here, I kept thinking about how he used to be—you know, confident and easy-going, always in the middle of everything. This version of him feels like he's carrying the weight of the world on his shoulders."

Rachel nodded, her expression growing serious. "He has been, in a lot of ways. It's been eight months since Dad died, and sometimes I feel like I'm watching my twin brother disappear a little more each day."

The pain in Rachel's voice was unmistakable. "I'm sorry," Amanda said quickly. "I probably shouldn't have gone out to your farm the way I did. I should have called. I was all gung-ho and just assumed he would help with the float like he'd done in the past. I hope I don't sound like I'm complaining."

"Don't apologize," Rachel said firmly. "You're not complaining—you're caring. And honestly, I'm glad you went out there. Brandon needs more people in his life who are willing to push back when he tries to disappear into that farm."

Amanda stared into her coffee cup as she tried to sort through the complicated tangle of emotions the morning had stirred up.

"There's something else... this is so embarrassing and so not the right time," she said finally, her voice quieter now.

Rachel leaned forward, her expression expectant and slightly concerned. "What?"

"I'm still attracted to him." The words tumbled out in a rush, and Amanda felt heat rise in her cheeks as soon as she'd said them. "Which is ridiculous, right? I mean, I had a crush on him in high school, but that was twelve years ago. I'm a grown woman with a successful business and a life of my own. I shouldn't be reacting to your brother like I'm eighteen years old again, especially with everything he's going through."

For a moment, Rachel just stared at her, and Amanda braced herself for teasing or disbelief. Instead, her friend's face broke into a gentle smile.

"Oh, honey," Rachel said softly. "You really thought those feelings were gone?"

"Yes," Amanda admitted, laughing shakily. "I mean, it's been over a decade. We've both moved on with our lives. He was married, for crying out loud. I dated other people. I convinced myself that what I felt for him in high school was just... teenage hormones or whatever."

"And now?"

"Now I'm thinking that it was never just a teenage crush. That maybe I've been comparing every man I've ever dated to your brother, and that's why nothing ever felt quite right."

Rachel reached across the table and squeezed Amanda's hand. "You know I love you, right? And I'm saying this with all the affection in the world—I've been waiting for you to figure this out for years."

"What do you mean?"

"I mean, you've been carrying a torch for my brother since we were in high school, and everyone can see it except you."

Amanda stared at her friend. "I think this is the wrong time and the wrong place to be feeling this way toward your brother. What is wrong with me? I need to get a grip on myself and move on."

"Nothing's wrong with you, Amanda. I think you're a woman who knows what she wants, even when she doesn't want to admit it to herself. And I think my brother would be lucky to have someone like you in his life, especially now when he needs it most."

The conviction in Rachel's voice surprised Amanda. She'd expected teasing or gentle mockery, not this straightforward encouragement.

"Rachel, he could barely look at me this morning. He hardly spoke. He basically shoved me aside and told me to coordinate everything through you or your mom."

"Stop and think about what has happened in his life this past year. Samantha left him just before Christmas—told him she couldn't handle the isolation of farm life and that she'd married the wrong person. She was gone before he could even process what was happening."

Amanda winced. She'd known about the divorce, of course, but hearing the details again made her chest ache for the pain Brandon must have felt.

"And then a few weeks later, Dad had his heart attack," Rachel continued. "Brandon was the one who found him in the barn. He tried CPR, called the paramedics, and did everything he could, but Dad was already gone. In the span of a month, he lost his wife and our dad."

"I can't imagine," Amanda said quietly, and she meant it. The thought of Brandon dealing with that kind of compounded loss made her want to drive back to the farm immediately and wrap him in the kind of hug that said she was here to lean on and wasn't going anywhere.

"He feels guilty about Samantha leaving. He keeps blaming himself, thinking that if he'd been a better husband or if he'd paid more attention to what she needed, she wouldn't have left. And then Dad died, and I think part of him sees that as proof that he can't protect the people he loves."

"So when I assumed he would help with the parade float..."

"You were asking him to care about something again," Rachel finished. "And I think that terrifies him right now."

Amanda sat back in her chair, pieces of the morning's conversation falling into place. Brandon's resistance hadn't been personal rejection—it had been self-protection. He'd given her exactly what the festival needed while keeping himself safely on the periphery, uninvested and therefore unhurt if anything went wrong.

"He's barely been to church since the funeral... I know you've noticed," Rachel added. "Mom and I have been worried about that too. He says he's too busy with the farm, but I think he's angry at God."

The mention of Brandon's struggle with faith hit Amanda particularly hard. She remembered the boy who had participated in youth group activities and the man who had volunteered for church service projects without being asked. The idea of his feeling disconnected from the faith community that had once been such an important part of his life made her heart ache.

"What can I do? I mean, if he needs space, I can work with you and your mom for festival planning. I don't want to push him into something he's not ready for."

Rachel was quiet for a moment, studying Amanda's face with the kind of intense focus that suggested she was weighing her words carefully.

"I think," she said finally, "that the worst thing you could do right now is give up on him."

"What do you mean?"

"I think Brandon needs a friend more than anything. Sadly, he's used to people walking away when things get difficult. Samantha did it. Some of his friends have done it, not out of malice but because they don't know how to handle grief or where Brandon is in his life right now. Even I've been guilty of tiptoeing around him instead of calling him out on his behavior." Rachel leaned forward, her voice taking on a tone of conviction. "You went out to the farm this morning and asked him to be part of something meaningful. You probably scared the daylights out of him, I imagine."

"So I should... what? Keep bothering him until he agrees to help?"

"I think you should keep being you," Rachel said simply. "Keep showing up. Keep believing that the man you know is still in there somewhere, just buried under a lot of pain and fear. And maybe, if you're patient enough and persistent enough, he'll remember how to trust again. He needs a friend right now, Amanda... someone besides Mom or me, and that someone might just be you."

Amanda felt tears prick at her eyes, though she wasn't entirely sure why. Maybe it was the hope and encouragement in Rachel's voice or the overwhelming vision that kept replaying in her mind of how deeply Brandon was hurting.

"What if I'm not what he needs? I mean... set aside the attraction I still feel for him... what if I can't be the person to bring him back to life or help him find a little joy again?"

"Then you'll find out," Rachel said gently. "Amanda, you're one of the kindest, most genuine people I know. You've built a successful business, you're involved in your community, and you have a faith in God that sustains you through difficulties. Try. Don't give up on him... please?"

"Rachel, I'm not sure if I'm brave enough for this. He's really hurting, and caring about someone who's carrying that much pain... it's scary."

"The best things usually are. Besides, when has Amanda Baker ever backed down from a challenge?"

Despite everything, Amanda laughed. "You make it sound like I should storm back out to the farm with all my craziness until he surrenders."

"Now there's an idea," Rachel said with a grin. "Though I was thinking more along the lines of gentle persistence. You know, the kind that lets him know you're not going anywhere without making him feel pressured."

They sat in comfortable silence for a moment, the familiar sounds of the candy shop providing a soothing backdrop to Amanda's racing thoughts. Outside the window, she could see the usual Saturday morning activity on Main Street—tourists browsing shop windows, locals running errands, and the normal rhythm of life in Laurel Ridge continuing as it had for generations.

"I should probably head out and let you get back to work," Amanda said finally, though part of her wanted to stay in this cozy space with Rachel's encouragement surrounding her like a warm blanket. "I need to run by the grocery store and then head home to work some more on plans for the festival. And I really need to think about this situation with Brandon, too. The changes in him are bothering me, Rachel. He's really weighing heavy on my heart. I hurt from witnessing where he is emotionally this morning."

Rachel stood as her friend gathered her purse. "Don't give up on him. Keep encouraging him. Keep trying to involve him in the festival planning. And don't be surprised if he finds reasons to check on what is going on when we start working on the float. He might be keeping his distance emotionally, but he won't be able to resist making sure everything goes smoothly. It's who he is... trust me on this."

"You think so?"

"I know my brother," Rachel said confidently. "He can try to stay uninvolved all he wants, but when it comes down to it, he won't be able to watch from the sidelines if he thinks the festival might fail. His sense of responsibility won't let him... I have faith he'll come back around, and I believe you're the person to help nudge him along."

Amanda hugged her friend goodbye.

"Thank you. For listening, for understanding, for... just being you."

"That's what best friends are for," Rachel replied. "And Amanda? Sometimes, the people we need most come into our lives when we're least ready to recognize them. Maybe this timing isn't a coincidence. I sincerely believe that."

As Amanda stepped back onto Main Street, Rachel's words echoed in her mind along with everything else they'd discussed. The afternoon sun felt warmer now, and the familiar sights of her hometown looked somehow more hopeful than they had an hour ago.

She couldn't decide if Rachel's parting comment was encouragement or a warning, but either way, something had shifted inside of her. The seed of hope Rachel had planted was taking root, and Amanda found herself walking back toward her car with a lightness in her step that had been missing since she'd driven away from Whitaker Farms earlier.

Maybe she didn't have all the answers about what was happening with Brandon. Maybe she was setting herself up for disappointment by caring about someone who was still healing from deep wounds. But whatever came next, she wouldn't face it alone. She had Rachel's friendship, her own determination, and the belief that sometimes the most important journeys began with a single act of faith—like showing up at someone's farm on a Saturday morning and refusing to accept that the emotional walls they had built were permanent.

Chapter 4

The scent of his mother's chicken casserole hit Brandon the moment he stepped through the farmhouse's back door, rich with the aroma of onions, cream of chicken soup, and the crispy fried onions she always sprinkled on top. The familiar smell wrapped around him, and the day's tensions began to ease from his shoulders.

"Hi sweetie," Helen called from the kitchen. "Rachel just pulled the apple pie from the oven."

"And before you ask, yes, I used Dad's favorite recipe." Rachel's voice followed from deeper in the kitchen.

Brandon paused in the mudroom to hang his work jacket on the peg that had been his since childhood, right next to the one that had been his father's. The sight of the empty peg still caught him off guard sometimes, even after eight months. He pulled off his boots and set them neatly beside the door, another habit James Whitaker had instilled in all his children.

The farmhouse kitchen welcomed him with its familiar comfort—honey-colored cabinets that his father had built by hand years ago, countertops worn smooth by decades of meal preparation, and the large oak table that had been the center of family life for as long as Brandon could remember. Afternoon light filtered through the gingham curtains his mother had sewn herself, casting everything in a warm light that spoke of home.

Rachel stood at the counter, sliding a perfect golden-brown pie onto a cooling rack. Her dark hair was pulled back in a messy bun secured with what looked like a pencil, and she wore an apron over jeans and a sweater that had seen better days. She looked up when he entered, her face lighting up with the kind of unguarded joy that had always been pure Rachel.

"There's my favorite farmer," she said, wiping her hands on her apron. "Geez, Brandon, you look like you've been wrestling with some pretty tough chores today."

"Something like that." Brandon accepted the quick hug she offered. "Smells incredible in here."

"Mom's been cooking all afternoon," Rachel said, nodding toward where Helen stood at the stove, stirring something that smelled like heaven. "I think she's trying to feed half the county."

Helen Whitaker turned from the stove with a smile that reached her eyes, the same warm blue eyes that both her children had inherited. At sixty-two, she moved with the careful grace of someone who had spent decades managing a busy farm and family, but Brandon noticed the way she favored her left hip when she thought no one was looking. Her silver hair was pulled back in its usual neat bun, and she wore the floral apron he'd bought her for Mother's Day three years ago.

"Can I help with anything?" he asked.

"Absolutely not," Helen said firmly. "You've been working since before dawn. Sit down and let me take care of you."

Brandon settled into his usual chair at the kitchen table, the one that faced the window overlooking the back field. The view had always been his favorite—rolling hills of farmland dotted with oak trees around the outer edges, fence lines that stretched toward the mountains in the distance, and the sense of space and permanence that had drawn his family to this land three generations ago.

But his eyes inevitably drifted to the empty chair beside him, the one where his father had sat for every Saturday dinner, every holiday meal, and every lively breakfast. Helen had left it there, neither removing it nor acting as if someone might still fill it. It was simply there, a silent acknowledgment of the man who had shaped all their lives.

"So," Rachel said, settling into her chair with a glass of sweet tea, "how did your meeting with Amanda go this morning?"

The casual question caught Brandon off guard, though it probably shouldn't have. Rachel had always possessed an uncanny ability to zero in on exactly the topics he'd rather avoid.

"Fine," he said, reaching for his glass of tea. "She came by to discuss festival logistics."

"Logistics," Rachel repeated, her tone suggesting she found his choice of words amusing. "That sounds appropriately businesslike. Did she ask for anything specific?"

Brandon took a sip of tea, buying himself time. His mother's sweet tea was perfect, as always—just sweet enough to complement the tartness of fresh lemons.

"The usual stuff. Pumpkins, mums, hay bales."

"And?" Rachel prompted.

"And nothing. I told her we'd supply what she wants for the festival."

Helen brought a basket of fresh cornbread to the table, the golden squares still warm from the oven. The smell made Brandon's mouth water, reminding him that he'd skipped lunch.

"Amanda's such a sweet girl," Helen said, settling into her chair. "Always has been."

"She is. She's done well with her gift shop too," Rachel added, buttering a piece of cornbread. "I swear half my customers talk about her shop like it's the best thing in the world, and honestly... it is. She has an eye for what people want."

Brandon reached for the cornbread, hoping the conversation would shift to safer ground. "How was business today at the candy shop?"

"Nice try," Rachel said with a grin that told him she wasn't going to be distracted that easily. "We're not done talking about Amanda yet."

"There's nothing to talk about. She asked for festival supplies. I agreed to provide them. End of story."

"Is it, though?" Rachel tilted her head, studying him with the kind of sisterly perception that had always made him feel like she could see straight through him. "Because according to what I heard, she has some pretty creative ideas for this year's festival."

Brandon's hand stilled on his cornbread.

"She has plans for making this year special. She really wants the decor to make a statement." Rachel's eyes sparkled with mischief. "I also heard that someone might have been a little less than enthusiastic about the parade float."

Heat crept up Brandon's neck. "The festival doesn't need to be turned into some kind of spectacle."

"Spectacle?" Helen's eyebrows rose. "Amanda's not the type to suggest anything inappropriate. What kind of ideas does she have?"

Brandon shifted in his chair, suddenly feeling like he was fifteen again and trying to explain why he'd come home past curfew. "I don't really know. Told her she needed to speak with either of you about the parade float."

Rachel and Helen exchanged one of those meaningful looks, the kind that usually meant he was about to receive some bit of wisdom whether he wanted it or not.

"Brandon," Helen said gently, "your father always loved helping with the festival floats. Remember how he'd spend hours in the barn, making sure every detail was perfect? He used to say it was one of his favorite parts of fall."

"That was different."

"How?"

"He... he enjoyed that kind of thing. People. Community involvement. I'm not..." Brandon trailed off, not sure how to finish the sentence without sounding like he was making excuses.

"You're not what?" Rachel asked as she leaned forward. "Not capable of helping your neighbors? Not interested in being part of the community that's supported this family for generations? Not interested in helping decorate a simple parade float?"

"Drop it, Rachel. This farm doesn't run itself." Brandon's voice came out sharper than he intended.

"No one's asking you to neglect the farm," Helen said quietly. "But shutting yourself off from people won't make the grief any easier to bear, son."

The words hit their mark, and Brandon felt his defenses rise automatically. "I'm not shutting myself off. I don't have time for elaborate festival planning on top of everything else."

"Or maybe," Rachel said, "you're afraid that getting involved might mean letting people close enough to matter. And we all know how well that worked out last time."

The reference to Samantha hung in the air like smoke from a smoldering fire. Brandon's jaw tightened, and he set his cornbread down.

"Leave it alone, Rachel."

"I'm just saying," she continued, undeterred by his warning tone, "Amanda's not the type to cut and run when things get difficult. She's been part of this community her whole life. She's not going anywhere. And by the way, brother dear... you were rude to her this morning."

"I said leave it alone."

Helen reached across the table and placed her hand over his, her touch gentle but firm. "We're not trying to upset you, sweetheart. We just hate seeing you so isolated. Your father wouldn't want that for you."

"Dad's not here to want anything," Brandon said, the words coming out bitter.

The silence that followed was deafening. Helen's hand tightened over his, and he saw the flash of pain in her eyes before she quickly composed herself.

"You're right," she said quietly. "He's not. But I am. And I'm telling you that hiding away on this farm, avoiding anything that might require you to trust or hope again, isn't living. It's just existing."

Brandon stared down at their joined hands, his mother's weathered fingers covering his work-calloused ones. The gesture was so familiar, so full of love and concern, that it made his throat tight.

"I'm not hiding," he said, but even to his own ears, the words sounded hollow.

"Then prove it," Rachel said gently. "Help us with the parade float. Just show up. Be a part of something good. That's all anyone's asking."

"I'll think about it," he said, then looked at his mom. "Sorry, Mom, I'm not in the best of moods."

"It's fine. Now... let's say grace," Helen said, extending her other hand to Rachel.

Helen offered a simple prayer of gratitude for the food, for family, and for the blessing of another day together. Brandon found himself listening to the familiar words with new attention, hearing the subtle emphasis she placed on gratitude and togetherness.

The rest of dinner passed in easier conversation—Rachel's stories from the Sweet Shoppe, Helen's plans for her fall garden and the mums she grew in the greenhouses on the farm, and Brandon's updates on various things around the farm. But underneath the comfortable routine, he could feel his mother and sister watching him, weighing his responses, clearly not finished with their campaign to draw him back into the land of the living.

When the apple pie was served—perfectly golden and fragrant with cinnamon, just the way his father had loved it—Rachel couldn't resist one more gentle push.

"You know," she said, taking a bite of pie, "I was thinking about what Amanda said earlier when I talked to her on the phone, about making this year's festival special and a little different. Maybe that's exactly what this town needs."

"The festival is always special," Brandon said.

"Is it, though? Or has it become just another obligation, something we do because we've always done it?" Rachel set down her fork and looked at him directly. "Maybe Amanda's right. Maybe it's time for something different. You know, jazz things up. Change things up a bit... I think we could all use some changes."

Helen nodded thoughtfully. "Change isn't always bad, sweetheart. Sometimes it's exactly what we need to move forward."

Brandon knew they weren't just talking about the festival anymore. They were talking about him, about the walls he'd built around himself, and about the way he'd been going through the motions of living without actually engaging with life.

"I already said I'd think about helping out," he said finally, because it was easier than arguing and because part of him knew they were right.

After dinner, Brandon helped clear the table and wash dishes. Helen washed, he dried, and Rachel put everything away in its proper place. The routine was soothing, requiring no conversation, just the comfortable presence of family working together.

When the last dish was dried and put away, Brandon kissed his mother's cheek and gave Rachel a hug.

"Thanks for dinner, Mom," he said. "And for… everything."

Helen's smile was soft and knowing. "That's what family is for. We love you, Brandon. Don't forget that."

The evening air was crisp as Brandon stepped off the farmhouse porch and began the familiar walk down the gravel drive toward his own home. The half-mile trek had been his nightly routine for the past three years, ever since he'd finished building the cabin on the back portion of the family property. It had seemed like a good idea at the time—close enough to help with the farm and his aging parents, far enough away to have his own space and independence.

Now, the walk often felt longer than it was, especially on nights like this when his thoughts were tangled and his emotions raw.

The September night was clear, with a moon bright enough to cast shadows across the fields. Crickets chirped in the grass along the drive, and somewhere in the distance, an owl called out across the rolling hills. The surrounding sounds should have been comforting, but tonight they only emphasized the solitude that had become his constant companion.

Brandon's boots crunched on the gravel as he walked, the sound rhythmic and meditative. To his left, a field stretched toward the tree line, where the shapes of pumpkins were barely visible in the moonlight. To his right, the cornfield rustled softly in the evening breeze, the stalks heavy with ears that would be ready for harvest soon.

This land was in his blood, part of his identity in ways that went deeper than conscious thought. His great-grandfather had cleared these fields by hand, his grandfather had modernized the operation, and his father had expanded it into the successful enterprise it was today. Brandon was the fourth generation to work this soil, and if he had children someday, they would be the fifth.

If he had children.

The thought brought with it the familiar ache of dreams deferred, plans that had crumbled along with his marriage. Samantha had talked about children in the abstract, someday when they were more established, or someday when life was less demanding. But someday had never come, and by the time she left, Brandon had realized that her version of someday involved leaving the farm entirely.

He rounded the bend in the drive where the old oak tree stood sentinel, its massive trunk scarred by decades of weather but still strong, still growing. His father had built a tire swing on that tree when Brandon and Rachel were children, and even now, a piece of rope still hung from one of the lower branches, weathered but intact.

His cabin came into view as he crested a small hill, its windows glowing warmly in the darkness. The structure was simple but well-built—one large room that served as a living area and kitchen, a master en suite, two additional bedrooms, and an office.

It had been his sanctuary during the worst days of his life after Samantha left and his dad had passed, a place where he could retreat from well-meaning friends and family members. But lately, the sanctuary felt more like a prison, beautiful and comfortable but ultimately isolating.

Brandon climbed the three steps to his front porch and leaned against the railing, looking back toward the farmhouse. The lights were still on, and he could picture his mother and Rachel finishing their evening routines—Helen checking that all the doors were locked, Rachel probably raiding the kitchen for one more piece of pie.

They were worried about him. He could see it in their faces, hear it in their voices, and feel it in the careful way they chose their words around him sometimes. They loved him enough to push him, to challenge him, and to refuse to let him disappear entirely into his grief and disappointment.

Amanda's not the type to cut and run when things get difficult.

Rachel's words stung because they highlighted everything he'd lost when Samantha left. Trust. Hope. The belief that love could weather any storm. But they also highlighted something else—the possibility that not all women were like his ex-wife, that some people stayed when things got hard.

Brandon straightened and reached for his front door, then paused with his hand on the handle. Through the kitchen window, he could see his reflection in the glass—a man who looked older than his thirty years, carrying burdens that showed in the set of his shoulders and the lines around his eyes.

His father would barely recognize him now.

James Whitaker had been a man who embraced life, who found joy in simple pleasures, and who believed in the power of community and connection. He'd raised his son to be generous, to help others, and to see challenges as opportunities rather than threats.

Somewhere along the way, Brandon had lost that vision. Grief and betrayal had twisted him into someone defensive and closed-off.

Maybe Amanda's right. Maybe it's time for something different.

The words his sister had spoken at dinner echoed in his mind as he opened the door and stepped into his home. The space was neat and functional, everything in its place, but it felt empty in ways that had nothing to do with furniture or decoration.

Brandon moved to the kitchen and poured himself a glass of water, his movements automatic. Through the window above the sink, he could see the lights of the farmhouse in the distance, warm and welcoming. His family was there, loving him, supporting him, but also challenging him to be better than he'd been.

And somewhere in town, Amanda Baker was probably making lists and planning decorations and dreaming of ways to make this year's festival special. She was doing exactly what his father would have done—throwing herself into a project that would bring the community together, that would create joy and connection and shared purpose.

He had dismissed her without really listening. He'd chosen the path of least resistance, the minimum involvement, and the safest possible engagement. It was the choice of a man who had been hurt and was determined not to be hurt again.

But it wasn't the choice his father would have made. And it wasn't a choice the man he used to be would have made either.

Brandon pushed away from the counter and walked to his bedroom. As he got ready for bed, Brandon found himself thinking about his dad more. How he had built this farm, had created beautiful things, and had always been available to help others. He'd lived with an open heart, and even though that heart had been broken by loss and disappointment as well, he'd never stopped believing in the possibility of good things and his faith in God.

As he settled into bed and listened to the familiar sounds of the farm at night, Brandon thought about everything that had happened to himself and his family in less than a year. The losses. The silence where laughter used to be. The way he himself had become someone he barely recognized.

Maybe he should call Amanda tomorrow, apologize for the way he'd acted, tell her he'd reconsidered, and offer to help with the parade float. It would be a step in the right direction, possibly a way to find his place in a world that felt unfamiliar and unbalanced.

He rolled onto his side, pulling the quilt his grandmother had made closer to his chin. Outside, a coyote called across the valley, its voice lonely and wild in the darkness.

Chapter 5

Amanda pressed her pencil eraser against her lips, staring at the bewildering array of notebooks, sticky notes, and coffee-stained index cards scattered across her kitchen table. The remains of Sunday dinner sat pushed to one side, forgotten in favor of the festival planning chaos that had taken over her dining space.

"Okay, so we've got twelve volunteers confirmed for Wednesday night," Rachel said, consulting the legal pad in front of her. She sat cross-legged in Amanda's kitchen chair, having kicked off her shoes and tucked her feet underneath her like they were still teenagers planning a sleepover. "But knowing this town, we'll probably have twice that many show up because everyone will decide at the last minute that they want to help."

Martha chuckled from her spot at the head of the table. "Honey, organizing Laurel Ridge volunteers is like herding cats—if cats could argue about the best way to arrange hay bales and had strong opinions about the proper shade of orange for autumn displays."

"Don't forget cats that bring their own ideas about what the parade float should look like," Amanda added, making a note in the margin of her planning notebook. "Mrs. Henderson has already called twice with suggestions for incorporating her prize-winning chrysanthemums."

"And Earl mentioned something about wanting to make sure we include a tribute to local veterans," Rachel said, adding another name to her volunteer list.

Amanda leaned back in her chair and surveyed the disaster that was her usually pristine kitchen table. When Rachel and Martha had arrived three hours ago, she'd cleared the dining table, thinking they'd spend maybe an hour going over basic logistics. Instead, they'd ordered pizza, brewed multiple pots of coffee, and transformed her dining area into festival planning headquarters. The autumn centerpiece she'd arranged just yesterday—a simple wooden bowl filled with mini pumpkins and burgundy leaves—now sat relocated to the kitchen counter, displaced by their growing collection of planning materials.

"Maybe we could do different sections on the float," Amanda suggested, reaching for her coffee mug. The ceramic was warm against her palms, and she inhaled the rich aroma of the hazelnut blend Martha had brought from the diner. "A main harvest theme in the center, with smaller features along the sides?"

"That could work," Martha said thoughtfully. "We've got enough space on that trailer to create distinct areas. And it might actually make the construction easier if we're working with smaller sections instead of one massive display."

Rachel scribbled something on her legal pad, then looked up with the kind of mischievous expression Amanda had learned to recognize over years of friendship. "Of course, this is all assuming we can convince a certain stubborn farmer to help us. He knows more about the construction of parade floats than we do."

"Rachel," Amanda warned, but there was no real heat in her voice.

"I'm just saying, my brother's good with stuff like that. He knows what he's doing, whereas... we really don't. Remember the year he suggested that multilevel harvest scene with the waterfall of corn, Martha? That float won first place."

Martha nodded, her eyes twinkling with memory. "Your daddy was so proud of that design. He and Brandon spent hours figuring out how to make the mechanical corn dispenser work without jamming."

The mention of Brandon's father brought a moment of respectful quiet to the table. Amanda fidgeted with her pencil, remembering how reserved Brandon had been when she'd visited the farm yesterday.

"Girls, my brother is so lost. He's worrying me," Rachel said.

Martha reached across the table and patted Rachel's hand. "That boy has been carrying more weight than any one person should have to bear. Losing your daddy and his marriage in the same season would knock anyone sideways."

"He was a bear at dinner last night," Rachel continued, setting down her pen. "Mom made his favorite meal, I made dessert, and we tried to keep the conversation light."

Amanda felt something twist in her chest. "Did you bring up the festival?"

"I did. He didn't have much to say."

"When I spoke to him yesterday, it was like talking to someone who was there but not really present, if that makes sense. It was like talking to someone with a mask on, emotionless," Amanda said.

Martha made a small sound of understanding. "I've seen that look on his face at church—the few times he's been since the funeral. He sits in the back pew, goes through the motions, but there's no joy in him."

The three women sat with that observation for a moment, each lost in their thoughts about the man who had once been the heart of so many community activities.

"I keep thinking about what Dad would say," Rachel murmured, absently drawing circles on her legal pad. "He'd probably tell Brandon that grief is natural, but isolation isn't healing. Dad believed in working through pain, not around it."

"Your father was a wise man," Martha said gently. "But sometimes wisdom takes time to sink in, especially when someone's hurting as deeply as Brandon is."

Amanda stared at her coffee, watching steam rise from the surface in delicate spirals. "I want to help him, but..." She trailed off, not sure how to articulate the pull she felt toward Brandon's pain without bringing up the complicated emotions he stirred up in her.

"But you don't know how," Rachel said.

"Exactly. And I'm worried that pushing too hard will just make him retreat further. But ignoring the situation feels wrong too." Amanda looked up at her friends. "How do you reach someone who has locked the door from the inside?"

Martha leaned forward, her gaze kind but direct. "You don't try to pick the lock, honey. You just sit on the porch and wait. You let him know you're there." She paused, her eyes holding Amanda's. "That boy's world didn't just crack when Samantha left; it shattered when God called James home. Two anchors gone in one season. He's afraid that anything he holds onto now will just vanish, too."

The truth of it landed with a quiet thud in Amanda's chest.

"But you," Martha continued, her voice firm with conviction, "you're not vanishing. You have roots here. Your business, our church, your whole life. You're steady. You're not going anywhere—Lord willing."

"So, I just... keep showing up?" Amanda asked, feeling a fragile shoot of hope.

"Yes. You keep showing up," Martha said simply. "Not in a pushy way, but consistently. Treat him like the man he was, not the man his grief has made him. In time, he'll remember who that is."

"And if he doesn't? What if this withdrawn version is permanent?"

Rachel shook her head. "I don't believe that. I've seen glimpses of the old Brandon. He's still there."

Hope stirred in Amanda's chest. "So, I should keep trying to involve him in festival activities?"

"Keep inviting him," Martha corrected gently. "There's a difference between involving someone and inviting them. Involving implies they don't have a choice. Inviting gives them the option to say yes when they're ready."

Martha's distinction resonated with Amanda immediately. She thought about her approach at the farm yesterday—how she'd presented Brandon with her plans as if his participation was assumed rather than requested.

"I think I might have gotten that wrong yesterday," she admitted.

"Probably," Rachel said with characteristic honesty. "But that's okay. You can try again."

"How?"

Martha tapped her pen thoughtfully against the table. "You keep showing up for him. You keep inviting him to do things. You invite him to join in the parade float construction. You invite him to go for a walk. You invite him to join you for a cup of coffee or invite him to come have a slice of pie with you at my diner. You keep trying to engage with him. And most importantly... you, Amanda Baker, never give up on him."

Amanda hesitated, then nodded slowly.

"Keep giving him an open door, Amanda. If he wants to step through, he will. If not, keep the door open and try again another time," Martha continued.

Rachel's expression softened. "I like that. He might grumble, but I know my brother—he'll feel the tug of curiosity."

Amanda smiled, a flicker of hope stirring in her chest. "Then that's what I'll do."

"Good," Martha said with satisfaction. "Patience and persistence, honey. That's what that boy needs right now. He needs a friend, someone to just show up and be there. Someone who doesn't demand more than he's willing to offer where he is right now in his life."

The threesome spent the next hour finalizing details for the first volunteer meeting on Wednesday. They drafted lists of materials they knew they'd need for the parade float. They figured out timelines and prepared backup plans for the inevitable complications. By the time they'd covered every detail twice, the September evening had settled into full darkness outside Amanda's windows.

"I should head home," Rachel said, stretching as she gathered her notes. "Early morning at the shop tomorrow."

"Same for me. These old bones need a good night's sleep, girls," Martha said.

They spent a few minutes gathering papers and rinsing coffee mugs, in the simple rhythm of women who'd done this kind of work together many times before. Amanda felt the familiar warmth that came from being surrounded by friends who knew her well and loved her.

As they prepared to leave, Rachel paused at the front door, her hand on the handle.

"Amanda," she said, "about Brandon. It's not going to be easy trying to work with someone who's determined to keep everyone at arm's length. But don't give up on him, okay? I have a feeling this festival might be exactly what he needs."

Martha nodded in agreement. "And remember, honey, sometimes the best way to help someone heal is just to show up consistently."

Amanda hugged them both goodbye. She stood on her porch and watched their cars pull away, Martha's sedan followed by Rachel's compact SUV. Their taillights disappeared around the corner, leaving her alone with the quiet sounds of evening in Laurel Ridge—crickets chirping, a dog barking somewhere in the distance, and the gentle rustling of leaves in the oak tree that shaded her front yard.

She turned back toward her house, suddenly aware of how empty it felt after hours of laughter and conversation. The kitchen table still bore evidence of their planning session, with papers and pens scattered across the surface like the remnants of a creative explosion.

Instead of cleaning up immediately, Amanda poured herself a final cup of coffee and settled back into her chair. She pulled her planning notebook toward her and flipped through the pages they'd filled, noting the careful division of responsibilities, the backup plans, and the optimistic timeline that assumed everything would go smoothly.

Her handwriting mingled with Rachel's neat script and Martha's more elaborate cursive, creating a visual record of their collaboration.

Tomorrow she'd start making phone calls to confirm volunteers. On Tuesday, she'd order a few decorative supplies from one of her suppliers and coordinate with the local businesses that were contributing materials. Wednesday evening she'd host the first official volunteer meeting at Whitaker Farms, trying to channel Martha's patience and Rachel's enthusiasm.

She closed her notebook and carried her coffee mug to the kitchen sink. Through the window above the sink, she could see the lights from homes spread across the mountains outside Laurel Ridge proper, twinkling in the distance. Somewhere out there, Brandon was probably finishing evening farm chores.

The thought of his isolation struck her again, sharper now. She tried to imagine what it would feel like to move through each day without genuine connection, to sit at a table with people who loved you but feel unable to fully engage with them.

Standing at her kitchen sink, a silent prayer lifted from her heart...

Lord, just show me how to be a friend to him.

Chapter 6

Brandon ran the wide push broom across the main barn's concrete floor, the bristles scraping against the surface with a rhythm that matched his scattered thoughts. Dust motes caught in the late afternoon light streaming through the windows, and the familiar scent of hay and old wood surrounded him like a well-worn jacket. He'd been out here for the better part of an hour, moving folding chairs from storage and uncovering the parade float frame that had sat dormant under its tarp since last September. Basically, making the space presentable for whatever was about to unfold.

Just show up, Rachel had said during Saturday's dinner. *That's all anyone's asking.*

Well, here he was. Showing up and preparing the barn for the fall festival volunteer meeting.

The rumble of tires on gravel pulled his attention toward the open barn doors. A familiar blue sedan rounded the bend, easing over the rutted farm road. Brandon glanced at his watch. Early, of course. Somehow, he wasn't surprised. He set the broom aside and wiped his hands on his jeans, stepping toward the entrance as her car came to a stop near the barn.

Amanda's car door opened, and she emerged in a flurry of movement and color. She wore a burgundy sweater that complemented the September evening, her blonde hair pulled back in a ponytail that swished as she moved. He could see the energy radiating from her—the kind of purposeful excitement that seemed to be her natural state.

"Brandon!" she called out. "I was hoping I'd see you this evening."

She opened her trunk and began pulling out an impressive array of supplies—poster boards, plastic bins, binders, and what appeared to be several rolled-up pieces of fabric. The sheer volume of materials made Brandon shake his head in amazement.

"Need a hand?" he asked, walking toward her car.

"Sure," Amanda said, shooting him a grateful smile. "I may have gotten a little carried away with the visual aids. "

Brandon reached for one of the plastic bins, surprised by its weight. "What exactly is in here?"

"Sample decorations, fabric swatches, and photographs of other festival displays for inspiration. Oh, and paint samples. Lots of paint samples."

"Paint samples?"

"For the float background. I found these gorgeous autumn shades that would look perfect against the hay bales and jazz things up a bit, but I wanted to get everyone's input before making any final decisions." She paused in her gathering. "Unless maybe jazzing things up is too much? Should I keep things more traditional..."

The uncertainty in her voice had him looking her way again. This was the same woman who had arrived at his farm on Saturday morning with confidence and determination, but now she seemed to be second-guessing herself.

"Amanda," he said, setting down the bin he was holding. "I owe you an apology."

She blinked, clearly not expecting the change of subject.

"I was... I wasn't very welcoming when you came by last Saturday. You were excited about the festival, and I shut you down without even really listening." Brandon ran a hand through his hair, feeling awkward but knowing the words needed to be said. "I thought about calling you to apologize, but I just... well, I never got around to it."

Amanda's expression softened, and she shook her head. "You don't need to apologize. I showed up unannounced and probably overwhelmed you with all my ideas and plans. I should have been more considerate."

"You were excited about something that matters to you and the community. There's nothing wrong with that." He picked up the bin again, then reached for another box. "So why don't you show me these paint samples and tell me about this 'Harvest of Blessings' theme my sister mentioned?"

The smile that spread across her face was like a sunrise breaking through clouds—gradual, then brilliant. "Really? You want to hear about it?"

"I'm here, aren't I?"

"Well... the theme idea came to me during my morning walk on Sunday before church," Amanda said as they walked toward the barn, her voice taking on an animated quality. "I was thinking about what fall really means—not just the pretty colors and pumpkin spice everything, but the deeper meaning. It's harvest time, right? When we gather, we celebrate the good things we've been working toward all year."

Brandon noticed how her eyes lit up as she talked.

"But it's also when we pause to be grateful," she continued, setting her supplies down on one of the tables he'd arranged. "For the community that supports us, for the work that sustains us, and well... just for so many reasons."

She began unpacking her materials, her hands sure and quick as she organized poster boards and opened binders.

"So instead of just focusing on autumn imagery—which is beautiful, don't get me wrong—I thought we could create a float that tells the story of what we're truly harvesting. The relationships, the traditions, the ways we take care of each other."

Brandon found himself watching her hands as she worked, noting the care with which she handled each item. There was something compelling about her that made him want to listen.

"These are the color palettes I'm thinking will work," Amanda said, spreading out several paint chips in warm autumn tones. "Deep golds, rich burgundies, warm oranges. Nothing too bright or artificial-looking."

Before Brandon could respond, the sound of the farmhouse's back door closing reached them, followed by familiar voices. Helen and Rachel were making their way across the yard, Helen carrying a large thermos while Rachel balanced a large covered plate.

"The cavalry arrives," Rachel announced as they entered the barn. "Mom made coffee, and I brought cookies from the shop."

"Chocolate chip," Helen added, setting the thermos down on the table.

Amanda's face lit up with genuine pleasure. "That's so thoughtful. Thank you both."

Brandon watched his mother and sister greet Amanda with affection. Helen admired the poster boards while Rachel immediately began examining the paint samples with interest.

"These colors are gorgeous," Rachel said, holding up a chip in deep amber. "This would look beautiful on the float and work well with the theme."

"That's exactly what I was thinking," Amanda said, her enthusiasm building again. "And if we use this burgundy as an accent color, we can tie in some of the church's fall decorations."

More vehicles were arriving now—Martha's sedan, Pastor Andrew's pickup truck, and several cars Brandon recognized. The barn began filling with voices and laughter as people greeted each other and admired Amanda's setup.

Brandon retreated to the edge of the gathering, leaning against one of the barn's support posts where he could observe. It had been so long since he'd been part of anything like this that he'd almost forgotten the particular energy it created.

Martha appeared beside him, having navigated the crowd with the skill of someone who'd spent decades moving through groups of people.

"Quite a turnout," she said.

"Yep, Amanda did a good job organizing it," he said, watching as Amanda gestured toward one of her poster boards while explaining something to Pastor Andrew.

"She's got a gift for bringing people together," Martha observed. "Your mom mentioned that you set up the barn for tonight."

Brandon shrugged. "Just moved some chairs around."

"Still, I thank you. Saved us all a bit of work."

"Rachel asked me to... it's no big deal."

Amanda's voice rose above the general conversation and commotion happening in the barn. "All right, everyone. Thank you all for coming tonight. I know Wednesday evenings are busy, but I'm hoping what we accomplish here will make this year's Fall Festival something really special. I'd love to show you what Martha, Rachel, and I are thinking for this year's float."

The group naturally formed a semicircle around Amanda's display area. Brandon found himself with a clear view as she began presenting her vision, her hands moving expressively as she described each element.

"This year's theme is 'Harvest of Blessings,' and I want our parade float to reflect not just the abundance of the season, but the abundance of community we have here in Laurel Ridge. The central focus will be a traditional harvest scene," she explained, pointing to sketches and photographs she'd mounted on poster board. "But instead of just static displays, I want to create elements that tell our story as a community."

She moved to another board, this one covered with fabric swatches and detailed drawings.

"Here's where it gets interesting. I'm thinking we create different 'blessing stations' along the float. One section celebrates our local businesses, another highlights some of our founding families, and a third honors the ways we support each other through difficult times."

Brandon watched the surrounding faces, noting the way people leaned forward with interest, the nods of approval, and the questions that showed genuine engagement with her ideas.

"Now, the technical challenge," Amanda continued, "is going to be creating a structure that's stable enough to support people and decorations but light enough to actually move down Main Street. I really need everyone's help with this. This is my first time working on a float for the parade, and I'll admit... I'm clueless when it comes to some of the more technical aspects. Coming up with ideas and decorating... no problem, but building? Well, that's another story."

She gestured toward the parade float frame that Brandon had uncovered earlier—a basic trailer with a wooden platform that had served as the foundation for previous years' displays.

"I was thinking we could build risers at different heights, maybe use some kind of lightweight framing system..."

"You'd want to use metal tubing," Brandon said.

Every head in the group turned toward him, and he felt heat rise in his neck. But Amanda's expression was expectant and encouraging, so he continued.

"PVC would be too weak for people to stand on, and wood framing would be too heavy. But if you use aluminum tubing with proper cross-bracing, you could create multiple levels that would be both stable and manageable."

Amanda tilted her head. "Aluminum tubing? Cross-bracing? Zero knowledge in that department, Brandon. So... could we anchor it to the trailer in some way? What's going to keep it from moving?"

"Drill into the deck and use flanged bases for the uprights." Brandon said as he moved closer to the group, caught up in the problem-solving aspect. "You'd want to plan your weight distribution carefully, though. Keep the heaviest elements toward the center and front."

"What about weather protection?" asked Mrs. Davenport, one of the longtime volunteers. "Last year we had an unexpected rain shower right before the parade."

"Treated canvas," Brandon replied. "Or you could use those portable canopy frames as a backup. Easy to set up if you need weather cover."

Amanda was scribbling notes as he talked, and when she looked up, her smile held genuine admiration.

"This is exactly the kind of expertise we need," she said. "Would you be willing to help with the technical planning? Maybe? I can handle the creative elements, but I'm definitely out of my depth when it comes to engineering."

The question hung in the air, and Brandon was aware of the subtle shift in the room's energy. His mother and Rachel were carefully not looking at him, while Martha studied her coffee cup with sudden intense interest. Even Pastor Andrew seemed to be holding his breath.

"Sure. I'll... I'll figure out what you need," he said finally.

Amanda's face brightened. "Wonderful."

The meeting continued for another hour, with various volunteers claiming responsibility for different aspects of the project. Lists were made, schedules coordinated, and contact information exchanged. Meetings for decorating the parade float were planned for every Monday and Wednesday evening from now until festival time in October. Brandon found himself drawn into several technical discussions, his knowledge of construction and engineering making him a natural resource for solving practical challenges.

When the meeting finally wound down and people began gathering their things, Brandon automatically helped Amanda pack up her supplies. The barn had grown quiet except for the soft murmur of conversations and the distant sound of cars starting up in the parking lot.

"I can't believe how well that went," Amanda said, carefully rolling up her poster boards. "I was so nervous I'd forget something important, but everyone was so helpful. And your engineering suggestions—I appreciate you jumping in like you did."

"You had the hard part figured out. You know what you want the float to look like," Brandon replied, stacking her binders. "Vision's harder than mechanics."

Amanda paused in her packing, studying his face. "You don't give yourself enough credit."

"What do you mean?"

"I mean, you solved a problem this evening that could have taken me hours of searching the internet to find a solution, and you did it all while acting like it was no big deal. I appreciate that."

Brandon picked up the easel contraption she'd used to hold one of her display boards, focusing on its folding mechanisms rather than responding.

They carried her supplies out to the car in silence, their footsteps crunching on the gravel. The September evening had turned cool, carrying hints of autumn in the mountain air.

"Thank you," Amanda said as they loaded the last of her materials into the trunk. "For everything tonight. For apologizing earlier, for making space in the barn for us to meet, and for sharing your ideas." She smiled, and something in the warmth of it made Brandon's chest tighten. "I have a feeling this festival is going to be better because of your input tonight."

Brandon nodded, not trusting his voice. Amanda climbed into her car, rolled down the window, and waved as she pulled away.

He stood in the driveway longer than necessary, the sound of her engine fading into the night. The barn behind him glowed with warm light, and he could hear his mother and Rachel finishing their cleanup inside, their voices mixing with Martha's distinctive laughter.

Brandon walked slowly back toward the barn, then stopped at the open doors. Something about Amanda's smile lingered in his mind—not just its warmth, but the way it had reached her eyes when she looked at him. Like she saw something worth looking at.

The thought unsettled him more than he cared to admit.

Chapter 7

The wrench slipped from Brandon's grip for the third time in ten minutes, clattering against the concrete floor of the barn with a metallic ring that echoed off the high rafters. He muttered under his breath and crouched to retrieve it, his patience wearing thin with the stubborn hydraulic fitting that refused to cooperate. The old hay baler had been giving him trouble all week, and with the first cutting of winter hay coming up, he couldn't afford to have equipment sitting idle.

He'd been elbow-deep in its mechanical guts for the better part of an hour when Amanda's voice called out from the barn's entrance.

"Brandon? Are you in here?"

He looked up from the maze of hoses and fittings, grease smeared across his forearms and a wrench still in his hand. Amanda stood silhouetted against the morning sunlight, her blonde hair caught in a loose braid that hung over one shoulder. She wore jeans, boots, and a light green sweatshirt that brought out the blue in her eyes, and she clutched her phone in one hand like she was ready for business.

"Over here," he called, wiping his hands on a shop rag as he straightened. "What brings you out this way?"

"I called your mom this morning and asked if I could come out and get a better sense of what you have available for the festival decorations this year. She said to find you and that you'd be happy to give me a tour."

Brandon shot a mental note of thanks to his mother for volunteering his time without asking. "Did she now?"

"She seemed pretty confident you wouldn't mind." Amanda's expression flickered with uncertainty, and she shifted her weight from one foot to the other. "Unless you're too busy? I mean, I can see you're working on something important, and I don't want to interrupt—"

"It's fine." The words came out before Brandon could think of a reasonable excuse to avoid spending his morning playing tour guide. "This can wait. The baler's not going anywhere."

Amanda's face brightened immediately. "Perfect. I promise I won't keep you too long."

Brandon set down his wrench and reached for a clean rag to finish wiping his hands. "Probably easier to drive around and look at everything. The golf cart's parked outside—we can cover more ground that way."

"Sounds good."

They walked out into the late September morning; the air was crisp, carrying the scent of ripening crops. September in West Virginia was Brandon's favorite time of year—cool mornings, warm afternoons, and the satisfaction of watching months of work come to fruition in the fields.

The golf cart sat beneath a maple tree that was just beginning to show touches of gold at the tips of its leaves. Brandon climbed behind the wheel while Amanda settled beside him, immediately pulling up what looked like a detailed note-taking app on her phone.

"All right," she said, her fingers already moving across the screen. "Where should we start?"

"Pumpkin fields," Brandon said, turning the key. The electric motor hummed to life with barely a whisper. "That's probably what you'll need most."

He drove them down a gravel path that wound between the main barn and the first of the farm's pumpkin patches. As they crested a small rise, the field spread out before them like something from a postcard—rows upon rows of orange orbs nestled among broad green leaves, stretching toward the tree line in the distance.

Amanda let out a soft gasp. "Brandon, ohhhh... I just love this time of year."

Brandon glanced over at her, surprised by the genuine wonder in her voice. Amanda had been to the farm plenty of times over the years to visit Rachel, but she was looking at the pumpkin patch like she'd never seen anything quite like it.

"We've got over twenty-five acres in pumpkins this year," he said, stopping the cart at the edge of the field. "Mix of jack-o'-lantern varieties, sugar pumpkins, and miniatures."

Amanda was already climbing out of the cart, her attention completely focused on the field. She walked a few steps into the rows, careful not to disturb the vines, and crouched down beside a cluster of perfectly round orange pumpkins.

"These are beautiful," she said, running her hand gently over the surface of one. "So smooth and uniform. How do you get them to grow like this?"

Brandon joined her at the edge of the field, surprised by the genuine curiosity in her question. "Soil preparation, proper spacing, consistent watering. And you have to turn them regularly so they develop even color."

"Turn them?"

"Every few days, you rotate each pumpkin slightly. Otherwise, they develop flat spots where they sit against the ground." He demonstrated with a nearby pumpkin, showing her the careful technique that prevented damage to the vine.

Amanda watched intently, then tried it herself on the next pumpkin.

"Like this?" she asked, glancing up at him for confirmation.

"Yep, that's all there is to it. You're a natural-born pumpkin turner."

She beamed at the simple praise, and Brandon felt warmth spread through his chest. When was the last time someone had been so genuinely interested in the details of his work? Samantha had tolerated his farming talk, but she'd never asked questions or shown real curiosity about the processes that consumed his days.

"So for the festival," Amanda said, pulling out her phone to make notes, "how many pumpkins could we realistically use for downtown decorating? I'm thinking displays at every storefront, plus larger arrangements in the town square."

Brandon did quick calculations in his head, drawing on years of experience with the festival's needs. "Previous years, we've donated maybe two hundred pumpkins total. Small ones for individual displays, medium for groupings, and larger for centerpieces."

"What if I wanted to go bigger this year? Really make Main Street spectacular?"

The enthusiasm in her voice was infectious.

"This area here is all sugar pumpkins. That section over there has miniatures; they're smaller than the sugar pumpkins here in this field.

And the backfield has the big carving pumpkins." He paused, studying her excited expression. "How much bigger are we talking?"

Amanda's eyes sparkled with mischief. "What if I said I wanted enough pumpkins to create a harvest wonderland? Make a big statement. Pumpkins everywhere you look when you're at the festival."

Despite himself, Brandon smiled. "Then I'd say you're talking about doubling our usual donation. Maybe more."

"And that would be... possible?"

"It would be possible," he confirmed and was rewarded with Amanda clapping her hands together in delight.

The sound was so spontaneous, so full of joy, that Brandon actually laughed—a real laugh that surprised them both. When was the last time he'd laughed like that?

"Okay, wonderful," Amanda said, typing rapidly on her phone. "So let's say four hundred pumpkins, various sizes. What about gourds?"

They spent the next thirty minutes driving and walking through the gourd fields, where Amanda exclaimed over the variety of shapes, colors, and sizes. She took pictures of different specimens, asked detailed questions about growing techniques, and filled several screens on her phone with notes about quantities and varieties.

Brandon watched her move through the rows with growing fascination. She had a way of seeing beauty in the most ordinary things—the curve of a butternut squash, the intricate patterns on an acorn squash, the unusual coloring of a carnival gourd. Her appreciation wasn't performative or exaggerated; it was a genuine wonder at the natural world.

"These warty gourds are my favorite," she said, carefully lifting one to examine its unusual surface. "They look like something from a fairy tale."

"Most people think they're ugly," Brandon said.

"Then, most people have no imagination." Amanda set the gourd down gently and looked up at him with sparkling eyes. "I think they're perfect. Character is more interesting than conventional beauty, don't you think?"

The comment struck him oddly, as if she was talking about more than gourds. He found himself really looking at her for the first time in years—not just seeing Rachel's best friend or the festival coordinator, but Amanda Baker herself.

Her face was animated as she talked, her hands moving expressively to emphasize her points. There was intelligence in her questions, warmth in her laughter, and a zest for life that seemed to bubble up from some inexhaustible source. When had she become so... compelling?

The realization unsettled him more than he cared to admit.

"Next stop?" Amanda asked, oblivious to his internal confusion.

"Mums," Brandon managed, starting the golf cart again.

The chrysanthemum greenhouses were his mother's domain, long structures filled with chrysanthemums in every shade from deep burgundy, orange, bronze, purple, and bright yellow. The air inside was humid and fragrant, filled with the earthy scent of growing things and the subtle sweetness of the flowers themselves.

"Oh my goodness," Amanda breathed as they entered the first greenhouse.

Rows of mums in various stages of bloom stretched the length of the building. Some were compact and button-like, others full and shaggy, and still others formed perfect pompoms of color. Helen had been growing mums for over twenty years, and her expertise showed in the quality and variety.

"Your mom is an artist," Amanda said, walking slowly down one of the aisles. "These are gorgeous."

"She'll be pleased to hear that. The mums are her pride and joy." Brandon watched Amanda examine the flowers with the same careful attention she'd given the pumpkins and gourds. "We usually donate about fifty plants for the festival. Mix of colors and sizes."

"Could we do more this year? Maybe a hundred? I'm envisioning mum displays on every corner, plus major arrangements for the parade route."

"I don't see why not. Mom always grows extras anyway. You really want to go all out this year, don't you?"

Amanda was taking more pictures, getting close-up shots of different varieties. "You better believe it. My goal is to make a statement this year. Ohhh...these bronze-colored mums are incredible. And the deep red... oh, Brandon, they're perfect for our color scheme."

She was so absorbed in the flowers that she didn't notice the way his name sounded different when she said it—less formal, more familiar. But Brandon noticed. The sound sent an unexpected jolt through him.

"What about these?" Amanda asked, pausing beside a group of particularly full, cream-colored mums.

"Those are Mom's specialty. She calls them her wedding mums."

"They're gorgeous. So full and romantic." Amanda touched one bloom gently. "Your mom has incredible talent."

"She'd love to hear you say that. Growing things is her passion project."

"I can tell. There's so much love in this place." Amanda gestured around the greenhouse. "You can feel it in how carefully everything is tended."

Her observation was so perceptive, so understanding of what made his family's operation special, that Brandon felt his guard slip, just a little. This was what he'd been missing with Samantha—someone who understood that farming wasn't just about crops and profits but about stewardship and care and the deep satisfaction of nurturing life.

They visited two more greenhouses, with Amanda taking notes and asking questions about timing, transportation, and care instructions. By the time they finished, her phone was full of pictures, and her enthusiasm had, if anything, increased.

"Okay, now what about the fodder shocks?" She said as they climbed back into the golf cart.

They drove toward the cornfields, where Brandon had been working for the past week to prepare for the farm's opening to the public. Some sections had been cut, and the stalks were bundled into neat shocks that stood like sentinels across the field. Other areas had been left standing to create the corn maze that was always a favorite attraction for visiting families.

"We cut the corn when it's still slightly green but mature," Brandon explained as they parked beside one of the harvested sections. "Dry it slightly, then bundle it. The shocks last for months if they're stored properly."

Amanda climbed out of the cart and walked toward the nearest bundle, which stood taller than she was. "They're like sculptures," she said, walking around one to examine it from all angles.

"Never thought of it that way."

Brandon looked at the fodder shock with fresh eyes, trying to see what Amanda saw. The bundles were practical, functional, and designed to preserve the cornstalks for decorative use.

"How many would you need?" he asked.

"For downtown? Maybe forty or fifty? I want to create groupings at major intersections, plus use some for the parade float."

"That won't be a problem. We usually make a few hundred for our own use when we open to the public."

Amanda was typing notes again, her fingers flying over her phone screen. "The festival will be incredible, Brandon. The quantities you're willing to supply... I'm going to be able to create something special and memorable."

The joy in her voice was unmistakable. When had he stopped noticing how infectious enthusiasm could be? When had he forgotten how good it felt to be part of creating something meaningful?

They spent another hour touring the rest of the operation—the fodder shock storage areas, the snack shack that would open to the public in a few weeks, and the various equipment sheds and barns. Amanda's note-taking became more detailed as they went.

They drove back toward the main barn complex, past fields that were full of farmworkers busy doing what they do, preparing for the busy season ahead. Amanda waved at several people as they passed, and each responded with a wave or tip of a hat.

"Everyone seems to know you," Brandon observed.

"Well, Brandon, owning a store in town helps. Plus, I've met many of the people that work here over the years when I come out to visit Rachel. Your farmworkers are some of the nicest people in Laurel Ridge."

The comment was casual, but it revealed something important about Amanda's character. She noticed people, remembered them, and treated everyone with the same warmth and respect. It was another softening of Brandon's defenses.

They arrived back at the main barn and walked inside. The barn was cool and spacious, with the parade float frame positioned in the center of the concrete floor. Amanda walked around it slowly, her mind clearly working through possibilities.

"This thing seems to have grown in size since Wednesday. I'll admit it seems so much bigger now that I'm really paying attention and thinking harder about how to make my vision come to life," she said, running her hand along the wooden platform.

"Dad built it a little bigger than standard flatbed trailers. He built it to last, though."

Amanda glanced at him, her expression softening. "I can see the quality in the construction. He did beautiful work."

Brandon nodded his thanks.

"So if I'm thinking about multiple levels for this float and different blessing stations," Amanda continued, "the layout would need to be planned carefully."

She pulled up a sketch on her phone. "I'm thinking the main harvest scene here in the center, then smaller tableaus along the sides."

Brandon studied the drawing, his engineering mind automatically working through the structural requirements. "You'd want your heaviest elements in the middle, for stability. Maybe put the blessing stations at the corners where they'd be most visible to the crowd."

"And using aluminum tubing for the framework, we could create different heights without making it too heavy, correct?"

She was gesturing as she talked, her hands sketching shapes in the air to illustrate her vision. Brandon realized he was watching her more than listening to her words, captivated by the animation in her face and the graceful movement of her hands.

This was dangerous territory. Amanda Baker was his sister's best friend and the festival coordinator who needed his help. But she was also a woman—an attractive, intelligent, passionate woman who seemed to genuinely appreciate everything around her.

The recognition hit him like a physical force, and for a moment, he couldn't breathe properly.

"Brandon?" Amanda was looking at him with concern. "You okay?"

"Fine," he managed. "Just thinking."

But he wasn't fine. He was terrified because, for the first time in months, he felt something besides grief and disappointment. He felt interested. He felt attracted. He felt alive in a way that Samantha's leaving had convinced him might be gone forever.

"The framework... would, um... need to be modular," he said, forcing himself to focus on the technical aspects. "Easy to assemble and disassemble for transport."

"Right. And we'd need to consider how people would get on and off the float during the parade." Amanda was back in problem-solving mode, oblivious to his internal crisis.

They spent another twenty minutes discussing practical details—power sources for any electrical elements, weather protection, and safety considerations for the people who would be riding the float. Amanda took more notes and asked questions that impressed him.

"I think that covers everything on my list," she said finally, looking up from her phone with satisfaction. "This is all going to be spectacular, Brandon. I can't thank you enough for taking the time to show me around the farm this morning and help me work through a few more details for the parade float."

Before he could respond, the sound of footsteps on gravel announced a new arrival. Helen appeared in the barn doorway, her face brightening when she saw them.

"There you two are," she said, smiling warmly at Amanda and shooting Brandon a quick, assessing glance. "How did the grand tour go?"

"Wonderful," Amanda said. "Brandon showed me everything, and I think we're going to have a fantastic fall festival this year."

"Well... that's nice to hear," Helen said. "I was just coming to see if you'd like to stay for lunch. I made far too much chicken salad, and I could use some company."

"That's so kind of you," Amanda said without hesitation. "I'd love to."

Helen beamed. "Wonderful."

Amanda fell into step beside Helen, the two women chatting easily as they headed across the yard. Halfway to the house, Amanda glanced back over her shoulder to where Brandon still stood in the barn doorway.

"Well, come on," she called, her voice carrying a hint of laughter. "Let's go have lunch."

Brandon shook his head, watching as she turned back to his mother and continued their conversation without missing a beat. He'd spent the morning showing her around the farm he'd known all his life, but somehow she'd managed to show him things he'd never noticed—the way morning light could make ordinary pumpkins look magical and the way genuine enthusiasm could transform routine farm life into something that felt almost celebratory.

And now this woman was walking toward his mother's home, chattering about festival plans and harvest decorations with the same energy she'd brought to everything else this morning.

Brandon started following them toward the house, unsure what whirlwind he'd found himself caught up in now.

Chapter 8

Amanda was elbow-deep in Helen's kitchen, spreading chicken salad on slices of homemade bread while Helen was busy cutting pickles.

"Hand me that platter in front of you, dear," Helen said, gesturing toward a cheerful yellow ceramic dish that sat on the counter beside the window.

Amanda reached for the platter, noting the way the afternoon light streamed through the gingham curtains. "I've always loved your kitchen. It's always felt like the heart of your home."

"It is," Helen agreed, arranging the sandwiches on the platter with care. "James used to say the kitchen was where all the important conversations happened. Business talk happened in the barn, but family talk happened right here in this kitchen."

The mention of her husband carried no sadness, just happy memories, and Amanda smiled at the image of family gatherings centered around this warm, welcoming space.

"There's something about kitchens that makes people want to linger, isn't there?" Amanda said, helping Helen load a tray with glasses.

"Food and fellowship," Helen nodded. "The Bible's full of both for good reason."

They worked together naturally, Helen filling glasses with sweet tea while Amanda gathered napkins and utensils. Through the window, Amanda could see Brandon sitting on the back porch, his long frame relaxed in one of the wooden chairs that faced out toward the fields.

"He's been different since Wednesday night," Helen said quietly, following Amanda's gaze. "More present, if that makes sense. Still quiet, but not quite so... distant."

"Hmmm, well maybe talk of the festival has put him in better spirits. It's nice when the whole community gets involved in something together."

Helen gave her a look that was both knowing and gentle. "Indeed it is."

They carried the food and drinks out onto the back porch, where a simple wooden table sat surrounded by chairs that had clearly seen years of family meals and conversations. The view stretched across the farmyard toward rolling fields and distant mountains, with the late September breeze carrying scents of hay and ripening crops.

"This is perfect weather for eating outside," Amanda said, setting down the tray of glasses. "I've always loved sitting on this back porch and enjoying the view."

"Mom likes to have her morning coffee out here and watch the sunrise over the corn." Brandon said.

"Best way to start the day," Helen said, settling into her chair. "Brandon, would you say grace for us?"

Amanda saw something flicker across his face—surprise, maybe, or hesitation.

"Of course," he said after a moment.

They bowed their heads, and Brandon's voice, when it came, was quiet but steady. "Lord, thank You for this food and for the hands that prepared it. Thank You for the good company and for the blessings of this day. Amen."

"Amen," Amanda and Helen echoed.

The prayer was simple, unadorned, but Amanda found herself touched by the sincerity in Brandon's voice. There was something beautiful about sharing a meal that began with gratitude.

Amanda took a bite of her sandwich, surprised by how perfectly seasoned the chicken salad was. "Helen, this is incredible. What's your secret?"

Helen beamed. "A little dill, a touch of lemon juice, and good-quality mayonnaise. Nothing fancy."

"It tastes like something my grandmother would have made," Amanda said. "That perfect balance of flavors that I can never seem to get quite right when I make chicken salad."

"Well, the real secret is making it the day before you plan to eat it," Helen said. "Gives all the flavors time to marry properly."

"I'll have to remember that," Amanda said. "I love cooking, but I'm always looking for ways to improve. Running the shop keeps me pretty busy, so anything that can be made ahead is a blessing in disguise."

"How long have you owned Indulgences? It's been what... three or four years now?" Helen asked.

"Five years this coming December," Amanda replied. "Time flies, but it's been the most rewarding five years of my life. I love being able to help people find exactly the right gift for someone they care about."

Brandon leaned back in his chair, and Amanda noticed the way he seemed to be listening.

"What made you decide to buy the shop?" he asked.

"I'd been working there for about four years, learning the business from Mr. and Mrs. Baxter—the previous owners," Amanda said. "When they decided to retire, they offered to sell it to me first before putting it on the market. It felt... I don't know, like God was opening a door."

"That's a big decision for someone so young," Helen observed.

"It was terrifying," Amanda admitted with a laugh. "I spent weeks praying about it, making lists of pros and cons, and talking it over with anyone who would listen. I almost drove my parents crazy trying to make up my mind about what to do. I'm sure Rachel probably got sick of hearing about it."

"I doubt that," Brandon said. "Rachel loves having someone to give advice to."

The comment was made with obvious affection for his twin sister, and Amanda felt herself smiling at the picture it painted of the family dynamics.

"She does love to give advice," Amanda agreed. "But she's also incredibly supportive. When I was agonizing over the decision, she finally said, 'Amanda, you already know what you want to do. Stop overthinking it and trust God's timing.'"

"Smart girl," Helen said. "Takes after her mother, of course."

Brandon shook his head, but Amanda caught the hint of a smile at the corners of his mouth.

"So you took the leap," Helen continued.

"I did. And it's been wonderful. Challenging, absolutely, but amazing. I love being part of the community in this way, being the place people come when they want to show someone they care."

"You've certainly made a success of it," Helen said. "Every time I'm in town, I see people coming and going from your shop. And the window displays you create are just beautiful. And I have to admit, your shop is one of my favorites... and not because I've known you since you were a little girl. I mean that from the bottom of my heart."

"Thank you. Changing the displays with the seasons is one of my favorite things to do. I enjoy finding new ways to showcase the merchandise." Amanda paused to take another bite of her sandwich. "Though I have to give credit to my staff. April, my manager, has been instrumental in keeping everything running smoothly. And Natalie, my assistant manager, has such good instincts about what customers are looking for."

"It's nice to have people you can trust," Brandon said.

There was something in his voice that made Amanda glance at him more closely.

"It is," she agreed. "Though it took time to build that trust. I have five employees now, and I trust all of them. Running a successful business is a group effort. I'm at the point now where I have fewer worries about taking a day off or time away from the shop. But I'll admit I sometimes struggle with letting go of control. I want everything to be perfect, which isn't always realistic. I've been working really hard to let things go and have faith."

"Perfectionism is a hard habit to break," Helen said. "I spent years thinking I had to do everything myself to make sure it was done right."

"What changed?" Amanda asked.

Helen glanced at Brandon with a smile. "This one and his sister, mainly. It's hard to maintain control when you've got twin toddlers running in opposite directions. You learn to prioritize what really matters and let the rest go."

"I'm still working on that lesson, and it's hard," Amanda said.

"We all are, dear. It's a lifelong process."

The conversation continued to flow naturally around topics both large and small. Amanda was fully relaxed and enjoying the simple pleasures of good food and simple company on a beautiful afternoon.

The September air carried just enough coolness to make sitting outside pleasant without being chilly. In the distance, the sound of gentle wind through the corn created a soft rustling sound that felt like nature's own background music.

"This is my favorite time of year," Amanda said, gesturing toward the view spread out before them. "There's something about early fall that feels so full of possibility."

"Harvest time," Helen agreed. "When you get to see the results of all the spring planting and summer tending. And watch the world around you change in color."

"Yes. And there's beauty in every stage—the changing leaves, the abundance of crops, even the preparation for winter." Amanda paused, realizing she was getting carried away. "Sorry, I tend to get a little enthusiastic about the seasons."

"Don't apologize," Brandon said. "It's nice to hear someone appreciate it."

"It's impossible not to appreciate this," she said, gesturing toward the fields. "You and your family have created something really beautiful here."

"Dad always said farming was a partnership," Brandon replied. "You do your part, God does His, and hopefully you end up with something worth having."

"I always loved listening to your dad talk; he was so full of knowledge and wisdom."

"He was," Helen agreed softly. "He'd have liked seeing the farm used for the festival again this year. He always believed in being part of the community. If he were still with us, he'd be right out there in the thick of it all. He'd be your right-hand man, Amanda."

Brandon nodded, and Amanda saw the shadow that crossed his face at the mention of his father. But it wasn't the sharp pain she might have expected—more like the gentle ache of missing someone beloved.

Helen reached over and patted her son's hand briefly—a gesture so natural and loving that Amanda felt her throat tighten with unexpected emotion.

"I'm sure he's up in heaven smiling down on us right now," Helen said firmly.

They finished their meal as the afternoon light began to shift, painting everything in deeper golden tones. Amanda helped clear the table, carrying dishes back into the kitchen while Helen gathered the remaining food.

"Thank you so much for lunch," Amanda said as she filled the sink full of hot soapy water.

"The pleasure was all mine," Helen replied. "I've really missed having you visit us out here on the farm more often. I miss when you kids were younger. Now you all have busy lives... so I understand... but I do miss you."

"Well, hopefully we'll have lots more opportunities to spend time together as we work on the festival," Amanda said.

Her phone buzzed in her back pocket, and she grimaced apologetically. "I'm sorry, let me just check this."

She pulled out her phone and saw a text from April: Hey! Sorry to bother. Big fall shipment just arrived. The store is packed with customers, and I could really use some help. Any idea when you'll be back?

Amanda's heart sank as she read the message. The afternoon had been so perfect, so peaceful, and the last thing she wanted was to rush back to the busy demands of retail management.

"Well," she said, looking up at Helen apologetically. "I'm so sorry, but I need to get back to the shop. A shipment arrived, and they're swamped."

"Of course, dear. Don't worry about the dishes."

"Go help your employees," Brandon said, appearing in the kitchen doorway. "Mom and I can handle a few dishes."

"Are you sure?"

"Go," Helen said, shooing her toward the door. "We'll be fine."

Amanda hugged Helen quickly. "Thank you for everything. This was wonderful."

"Don't be a stranger. You come visit me anytime you want," Helen said warmly.

Amanda waved to Brandon as she headed toward the door, then broke into a jog as she crossed the yard toward her car.

She climbed into her car and waved again toward Helen and Brandon, who were standing together on the porch watching her leave. Helen raised her hand in farewell, while Brandon simply nodded in acknowledgment.

As Amanda drove down the driveway, she smiled despite the interruption to her peaceful afternoon.

Back on the porch, Helen watched Amanda's car disappear, then turned to look at Brandon, his hands shoved deep in his pockets.

"She's a lovely girl," Helen said simply.

Brandon nodded, his gaze still fixed on the empty parking spot where Amanda's car had been.

Chapter 9

Brandon scraped the knife blade against the piece of hickory in his hand, curling a thin shaving that fell to the porch floor at his feet. The motion was automatic, practiced—something to occupy his hands while his mind wrestled with thoughts that refused to settle into any kind of order.

The sun had disappeared behind the western ridge twenty minutes ago, leaving the sky painted in shades of coral and purple that would have been beautiful if he'd been paying attention. Instead, he sat in the wooden chair on his cabin's front porch, working the knife with steady strokes while replaying the day's events like a man trying to solve a puzzle with half the pieces missing.

Amanda Baker.

He'd known her for years. Had seen her hundreds of times at church, around town, and visiting Rachel.

He tried to think back to high school. Amanda had been there, of course—Rachel's friend, the quiet girl who got good grades and stayed out of trouble. He could remember her at football games, sitting in the student section with Rachel and a few other girls, but she'd never been part of the crowd he'd run with. His world had revolved around sports and his teammates, parties after games, and the easy confidence that came with being the quarterback everyone expected to lead them to state championships.

Had he even spoken to her back then? Really spoken to her, beyond polite hellos when she came to the house to see Rachel?

Brandon searched his memory and came up empty. If they'd had actual conversations, they'd left no impression. She'd been background, part of the scenery of Rachel's life but not his.

After graduation, she'd gone to college somewhere upstate while he'd stayed on the farm, learning the business from his father and gradually taking on more responsibility. She'd come home for holidays and summer breaks, and he'd see her around town or at the farm when she visited Rachel, but by then he'd been focused on other things. Learning to run equipment, managing crop rotations, and expanding their seasonal business. And girls—there had been girls, local ones mostly, though nothing serious until Samantha.

When Amanda and Rachel had returned to Laurel Ridge after college, he'd been wrapped up in his own life; he could barely remember those years.

Even at church, before he'd stopped going regularly, she'd been part of the congregation but not someone he'd paid particular attention to. She sat with Rachel or her parents; she'd participated in church activities and volunteered for things he vaguely remembered. A good person doing good things, but not someone who registered on his radar.

And why would she? He'd been busy with his own concerns, his own plans. Then the whirlwind courtship with Samantha, then the brief marriage that had unraveled so quickly he still felt dizzy thinking about it. Then Dad's death, and the months since, when he'd barely been able to see beyond the boundaries of grief and the demands of keeping the farm running.

But even before all that, during the years when life had felt normal and manageable, he'd somehow looked right past Amanda Baker. Seen her without seeing her.

The uncomfortable truth was settling in his chest like a stone. He'd been self-absorbed. Wrapped up in his own world and in his own plans. He'd noticed people in his immediate circle and opportunities that served his interests.

What kind of man did that make him?

Why did today feel like meeting her for the first time?

Brandon paused in his whittling, examining the piece of wood in his hand. It was beginning to take the rough shape of a bird—nothing fancy, just something to keep his fingers busy while he thought. The hickory was smooth beneath his thumb, solid and real in a way that grounded him when everything else felt uncertain.

He tried to pinpoint the exact moment things had shifted in his perspective. Had it been when she'd crouched beside the pumpkins in the field, her face lighting up with genuine wonder at something he saw every day? Or when she'd asked about turning the pumpkins to prevent flat spots, listening to his explanation with the kind of focused attention that made him feel like his knowledge actually mattered?

Maybe it was the way she'd looked at the warty gourds, finding beauty where most people saw imperfection. *Character is more interesting than conventional beauty, she'd said.*

Brandon set down the knife and rubbed his eyes with the heel of his hand. The exhaustion he'd been carrying for months felt different tonight—less like grief dragging him under and more like someone waking up from a long sleep, confused about where they were and how they'd gotten there.

The truth was, he hadn't really looked at any woman since Samantha left. Not looked-looked, anyway. He'd noticed people in passing, he'd been polite in conversations, but he'd kept himself closed off so tightly that nothing got in. He'd told himself it was self-preservation, protection from further disappointment.

But what if it was more than that? What if he'd been so busy guarding against pain that he'd shut out the chance for... what? Joy? Connection? The possibility that not every woman would see his life as something to run from?

The memory of Amanda's expression when she'd walked through the mum greenhouse came back to him with startling clarity. She'd looked at his mother's flowers with the same appreciation he'd seen on Helen's face when she tended them—the recognition of artistry, of care, of love made visible through growing things. Amanda had understood without being told that the greenhouse represented more than just plants. It represented Helen's passion, her skill, and her quiet way of adding beauty to the world.

Samantha had never looked at anything on the farm that way. She'd seen the buildings, the fields, and all the crops, but she'd never seen the heart behind them. Everything had been evaluated in terms of how it affected her—how early she had to get up, how it limited their social options, and how it tied them to one place when she was eager to explore the world.

Amanda, within one morning, had seen what Samantha had missed in eleven months of marriage.

Brandon resumed his whittling, taking longer, more careful strokes. The bird was beginning to look like something recognizable—a cardinal, maybe, though he hadn't planned it that way. His hands seemed to have their own ideas about what the wood wanted to become.

He thought back to high school again, trying to remember Amanda from those days. She'd been Rachel's friend, of course—they'd been inseparable since grade school. But Brandon's memories of that time were dominated by football practice, dating, and the social whirlwind that seemed to surround him without much effort on his part. Amanda had been there, in the peripheral vision of his teenage self, but always in Rachel's shadow, never demanding attention or making herself noticed.

Had he really been that self-absorbed? The question made him uncomfortable. Probably. He'd been a typical teenage jock, captain of the football team, homecoming king, and a young man focused on having fun. The world had felt full of possibilities back then, and he'd assumed those possibilities would always be there waiting for him whenever he decided to reach for them.

The sound of footsteps on gravel drew him from his reverie. He looked up to see a familiar figure walking down the drive from the direction of the farmhouse—Rachel, carrying a covered plate and moving with the purposeful stride that meant she had something on her mind.

"I brought you some of Mom's leftover chicken pot pie. Figured you probably hadn't eaten anything since lunch," she said as she approached the porch.

She wasn't wrong. Brandon had returned to the barn after Amanda left, intending to finish the repair work on the hay baler, but he'd found himself unable to concentrate. Instead, he'd cleaned tools that were already clean, rearranged equipment that was already organized, and generally accomplished nothing while his mind replayed every moment of his morning.

"Thanks," he said, setting down his whittling as Rachel climbed the three steps to the porch. "You didn't need to walk all the way out here, though."

"It's a nice evening for a walk," Rachel replied, settling into the chair beside his after she placed the plate of food on his side table. "Besides, I wanted to see how your grand tour went today."

Brandon shot her a sideways glance. "Mom fill you in?"

"Some. She mentioned that Amanda was excited about the festival and her typical fun-loving self and that you seemed to enjoy showing her around. She also said you all had lunch together."

"It was just lunch," Brandon said, picking up his knife again. "And festival stuff."

"Uh-huh." Rachel was quiet for a moment, watching him work. "So what are you making there?"

Brandon looked down at the piece of wood in his hands. "Started out as just something to do with my hands, looking like a bird now."

"Dad used to whittle when he was thinking through problems. Remember? He'd sit on the porch after dinner, working on some little project while he processed his day."

He did remember. How many evenings had he watched his father's hands shape wood while they talked about crops, weather, and the thousand small decisions that kept a farm running?

"Guess some things stick," he said.

They sat in silence for a few minutes, the mountain evening settling around them. The air carried the scent of cooling earth and the faint sweetness of late-season wildflowers.

"Amanda's really excited about this year's festival," Rachel said eventually.

"She has a lot of ideas."

"Good ideas?"

Brandon considered the question. "Yeah. Different from what's been done before, but good. She sees possibilities I wouldn't have thought of."

"She is gifted," Rachel said.

"She was... different today," he said, then stopped, unsure why he'd volunteered the information.

"Different how?"

"I'm still trying to figure that out. Just... enthusiastic. About everything. The pumpkins, the mums, even the warty gourds that most people think are ugly." Brandon shaped another curl of wood with his knife. "She sees things differently from most people."

"She sees the good in things. Always has. It's one of the things I love most about her."

The simple statement held layers of meaning, and Brandon felt his sister watching him.

"Brandon," Rachel said carefully, "can I ask you something?"

He nodded, not trusting his voice.

"What's going on in your head right now? And don't say 'nothing,' because I know you too well for that."

Brandon set down his whittling and stared out into the distant mountains. The question was fair, but he wasn't sure how to answer it. How did you explain that you felt like you'd been sleepwalking through your life for months, maybe years, and someone had just shaken you awake?

"I don't know," he said finally. "That's the honest answer. I don't know what's going on."

"Does it have to do with Amanda?"

The directness of the question hit him square in the chest. Rachel had never been one to dance around difficult topics.

"Maybe. Yes. I think so."

Rachel shifted in her chair, turning to face him more fully. "Want to talk about it?"

Brandon was quiet for a long moment, trying to organize thoughts that felt as scattered as leaves in a windstorm.

"I feel like I'm seeing her for the first time," he said eventually. "Which is stupid, because I've known her for years. She's been around forever. She was always here when we were kids. But today, when she was walking through the fields, asking questions about the crops, getting excited about festival decorations... it was like meeting a completely different person."

"Or maybe, like meeting the same person you've always known, but with your eyes actually open this time."

The observation stung because it was true. How many opportunities had he missed over the years to really see the people around him? How many conversations had he half-listened to? How many moments of connection had he let slip by because he was focused on something else?

"I think I've been asleep," he admitted. "For months now, maybe longer. Going through the motions but not really... present. Does that make sense?"

"Perfect sense," Rachel said. "Grief does that. So does disappointment. And you've had more than your share of both of those lately."

Brandon nodded, grateful that she understood.

"The thing is," he continued, "I don't know what to do with... this. Whatever this is. Amanda's your best friend. She's part of our community, our church. If I... if things went wrong..."

"You'd be risking more than just your own feelings," Rachel finished.

Brandon looked at her for a minute, trying to formulate a response. Then he shook his head and turned away. "I have no idea what's going on in my head right now. Let's just drop it."

"Nope. Talk."

He didn't say anything while thoughts and emotions twirled in his head. Was he losing his mind? Were the thoughts and feelings coursing through him right? Wrong? Should he even be feeling this way about his sister's best friend?

"Look, Rachel... with Samantha, when it ended, she left town. Clean break. But Amanda..." He gestured toward the lights of Laurel Ridge visible in the distance. "She's not going anywhere. And neither am I, if I even allow myself to... I don't know what I'm trying to say. But if I mess up, or say something wrong, or do something wrong... we all have to live with the consequences."

Rachel was quiet for several minutes, considering his words. When she spoke, her voice carried the wisdom of someone who'd thought deeply about love and loss and the courage required to risk both.

"You know what Dad used to say about the farm?" she asked.

"Which thing? He had a lot of sayings."

"That the biggest risk wasn't crop failure or bad weather or equipment breaking down. The biggest risk was being so afraid of losing what you had that you stopped planting new seeds."

"I remember."

"He said you could protect yourself from disappointment by not investing in anything new, but the cost was never having anything grow." Rachel leaned forward slightly, her voice gentle but firm. "Brandon, you've been protecting yourself from loss by not investing in life. But the cost is everything you might have gained."

"I'm not ready? What if I don't know how to do this anymore?"

"Then you learn. You take it slow, you are honest about where you are right now in the moment, and you trust that if it's meant to be, it will work out. And if it's not meant to be, you'll still be better off for having tried than for having done nothing."

"I miss him," he said quietly. "I miss being able to talk to him about things like this."

"Me too," Rachel said. "But he raised us to think for ourselves, and he raised us with faith that God has good plans for our lives. Even when we can't see them."

"She has me thinking I may want to try," he admitted quietly. "That's what scares me the most. I hadn't wanted anything in so long that I'd forgotten what it felt like. And now..."

"Now you remember," Rachel said softly.

"Yeah. Now I remember."

They sat together as full darkness settled over the mountains, the comfort of shared silence replacing the need for more words. Brandon thought about the morning's events, about Amanda's laughter and the way she'd looked at his family's work with genuine appreciation. He thought about her enthusiasm for the festival, her vision for bringing the community together, and the way she'd made even mundane conversation feel meaningful.

Most of all, he thought about the moment when she'd looked at him directly, without the careful distance he'd grown accustomed to seeing in people's eyes. She'd looked at him like he was someone worth knowing, someone whose thoughts and opinions mattered.

It had been a long time since anyone had looked at him that way.

"I should head back," Rachel said eventually, standing and stretching. "Love you, Brandon."

"Love you too, sis. Thanks for the food. And for listening."

"I'll always listen." She said as she paused at the top of the porch steps, looking back at him. "Brandon? Just stay open to possibilities, okay? And for what it's worth, I think Amanda would be a good friend for you. I think you might be good for her too, when you're ready."

After Rachel disappeared into the darkness, Brandon remained on the porch, turning the wooden cardinal over in his hands. The night air was cool against his skin, and the sounds of the countryside surrounded him.

For the first time in months, the solitude didn't feel like protection. It felt like an opportunity to think, to process, and to figure out what came next in his life.

Chapter 10

Amanda stared at the empty wooden platform stretched out before her like a blank canvas that mocked every creative instinct she possessed. The parade float trailer sat in the center of Whitaker's barn, its bare boards reflecting the morning light that filtered through the high windows. She sat down on its edge, her legs dangling over the side, clutching a steaming cup of coffee that Rachel had pressed into her hands when she'd arrived twenty minutes ago.

"So," Rachel said, settling beside her with her own mug. "We're really doing this."

"We're really doing this," Amanda confirmed, though her voice carried more uncertainty than conviction. "I'd really like to get the framework going so that when we get together with the rest of the volunteers on Monday, it's full steam ahead. I mean, how hard can it be? People build parade floats all the time."

Rachel shot her a sideways glance. "People who know what they're doing build parade floats all the time. We're people who had a really good idea and volunteered before thinking it through."

Amanda laughed despite her growing awareness of the challenge before them. "I love that about us. We leap first and figure out the landing later."

"Dad always said that was either courage or foolishness, and the only way to tell the difference was by the outcome. I'm hoping we land on the courage side of that equation."

"Okay," she said, pulling out her phone with the determination of someone about to scale Mount Everest. "Google time. How hard can aluminum framework construction be?"

Rachel brightened and produced her own phone. "Between the two of us and the entire internet, we've got this."

For the next thirty minutes, they dove into research with the intensity of graduate students cramming for finals. Amanda's phone screen filled with articles about tube connectors, load-bearing calculations, and weight distribution principles that might as well have been written in ancient Greek. She squinted at diagrams that showed metal tubing arranged in geometric patterns that looked both simple and impossibly complex.

"Listen to this," she said, reading from her screen. "'The critical factor in multi-level platform construction is ensuring adequate cross-bracing to prevent lateral movement under dynamic load conditions.' Dynamic load conditions—that's just people moving around, right?"

Rachel looked up from her phone, her brow furrowed in concentration. "I think so? But what's cross-bracing? And how much cross-bracing is adequate? These articles assume you already know what you're doing."

Amanda scrolled further down the page. "Oh, here we go. 'Flanged base connectors provide superior stability when properly anchored to the primary support structure.' See? Flanged base connectors. That sounds totally manageable."

"What's a flanged-base connector?"

"I have absolutely no idea, but I'm sure it's something Earl carries at the hardware store." Amanda set down her phone and gestured around them. "Picture this—we'll create these beautiful stations at different heights, connected by... flanged things... and cross-braced with... more flanged things."

Rachel dissolved into laughter. "Amanda, you sound like you're making up construction terms."

"I'm not making them up! They're real terms. I just don't know what they mean yet." Amanda jumped down from the trailer and began pacing, her hands moving as she talked. "But think about it—every building project starts with someone not knowing what flanged base connectors are, and then they figure it out, and then they build beautiful things."

"You're talking about flanged base connectors like they're a philosophical concept."

"Maybe they are! Maybe construction is just applied philosophy with better tools."

Rachel slid off the trailer and joined her friend's pacing. "Okay, so we've established that we need flanged base connectors, cross-bracing, and what else?"

Amanda consulted her phone again. "Something called EMT conduit—that's the aluminum tubing Brandon mentioned last week. Junction boxes for electrical if we want lights. Weather-resistant anchoring systems." She paused, looking up from the screen. "Rachel, do you know what any of this means?"

"Not a single word. But I love your confidence about it."

Amanda stopped pacing and faced her friend, suddenly struck by the absurdity of their situation. "We're standing in a barn, reading construction terminology on our phones, planning to build something neither of us has ever built before, for a festival that the entire town is counting on."

"When you put it like that, it sounds completely insane."

"It is completely insane." Amanda's face broke into a grin. "And somehow that makes me more excited about it."

Rachel shook her head, but she was smiling too. "You know what? You're right. This is exactly the kind of impossible project that turns out amazing because we're too stubborn to admit it's impossible."

"That's the spirit!" Amanda raised her coffee mug in a mock toast. "To being too stubborn for common sense."

"To flanged base connectors, whatever they are."

They clinked mugs and dissolved into laughter again; the sound echoing off the barn's high rafters. Amanda felt the familiar rush of excitement that came with tackling a new challenge. Yes, she was out of her depth. Yes, she had no idea what she was doing. But she was doing it with her best friend, in service of something that mattered to their community, and somehow that felt like enough.

Rachel returned to her phone, scrolling through more articles. "Okay, look at this diagram. I think the basic idea is that you create a skeleton framework first, then attach platforms at different levels."

Amanda peered over her shoulder at the screen. "That doesn't look so complicated. It's like... adult Tinkertoys."

"Expensive adult Tinkertoys that have to hold people without collapsing."

"Details." Amanda waved dismissively, then caught herself. "Okay, important details. Safety details. Details we should probably understand before we start building."

Rachel attempted to sketch what she was seeing on her phone screen, using a pen and the notepad she'd brought with her. Her drawing looked like abstract art created by someone who'd never seen the thing they were trying to represent.

"Is that supposed to be the framework?" Amanda asked, studying the lines and angles.

"It's my interpretation of the framework. Very artistic, don't you think?"

"It looks like a spiderweb."

Rachel held up her sketch, examining it critically. "It does. But I bet it would hold together."

Amanda tried to demonstrate what she thought a flanged base connector might look like, using elaborate hand gestures that grew more dramatic as her explanation became more confused. "So you take the base part, which is flanged—you know, with flanges—and you connect it to the thing that needs connecting, and then it's... connected."

"That was beautifully circular logic."

"I should have been an engineer."

"We could just admit that we need help from someone who actually knows what they're doing," Rachel said. "Brandon did offer to help."

"We're smart women. We can figure this out. Let's not bother him until we're desperate."

"Sure, we can figure this out. Eventually. Probably. Maybe." Rachel looked around the barn, taking in the tools and equipment.

The sound of someone approaching drew their attention toward the barn's entrance. Brandon appeared in the doorway, his work shirt dusty and his hair slightly mussed from whatever morning chores had occupied his time. He stopped when he saw them, his expression shifting from purposeful focus to curious amusement as he took in their phones, scattered papers, and the confusion on their faces.

"Having fun?" he asked, and Amanda caught the hint of a smile tugging at the corners of his mouth.

The question struck them both as hilariously understated given their current predicament, and they burst into laughter again. Amanda tried to compose herself, but every time she looked at Rachel's spider-web sketch or thought about her own dramatic flanged-base-connector demonstration, another wave of giggles overtook her.

Brandon waited patiently, leaning against the door frame with the air of someone accustomed to waiting out his sister's fits of hilarity.

"We're doing research," Amanda managed when she could finally speak. "Very serious, professional research into parade float construction techniques."

"I can see that," Brandon said gravely. "How's it going?"

"We've learned that flanged base connectors are very important," Rachel said, holding up her sketch. "And that cross-bracing prevents lateral movement under dynamic load conditions."

"Impressive." Brandon approached the trailer. "Mind if I take a look at what you've found?"

Amanda handed over her phone, suddenly self-conscious about her browser history full of basic construction questions. Brandon scrolled through the articles she'd bookmarked, nodding occasionally as he read.

He handed her phone back and walked over to a tool cabinet against the barn wall and returned with several pieces of metal tubing, various connectors, and small metal plates with holes in them. Amanda watched as he arranged the pieces on the trailer platform.

"This is EMT conduit," he said, holding up a length of aluminum tubing. "Electrical metallic tubing. It's lightweight, strong, and easy to work with for this kind of project."

He showed them several types of connectors, explaining how each one worked and when you'd use it. His voice was patient, informative, and completely free of the condescension Amanda sometimes encountered when asking men to explain things she didn't know.

"And this," he said, picking up one of the metal plates, "is a flanged base connector. The flange is just this flat part that spreads the load and gives you a surface to bolt it down to your platform."

Amanda stared at the simple piece of metal in his hand. "That's it? That's the mysterious flanged base connector?"

"That's it."

"It's so... practical," Rachel said, sounding slightly disappointed. "I was expecting something more exotic."

"Construction is usually more practical than exotic," Brandon said with a smile. "Though the end result can be pretty spectacular."

He spent the next twenty minutes walking them through the basics of framework construction, using the actual materials to demonstrate concepts they'd been struggling to understand from diagrams.

"The key is planning your load paths," he explained, sketching a quick diagram on Rachel's notepad. "You want the weight to flow down through the strongest parts of your structure to the trailer platform."

"Like a tree," Amanda said, suddenly understanding. "The branches support the leaves, but the trunk carries all the weight to the roots."

"Yep. Just like a tree." Brandon looked up from his sketching, meeting her eyes directly. "Good analogy."

The compliment caught Amanda off guard, leaving her smiling. When was the last time someone had praised her ability to grasp new concepts? At the shop, she was the expert. Here, she was the student—and Brandon's approval meant more than it probably should have.

"So what you're saying," Rachel interjected, "is that my spiderweb framework design might not have been structurally sound?"

Brandon glanced at her sketch and managed to keep his expression diplomatically neutral. "It shows creativity. Structural engineering usually requires a little less... artistic interpretation."

"Diplomatic," Amanda laughed. "You should be a teacher."

Brandon grinned.

"Look, how about if we all just drive into town? Get the materials, come back, and start on the basic framework," he said, setting down the metal tubing he'd been holding.

Amanda blinked, certain she'd misheard.

"You'd do that?" she asked.

He shrugged. "It's been a while since I built something that wasn't just farm related."

Rachel's face lit up with obvious delight. "Let's go, brother. I was dreading trying to explain flanged base connectors to Earl at the hardware store."

"Earl would have figured out what you needed... eventually," Brandon said with a grin.

"Are you sure?" Amanda asked. "I mean, I know you're busy with harvest preparations and everything."

"I'm sure. Let me go wash up and grab the truck keys. We can be at Earl's in twenty minutes and back here with supplies before lunch."

As he headed toward the barn doors, Rachel caught Amanda's eye and grinned. "Well, that was interesting."

"No doubt," Amanda said quietly, watching Brandon's retreating figure.

Ten minutes later, the three of them were walking toward Brandon's pickup truck, parked in the gravel area near the barn. Rachel claimed the middle seat, which put Amanda by the passenger window, watching the familiar landscape of Laurel Ridge roll past while listening to the comfortable sibling banter in the cab of the truck.

"Remember when we tried to build that tree fort when we were twelve?" Rachel was saying. "Dad found us with a pile of boards and a hammer, trying to nail everything together without any kind of plan."

"We had a plan," Brandon protested. "It just wasn't a good plan."

"Our plan was 'hammer boards together until they look like a fort.'"

"See? A plan."

Amanda laughed. "Did the fort work?"

"Define 'work,'" Rachel said. "It held together long enough for us to climb into it once before it collapsed."

"Dad made us tear it down and start over," Brandon added. "This time with blueprints, measurements, and proper joinery techniques."

"And the second time?"

"Still standing," they said simultaneously, then looked at each other and laughed.

Earl's Hardware occupied a corner building on Main Street, its green awning and hand-painted sign promising "Everything You Need to Fix Anything That's Broken."

Brandon led them through the store with the confidence of someone who'd been navigating its narrow aisles since childhood. He knew exactly where to find the EMT conduit, what aisle held the connectors, and which section contained the specialized hardware they'd need for the project.

"Mornin', Brandon," Earl called out from behind the counter. "Haven't seen you in here for a while."

"Mornin', Earl. Working on a project for the Fall Festival."

Earl's weathered face brightened with interest. "Festival project? What are you building?"

Brandon gestured toward Amanda. "Amanda's chairing the committee for the parade float this year. She's got some creative ideas."

Amanda felt a flutter of nervousness as Earl's attention focused on her.

"Well now," Earl said, his tone warming with approval. "What are you planning?"

As Amanda explained her vision for the multi-level blessing stations, Earl nodded along with growing enthusiasm. He asked intelligent questions about weight requirements, weather considerations, and assembly logistics that made it clear he understood both the creative and practical aspects of what they were attempting.

"Sounds ambitious," he said when she finished. "But doable. Brandon here's got the right idea with the EMT framework. Light, strong, and forgiving if you need to make adjustments."

They spent the next hour gathering materials, with Brandon explaining the purpose of each item as they added it to their cart. Amanda took notes on her phone, determined to understand not just what they were buying but why they needed each component. Earl contributed suggestions based on years of helping people, and Rachel served as the voice of practical concern, asking questions about timeline and complexity.

By the time they loaded everything into the truck bed, Amanda felt like she'd received a master class in basic construction principles. More than that, she felt genuinely excited about the building process.

The project no longer seemed impossibly complex—just challenging enough to be interesting.

"Thanks, Brandon," she said as they drove back toward the farm. "I know you've got a million other things you could be doing."

"I'd rather help than watch the two of you struggle," he replied simply.

Rachel looked at her brother, then looked over at her best friend and grinned. "It's gonna be a good day."

Amanda smiled. "I do believe you're right, my friend."

Chapter 11

Amanda surveyed the barn floor—lengths of aluminum tubing gleaming under the afternoon light, an array of connectors that now made perfect sense instead of resembling mysterious construction artifacts, and tools arranged with the kind of precision that spoke of Brandon's methodical approach to any project.

"All right," Brandon said, crouching beside the parade float platform with a measuring tape in hand. "The key is getting these anchor points exactly right. Once we drill into the deck, there's no going back."

Rachel stood nearby, holding three different types of connectors and studying them with the intense concentration of someone trying to solve a puzzle. "So the flanged ones go on the bottom, the straight connectors join the vertical pieces, and these T-shaped ones are for..."

"Corners and direction changes," Amanda finished, pleased that Earl's impromptu hardware education was sticking. She pulled out her phone to reference the notes she'd taken, then looked up to find Brandon watching her with something that might have been approval.

"You're a quick study," he said simply.

Amanda smiled as she approached the platform. "I had good teachers. Plus, I'm motivated—this float is going to tell our town's story, and I want to make sure the structure can support the vision."

Brandon measured and marked the first anchor point, his movements economical and sure. "Tell me again about these blessing stations. I want to understand how you're planning to distribute the weight."

Amanda's enthusiasm bubbled up as she gestured around the platform. "The central area will feature our main harvest display—traditional autumn abundance with pumpkins, cornstalks, and some of your mother's beautiful mums arranged in vintage baskets. That's our heaviest section, so it stays in the middle for stability."

She moved to one corner of the platform, her mind's eye already seeing her vision taking shape. "Over here, we'll have the 'Community Business Blessings' station. I'm thinking of a creative display showcasing local shops—maybe miniature storefronts or product displays from different Main Street businesses. Lightweight but visually interesting."

"Smart," Brandon said, making another mark on the platform. "What about the other corners?"

"The 'Heritage Families' station will honor our founding families—the Whitakers, the Talbots, and the Hendersons. Historical photos, maybe some heirloom items people are willing to loan for the parade. And the third station, across the back..." Amanda paused, feeling suddenly self-conscious about the last element of her vision.

"And?" Brandon prompted, looking up from his measuring.

"The 'Love in Action' station. Celebrating the ways our community takes care of each other. The volunteer fire department, the church food pantry, neighbors helping neighbors during difficult times." She met his eyes directly. "The kind of love that shows up with casseroles and prayers and willing hands."

Something shifted in Brandon's expression—a softening around his eyes that made Amanda's breath catch slightly.

"Dad would have loved that," he said quietly. "He always said the measure of a community wasn't its size but its heart."

Rachel cleared her throat. "Right, well, Dad also would have told us to stop talking and start building, so..." She held up her handful of connectors. "Where do I put these mysterious metal things?"

Brandon laughed. "Let's start with the vertical supports. Amanda, can you hold this upright while I get the base connector positioned?"

The next hour passed in a rhythm of measurement, adjustment, and gradual assembly. Amanda found herself falling into an easy partnership with Brandon, anticipating when he needed an extra pair of hands and learning to read his gestures. When he pointed toward a specific type of connector, she knew which one he meant. When he needed someone to steady a piece while he tightened bolts, she was already in position.

Rachel provided running commentary on their progress, her observations ranging from genuinely helpful to hilariously off-base. "That looks very... structural," she announced when they completed the first corner assembly. "It's like an adult Erector Set, except with more potential for actual injury."

"The goal is no injuries," Brandon said mildly, testing the stability of their work.

Amanda ran her hand along the aluminum framework, impressed by how solid it felt despite being lightweight. "This is going to be perfect. I can already picture how the blessing stations will look at different heights."

"Speaking of heights," Brandon said, consulting the rough sketch Amanda had made, "you'll want your main harvest display elevated enough to be visible from street level, but not so high that it becomes top-heavy. I'm thinking we build the center platform about eighteen inches up, with the corner stations at twelve inches."

"Whatever you say. You know what you're doing."

Brandon's cheeks colored slightly at the praise. "Just common sense and stubbornness, mostly."

They were positioning the framework for the second corner when the sound of the farmhouse's back door reached them, followed by Helen's voice calling across the yard. "I thought you all might need some refreshments!"

Amanda looked up to see Helen approaching the barn, carrying a tray that held a pitcher and glasses, and a plate of cookies balanced carefully beside them.

"Wow, you didn't need to—" Amanda began.

"Nonsense," Helen said, setting the tray down on a nearby work-bench. "Hard workers need fuel, and I could hear the construction sounds all the way from the kitchen. Besides, I wanted to see how this project was coming along."

Rachel immediately gravitated toward the cookies. "Mom, you're an angel. All this measuring and connecting has made me hungry."

"Everything makes you hungry," Brandon said as he walked to the tray. "Thanks, Mom."

Amanda accepted the glass of lemonade Helen offered; the cold liquid was a welcome relief. The lemonade was excellent—tart enough to be refreshing, sweet enough to satisfy, and carrying a subtle flavor that spoke of fresh lemons.

"This is delicious," Amanda said. "And these cookies..."

She bit into one of Helen's offerings, and the warm flavors of brown butter and cinnamon immediately transported her to childhood visits to her grandmother's kitchen.

"Snickerdoodles," Helen said with satisfaction. "James's favorite. Brandon's too, though he pretends he's too grown-up to have favorites anymore."

"I never said that," Brandon protested, reaching for a second cookie. "I just said I was capable of eating other types of cookies too."

"Such broad culinary horizons," Rachel teased.

Helen walked closer to examine their work, and Amanda felt a flutter of nervousness.

"Well, this is impressive," Helen said, running her hand along one of the vertical supports. "Very professional-looking. Plenty of room for creative displays and a few people to ride along."

Relief flooded through Amanda. "Brandon's done all the work. I had all these ideas but no clue how to make them structurally sound."

"He gets that from his father," Helen said, and Amanda caught the quick look of pride she shot toward her son. "James always said the best projects combined vision with craftsmanship. Looks like you three have that covered."

Helen rolled up her sleeves. "Now, what can I do to help? These old hands still remember how to use tools."

"Mom, you don't need to—" Brandon started.

"I'm bored, and I want to help," Helen said firmly. "This is for our community, and besides, it's been too long since I worked on a project like this. James and I used to love building things together."

Amanda watched the interplay between mother and son, noting the way Brandon's resistance melted immediately into acceptance. Family dynamics fascinated her—the unspoken communications, the deep knowledge of each other's moods and motivations, and the way love expressed itself through everything from fresh cookies to gentle corrections.

"We're about to start on the corner platform assembly," Amanda said. "If you'd like to help with that?"

Helen beamed. "I'd love to."

The afternoon shifted into an even more comfortable rhythm with Helen's addition to their team. She proved to be every bit as capable as her son, her movements sure and economical as she helped position framework pieces and steady connections while Brandon worked with tools. Amanda found herself thinking that this must be what a true family business looked like—multiple generations working side by side, each contributing their own skills and perspectives.

"Hand me that level, would you?" Brandon asked, and Amanda wasn't sure if he was talking to her or his mother until she realized Helen was already reaching for a different tool.

Amanda grabbed the small yellow level from the workbench and passed it to Brandon, their fingers brushing briefly as he took it from her, sending an unexpected jolt of awareness through her.

"Thanks," he said as he checked the alignment of their latest assembly.

Get a grip, Amanda told herself. *It's a construction project, not a romantic scene in a movie.*

But as she watched Brandon work, she thought about how deeply attractive it was watching a man work.

"Perfect," Brandon announced, checking the level reading. "This corner's solid."

They moved around the platform in clockwise fashion, building each corner assembly and connecting them with horizontal framework pieces. Amanda's back was beginning to ache from bending and lifting, and she noticed Rachel wincing slightly as she stretched her arms over her head.

"How much more?" Rachel asked, surveying their progress. "Not that I'm complaining, but I think I've discovered muscles I forgot I had."

"Just the center platform, and we'll have the basic framework complete," Brandon said. "This is the trickiest part, though. Has to be level and stable enough to support the weight of your main display."

Amanda studied the space they'd created, mentally arranging pumpkins and cornstalks and her Helen's beautiful mums. The framework was taking shape exactly as she'd envisioned it, maybe even better.

"I can't believe we're actually building this," she said. "This morning it was just a bunch of metal tubes and mysterious connectors, and now..."

"Now it's a bunch of metal tubes and mysterious connectors arranged in a specific pattern," Rachel said. "Though I admit it's pretty impressive."

"Now it's the foundation for something beautiful," Helen corrected gently. "That's what a good framework does—it holds up the vision so everyone can see it."

They positioned the center platform framework pieces, and Amanda found herself working directly opposite Brandon as they guided the aluminum tubing into place. This close, she could see the concentration in his blue eyes and the slight furrow between his brows as he focused on getting the alignment exactly right.

"Steady," he murmured, adjusting his grip. "Hold it right there."

Amanda held her position, acutely aware of his hands just inches from hers on the metal framework. She could smell the faint scent of his cologne and see the small scar on his left hand that she'd never noticed before.

"Got it," Brandon said, securing the connection. He looked up, meeting her eyes. "Good teamwork."

Amanda managed to nod.

Rachel's voice cut through the moment. "Are you two going to stare at each other all day, or can we finish this thing before my arms fall off?"

Heat rose in Amanda's cheeks as she stepped back from the framework, suddenly self-conscious.

Focus on the project, she reminded herself. *That's why you're here.*

But as they worked through the final assembly steps, Amanda couldn't quite shake the awareness that had settled over her. Every time Brandon handed her a tool, every time he explained a construction technique, every time his laughter mixed with Rachel's more animated responses, she felt herself falling a little deeper in appreciation of the man he was.

Kind. Patient. Competent. Still grieving but not broken. Strong enough to carry heavy loads, gentle enough to teach without condescension, and apparently immune to the effect he was having on her equilibrium.

"There," Brandon said, standing back and surveying their work. "Basic framework complete."

Amanda stepped back as well, looking at what they'd accomplished in a single afternoon. The aluminum skeleton of her vision stood sturdy and purposeful on the parade float platform, ready to support whatever creative displays she and the volunteers could dream up.

"It's perfect," she said, and meant it. "I can already see exactly how everything will look."

Helen wiped her hands on a shop rag and smiled with obvious satisfaction. "You all did beautiful work. This is going to be quite a parade float."

"We did," Amanda agreed, then realized something. "I need to call a few people tonight. I forgot that Tom Bradley and his son offered to cut and assemble wooden platforms for the seating areas and other structures we need. I should let them know the framework's ready for them to take measurements."

"Tom does good work," Brandon said. "He'll have those platforms cut and ready to install pretty quickly, I imagine."

"Which means the volunteers will have everything they need to start decorating," Amanda said, excitement bubbling up again. "This is really happening."

Rachel stretched and groaned theatrically. "This is really happening, and I'm really going to be sore tomorrow. But look what we built!" She gestured proudly toward the framework. "I helped build that. With flanged base connectors and everything."

"You did," Amanda laughed. "And you'll never look at aluminum tubing the same way again."

"I'll never look at hardware stores the same way again," Rachel replied with a grin.

Amanda gathered her notes and phone, glancing around the barn to make sure they hadn't left tools scattered about.

Brandon was securing the toolbox, his movements methodical and careful. Helen was gathering the empty lemonade glasses, humming something under her breath that sounded like an old hymn. Rachel was taking a final photograph of their completed work with her phone, probably planning to share it with anyone who would listen to her construction adventure stories.

It had been, Amanda realized, a nearly perfect afternoon. Hard work, good company, tangible progress toward a goal that mattered. The kind of day that reminded you why small-town life was worth the sometimes claustrophobic familiarity, why community projects were worth the coordination headaches, and why some things were worth the risk of caring about them.

"Thank you guys so much," she said, addressing all three of them but looking directly at Brandon. "I couldn't have done any of this without your help."

"You could have figured it out," Brandon said quietly. "Might have taken longer, might have involved more trial and error, but you'd have found a way. I imagine you don't give up on things that matter to you."

The observation, delivered in his matter-of-fact tone, hit Amanda with unexpected force. Was that how he saw her? As someone who persisted until she found solutions? Someone who didn't give up?

"Monday evening should be interesting," Helen said, breaking into Amanda's thoughts. "The volunteers are going to be so excited when they see the float. You've given them something substantial to work with."

"I think they're going to love it," Amanda agreed.

As they walked toward the barn entrance, Amanda was reluctant to end their day together. The work had been satisfying, yes, but more than that, she'd felt useful and needed.

Brandon paused at the barn door, looking back at their completed framework. "You know, I think Dad would have approved."

"I think he would have loved it," Helen said softly.

The September evening was cooling as they stepped outside, and Amanda realized with surprise that she'd lost track of time completely. The afternoon had passed in a pleasant way that work sometimes did when you enjoyed both the task and the company.

"I'm gonna head home, call Tom about those platforms, and probably work on some more festival stuff this evening," she said, though part of her wanted to linger.

"Drive safely," Helen said, giving her a quick hug. "It's been good for all of us to work on something together again."

"Thanks for the lemonade and cookies," Amanda replied. "And for jumping in to help. I loved having you work with us."

Rachel bounced over for her own hug. "Love ya, Amanda!"

Amanda looked at Brandon. "Monday evening, six o'clock?"

"Six o'clock," he confirmed. "I'll make sure the barn's ready for the invasion."

She laughed at his choice of words. "Invasion might be exactly the right term. I think our group of volunteers is excited to begin decorating."

"Good," Brandon said, and Amanda thought she caught something that might have been anticipation in his voice. "Enthusiasm produces good things."

Chapter 12

Brandon cast his line into the deeper pool where the narrow river curved, the motion as automatic as breathing after twenty-plus years of fishing this same stretch of water. The sun filtered through the canopy of leaves overhead, creating shifting patterns of light and shadow on the water's surface. A red-winged blackbird called from the cattails on the opposite bank, answered by another somewhere downstream.

His father had taught him to fish here when he was seven, standing behind him on this same rocky outcrop, guiding small hands through the rhythm of cast and retrieve. *Patience, son. The fish will come when they're ready, not when you want them to.*

A bass rose near the far bank, concentric circles spreading outward from where it had taken an insect off the surface. This river held memories in every eddy and pool—summers when he and Rachel had caught crawdads under the rocks in a shallow area, camping trips when Dad had shown them how to cook fish over an open fire, and quiet mornings when fishing had been less about catching anything than about having space to think.

The sound of laughter drifted through the trees, distant but unmistakable. Brandon paused, listening. Rachel's laugh rang out clear, followed by another voice that made something jump in his chest. Amanda.

Brandon reeled in his line and set down his rod, turning toward the sound. Through the screen of trees, he could make out three figures making their way along the old deer path that connected his cabin to the river. Rachel led the way with her typical confidence, Helen followed with her careful attention to where she stepped, and Amanda brought up the rear, carrying what looked like pizza boxes.

"Brandon!" Rachel called out when she spotted him. "We brought lunch!"

He stood up from his rocky perch, brushing dirt off his jeans. "What are you all doing here?"

"Looking for you, silly," Rachel announced cheerfully as they reached the riverbank. "We went to church this morning, and afterward we were going to go out for lunch, but then I had the brilliant idea to order pizza and eat with my hermit brother instead."

Helen stepped carefully over a root, her eyes taking in the fishing setup. "I missed having you in church with me this morning," she said without reproach, just simple honesty. "But I know this is your place of peace too."

Amanda shifted the pizza boxes in her arms, looking uncertain. "I hope we're not interrupting. Rachel said you wouldn't mind, but if you'd rather have your alone time..."

"No," Brandon said, surprised by how quickly and firmly the word came out. "I mean, it's fine. I wasn't catching anything anyway."

"Good," Rachel said, "because I'm starving, and this pizza smells incredible. Where should we set up the feast?"

Brandon looked around the riverbank, then up toward his cabin visible through the trees. "The back porch."

"Perfect," Helen said.

Brandon started collecting his tackle, acutely aware of Amanda watching him work.

"Did you catch anything?"

"A few. I let 'em go." He gestured toward the pool where he'd been fishing. "I mostly fish to relax."

Amanda's expression softened with understanding.

They made their way up the gentle slope toward his cabin, Helen and Rachel chatting easily about church gossip and festival plans. Brandon found himself matching Amanda's pace without conscious thought.

"I've never seen your cabin," Amanda said as they approached the back porch. "Rachel mentioned how beautiful it is, but..."

"It's nothing fancy," Brandon said quickly. "Just functional."

"Sometimes functional is the most beautiful," Amanda replied.

The comment stayed with him as they climbed the three steps to his back porch. Rachel and Helen were already raiding his kitchen, gathering paper plates and napkins.

"Brandon, do you have any bottles of water?" Helen called.

"Should be some in the fridge," he replied, setting down his fishing gear.

Amanda placed the pizza boxes on the wooden table and looked out over the view—rolling land that stretched toward tree-covered ridges, the river winding through the bottom land, and in the distance, the blue haze of mountains that marked the horizon. Her face lit up with genuine appreciation.

"This is gorgeous," she said. "How do you ever leave this place?"

"Some days it's hard."

"I can imagine. If I had a view like this, I'd probably never get any work done. I'd just sit here and stare."

Rachel emerged from the house carrying paper plates and a handful of napkins. "That's exactly what he does. Mom and I worry he's going to turn into a piece of porch furniture."

"There are worse things," Brandon said mildly.

Helen followed with water bottles and a dish towel for cleaning up. "Brandon, would you like to say grace, or shall I?"

"You go ahead, Mom."

Helen's prayer was simple and heartfelt, thanking God for the food, for family time, and for the gift of unexpected fellowship. Brandon found himself listening to the familiar words with new attention, hearing gratitude for things he'd been taking for granted.

The pizza was excellent—loaded with pepperoni and sausage from Sue's Pizza in town, still warm despite the journey. They ate and talked easily; the conversation flowed from yesterday's framework success to tomorrow's volunteer session.

"I spoke with Tom Bradley after church this morning," Amanda said between bites. "He's coming in the morning to install the wood pieces on the float. Pastor Andrew is going to come and help him as well."

"That's good," Brandon said. "He'll have everything ready to go so you and the volunteers can really get working on the float."

She grinned. "I can't wait. It's going to be so much fun."

"What's your favorite part of the Harvest of Blessings theme?" Helen asked.

Amanda considered the question while she tore her pizza into smaller pieces. "The 'Love in Action' station, I think. There's something powerful about celebrating the ways people take care of each other. It's easy to focus on big gestures, but it's really the everyday kindness that holds communities together."

Brandon studied her face as she talked, noting the way her eyes brightened when she discussed something she cared about. There was depth to her enthusiasm and genuine conviction behind her festival vision.

"Like when Mrs. Hinkle organized meal delivery for the Fletcher family when Bill was in the hospital," Helen said. "Or the way the youth group shovels driveways for the elderly every winter."

"Exactly. Those are the stories worth telling." Amanda took a sip of water. "I want people to look at our float and feel proud of what we've built together here in Laurel Ridge."

"Dad would have loved that," Brandon said. "He always said the best measure of a place wasn't its buildings but its people."

Helen's eyes misted slightly. "He would have been right in the thick of tomorrow night's decorating session, probably taking over and driving everyone crazy."

"He wouldn't have been able to help himself," Rachel agreed with affection. "Remember when he decided the church nativity scene needed better lighting? He spent days rewiring the entire stable setup."

"And then it rained opening night and shorted out half the circuits," Brandon added, smiling at the memory. "But he had backup power supplies ready to go within minutes."

"Always prepared for everything," Helen said fondly.

"He was such a good man," Amanda said.

"He was," Brandon said simply. "Some days I still reach for the phone to ask him a question about the farm or to tell him something interesting that happened."

"That's love. The kind that doesn't stop just because someone's not physically here with us anymore."

The observation hit Brandon square in the chest. He'd been thinking of his continued desire for conversations with his father as a weakness or inability to let go. Amanda saw them as connection, love that transcended physical presence.

Helen began gathering empty plates, and Rachel jumped up to help, both women moving with the efficient coordination of family cleanup routines.

"This really is peaceful," Amanda said, gazing out toward the mountains.

"It's been... refuge, I guess. Especially this year."

"Everyone needs refuge sometimes. There's wisdom in knowing when to retreat and regroup." She paused, then added carefully, "And there's wisdom in knowing when you're ready to venture out and live again."

Brandon looked at her directly, struck by her insight. "I used to think I had everything figured out," he said, surprising himself with the admission. "Farm, family, future. All mapped out in neat little plans."

"And now?"

"Now I'm not sure planning is the answer. Maybe some things are too important to plan. Maybe they just have to... unfold."

Amanda nodded thoughtfully. "My grandma used to say that when we make plans, God laughs."

"I remember hearing my grandparents say the same thing."

"She also used to say that the best things in life usually happen when we're paying attention to something else entirely."

Rachel's voice drifted out from the kitchen. "Brandon, where do you keep your leftover containers?"

"Cabinet above the coffeemaker," he called back.

"We're leaving you the extra pizza," Helen said. "Save you some cooking later this week."

Amanda began gathering napkins and empty water bottles. "I should probably head out soon too. I promised my parents I'd stop by this evening."

Brandon felt an unexpected pang of disappointment. The afternoon had passed too quickly, the conversation too easily. He wasn't ready for their time together to end.

"How are your parents doing?" Helen asked as she wiped down the table.

"Good. Dad's working on a kitchen renovation for the Johnsons, and Mom's been sewing up a storm, making baby quilts to donate for the church auction during the festival."

"I bet they're proud of you for stepping up and volunteering to help with the festival," Brandon said. "It's an ambitious job for sure."

Amanda's cheeks colored slightly at the praise. "I just hope I can pull it off. There are so many moving pieces."

"You will," Rachel said, returning from inside the cabin. "And we're all going to help make sure it happens."

They stepped down off the porch, and Brandon walked beside Amanda toward the farmhouse.

"Thanks for letting us crash your fishing expedition," Amanda said.

"No problem; it was worth the pizza and the company."

When they reached Amanda's car, Helen hugged Amanda goodbye, followed by Rachel's more exuberant embrace. Brandon stood slightly apart, unsure.

Amanda solved the dilemma by stepping forward and touching his arm briefly. "See ya tomorrow?

"Yep, I'll be sure and watch for Tom tomorrow and offer him a hand with installing the wood pieces on the float.

"Good." Her hand lingered for just a moment before she stepped back. "Enjoy the rest of your weekend."

Brandon watched her car disappear down the driveway, then hugged his mom and sister before heading home.

He climbed the porch steps and settled into his usual chair, looking out over the view that had been his constant companion.

A hawk circled overhead, riding thermals up from the heated valley floor. Brandon watched its lazy spirals against the deepening blue sky and thought about patience, about timing, about the way some things couldn't be rushed or planned but simply had to be allowed to unfold in their own season.

Maybe Amanda's grandmother had been right. Maybe the best things did happen when you were paying attention to something else entirely. And maybe, just maybe, he was finally ready to pay attention to whatever came next.

Chapter 13

Brandon set his sandwich down on the plate—turkey and Swiss on his mother's homemade wheat bread—and reached for his glass of sweet tea. The ice had mostly melted in the September warmth, but the drink still carried enough chill to be refreshing. Across the small porch table, Helen worked on her own sandwich, humming something under her breath that might have been an old hymn or might have been nothing at all.

The early Monday afternoon stretched around them, peaceful in the way that only farm life could provide. Somewhere in the distance, employees were working in the back fields, their voices carrying occasionally on the breeze but too far away to make out actual words.

"Tom and Pastor Andrew should be here soon," Helen said, glancing at the kitchen clock visible through the window.

Brandon nodded, taking another bite of sandwich. The bread was perfect—soft but substantial, the kind that only came from years of perfecting a recipe. His mother had been making this same bread for as long as he could remember, every Tuesday and Friday without fail, filling the farmhouse with the warm scent of yeast and flour.

"I made extra sandwiches," Helen continued, a note of satisfaction in her voice. "Just in case they haven't eaten."

"They're bringing wood pieces for the float, Mom. Not moving in. I doubt they'll need—"

The rumble of a diesel engine cut through his protest, and Helen's face brightened with the particular expression she wore when company arrived. Brandon recognized the sound of Tom Bradley's truck; the distinctive rattle of the toolbox in the bed was unmistakable after years of hearing it pull into their drive for various projects.

"Perfect timing," Helen said, already standing and smoothing her apron. "I'll get those extra sandwiches."

Brandon watched his mother disappear into the house, then turned his attention to the truck pulling up near the barn. Through the windshield, he could make out Tom's weathered face beneath his ever-present John Deere cap, and beside him, Pastor Andrew Whitman's younger profile.

Both men climbed out as Brandon descended the porch steps. Tom Bradley stood about five-foot-ten with the solid build of someone who'd spent forty years in construction. His handshake had the kind of strength that came from actual work, not gym equipment, and his face carried lines that spoke of both laughter and long hours in the sun.

"Brandon," Tom said, extending his hand. "Good to see you, son."

"Tom." Brandon shook the offered hand, then turned to Pastor Andrew. "Pastor."

Andrew Whitman was everything a young pastor should be—earnest, energetic, and genuinely interested in his congregation's lives. At thirty-four, he still had the slight build of his seminary days, though church potlucks had started filling him out some. His handshake was firm but not competitive, and his smile reached his eyes in a way that suggested authentic warmth rather than professional courtesy.

"Brandon, thanks for having us out," Andrew said. "Tom's been telling me about the float framework you all built. I'm eager to see it."

"You boys haven't eaten lunch yet, have you?" Helen called from the porch. "I've got sandwiches made, and there's fresh sweet tea."

Tom's face lit up. "Helen, you didn't need to—"

"Nonsense. Can't have you working on empty stomachs. Come on up here and eat something before you start hauling all those heavy pieces around."

Brandon caught the look that passed between Tom and Andrew—the universal expression of men who knew better than to argue with a determined woman. They followed Helen's directive, climbing the porch steps with the obedience of schoolboys.

Soon they were settled around the porch table, Helen's extra sandwiches distributed on paper plates. The sweet tea had been replenished in the pitcher with fresh ice, and Helen had added a plate of cookies that Brandon hadn't even known existed until she set them on the table.

"These are incredible, Helen," Andrew said after his first bite of sandwich. "Is this homemade bread?"

"Made it Friday," Helen said with modest pride. "Nothing fancy, just wheat bread."

"Nothing fancy, she says," Tom shook his head. "My wife's been trying to get bread to turn out like this for twenty years. Says Helen must have made a deal with the angel of baking."

Helen laughed, the sound carrying across the yard. "Tell Sharon the secret is patience. You can't rush good bread any more than you can rush a good tomato."

The conversation flowed easily around the table, the way it did when people who'd known each other for years gathered without agenda or urgency. Tom asked about the farm's preparation for pumpkin season, Helen inquired after Tom's daughter, who'd just started her junior year at Marshall University, and Andrew mentioned the upcoming blessing of the animals service that always drew interesting participants.

"Last year someone brought a snake," Andrew said, shaking his head with remembered amusement. "My wife about climbed into the pulpit when it started moving during the prayer."

"That was Eddie Morrison's boy," Tom said. "Kid's got a whole collection. His mama was mortified."

"God created serpents too... though I'll admit, I wish he never had created those vile things... I can't stand snakes," Helen said with a shudder. His mother had never been fond of snakes, blessing or no blessing.

"Speaking of blessings," Tom said, wiping his mouth with a napkin, "Amanda's vision for this float is something else. She must have been out to my workshop three times in the last week, measuring and sketching and adjusting her plans. That girl's got more energy than a whole kindergarten class."

Brandon's hand stilled on his glass. Just the mention of Amanda's name sent an unexpected current through him, like touching an electric fence.

"She's certainly dedicated," Andrew agreed. "She came by the church office several times too, wanting to coordinate the blessing stations with our ministry themes. I don't think I've ever seen anyone put so much thought into a parade float or the décor she's envisioning for the town."

"That's Amanda," Helen said fondly. "Even as a little girl, when she and Rachel would plan their pretend tea parties, Amanda would have every detail perfect. Matching napkins, flowers arranged just so, even a proper menu written out in her best handwriting."

Brandon found himself picturing a young Amanda, maybe eight or nine, with blonde hair in pigtails, arranging miniature place settings with the same focused intensity she now brought to festival planning. The image was unexpectedly endearing.

"Her daddy's the same way," Tom observed. "Amos Baker's the most meticulous carpenter I know. Measures three times, cuts once, and the cut's still perfect. Apple didn't fall far from that tree."

"Speaking of Amanda," Andrew said, his tone casual but his eyes finding Brandon's, "she mentioned you've been incredibly helpful with the technical aspects of the float construction."

Brandon shrugged, uncomfortable with the praise. "Just basic framework. Nothing complicated."

"That's not what I heard," Tom said with a knowing grin. "Amanda said you solved problems in five minutes that would have taken her hours to figure out on the internet. Said you were a natural teacher too."

Heat crept up Brandon's neck. "She was a quick learner."

"I'm looking forward to seeing what you all created," Andrew said. "The whole town's buzzing about this year's festival. Feels like there's new energy around it."

"Change can be good," Helen said, though Brandon caught the quick glance she shot his way. "Sometimes we need someone with fresh eyes to help us see possibilities we've been missing."

The observation hung in the air for a moment, carrying more weight than a simple comment about festival planning. Brandon focused on finishing his sandwich.

"Well," Tom said, pushing back from the table, "that truck isn't going to unload itself. Thank you for lunch, Helen. Hit the spot perfectly."

They all stood, Helen gathering plates while the men headed toward Tom's truck.

The truck bed was packed with precisely cut wooden platforms, each piece labeled in Tom's neat handwriting—"Blessing Station 1," "Seating Platform A," "Corner Support Right." The craftsmanship was evident even in these functional pieces, with edges sanded smooth, corners perfectly squared, everything speaking of Tom's decades of experience.

"Your dad would have loved this," Tom said quietly as they began unloading the first platform. "James always said the festival brought out the best in Laurel Ridge."

Brandon's hands tightened on the wood, but he managed to keep his voice steady. "He did love it. Used to start planning his contributions in August."

"I remember the year he convinced half the town to help build that massive harvest arch for Main Street," Tom chuckled. "Must have been fifteen feet tall, covered in corn stalks and pumpkins. Took a dozen men to move it into place."

"I remember that," Andrew said, lifting his end of the platform. "I'd just started dating Lily, and she made me volunteer to help. First time I met your father, actually. He spent twenty minutes explaining the proper way to secure corn stalks so they wouldn't shed everywhere."

Brandon smiled at the memory. "Dad had opinions about everything. And he wasn't shy about sharing them."

"Good opinions, though," Tom said. "Man knew what he was about."

They worked in a comfortable rhythm, unloading platforms and supports, carrying them into the barn where the float framework waited. Brandon found himself relaxing into the familiar pattern of physical work shared with other men, the simple satisfaction of moving objects from one place to another, progress measured in emptying truck beds and filling barn space.

"Quite an operation you've got here," Andrew observed, looking around the barn's interior. "This is impressive."

The aluminum framework rose from the trailer base like the skeleton of some benign creature, all clean angles and purposeful engineering. Tom walked around it slowly, running his hand along the supports, testing connections with the practiced eye of someone who understood structural integrity.

"This is solid work," he pronounced. "Amanda said you designed this, Brandon?"

"Just followed basic engineering principles. Nothing special."

"Nothing special, he says," Tom shook his head. "This framework could hold three times the weight Amanda's planning to put on it. That's not basic—that's professional grade."

Andrew was studying the structure with interest. "The different levels for the blessing stations—that was Amanda's idea?"

"All her," Brandon confirmed. "She's got this vision of telling Laurel Ridge's story through different heights and perspectives. Like a three-dimensional scrapbook or something."

"That's actually beautiful," Andrew said thoughtfully. "Height as a metaphor for spiritual growth. The higher you climb, the better your perspective becomes."

Tom started measuring the platforms against the framework, making small marks with a pencil he pulled from behind his ear. "These should fit perfectly. Might need some minor adjustments, but nothing my saw can't handle."

As they worked to position the first platform, Andrew mentioned casually, "This reminds me of yesterday's sermon on building solid foundations. Paul's first letter to the Corinthians, where he talks about being careful how we build."

Brandon's hands stilled for just a moment. Yesterday's sermon. A sermon he hadn't heard because he hadn't been in church. Again.

Andrew continued, seemingly oblivious to Brandon's reaction. "The passage talks about how each person's work will be shown for what it is. Some build with gold and silver; some with wood and hay. But it's really about the foundation underneath it all."

"Good message," Tom said, tightening a clamp. "Sharon mentioned it at lunch. Said it made her think about what we're building in our own lives, not just our houses."

Brandon focused on holding the platform steady, but he could feel Andrew's eyes on him.

"I haven't been there to hear your sermons lately," Brandon admitted.

"I know," Andrew replied simply. No accusations, no disappointment, just acknowledgment.

"Forgot my level," Tom said. "Be right back."

The barn fell quiet, and Andrew leaned against the trailer, his posture relaxed but his attention clearly focused.

"How are you doing, Brandon? Really doing?"

The directness of the question made Brandon look away. He'd gotten used to people dancing around his grief, making vague inquiries about "how things were going" without really wanting answers. Andrew's tone suggested he actually wanted to know.

"I'm managing."

"Managing and living aren't the same thing."

Brandon looked up sharply, but Andrew's expression held no condemnation, only genuine concern.

"No," Brandon admitted. "They're not."

Andrew nodded, letting the acknowledgment sit between them for a moment. "You know, I've been meaning to ask you something about the farm. Lily's sister is coming to visit with her kids next week. They're from Cincinnati, and the children have never really experienced a working farm. I was hoping to bring them out when you open to the public, but I realized I don't really know much about what you offer here. Would you mind giving me a tour? Help me understand what would be best for city kids who think milk comes from grocery stores?"

The request was reasonable, pastoral even—Andrew looking out for his extended family. But something in the timing, the way he asked it just as Tom conveniently remained absent, suggested a deeper intention.

"Sure," Brandon heard himself say. "We can walk through the areas we've set up for visitors."

They left the barn, stepping into the afternoon sunlight that had deepened from bright white to mellow gold. Brandon led them toward the corn maze entrance, where a wooden sign Rachel had painted announced, "Get Lost and Find Your Way!" in cheerful orange letters.

"We've been working on this for weeks," Brandon explained, his tour guide reflexes taking over. "Eight acres total, with three different routes. The children's path is shorter, maybe twenty minutes if they don't get too turned around. The adult maze can take an hour if you really get lost."

"Must take incredible planning," Andrew observed, studying the entrance where corn stalks rose well above head height.

"Dad designed it on graph paper every year. This year I just..." Brandon paused, realizing what he was about to admit. "I just copied last year's pattern. Couldn't seem to come up with anything new."

"Sometimes maintaining what exists takes all the energy we have," Andrew said gently. "There's no shame in that."

They walked along the edge of the maze toward the pumpkin fields, where orange globes dotted the landscape like oversized jewels scattered across green velvet. The public picking area had been marked off with cheerful ribbon, and small wagons waited in neat rows for families to use in collecting their choices.

"The kids will love this," Andrew said, with genuine enthusiasm in his voice. "There's something almost magical about choosing your own pumpkin straight from the field."

"Amanda said the same thing," Brandon said without thinking, then felt heat rise in his face at having volunteered the information. "Thursday. I gave her a tour so she could plan festival supplies. She got excited about everything. Even the warty gourds that most people think are ugly. Said character was more interesting than conventional beauty."

Andrew smiled slightly but didn't comment, instead asking, "Where do the hayrides load?"

They continued walking, Brandon explaining the logistics of managing public visits while maintaining a working farm. They reached the hayride loading area, where wooden benches had been secured to wagons that would soon carry families through the scenic parts of the property. Brandon explained the route, the safety measures, and the way his mother would provide apple cider at the halfway point on weekends.

"Your family's brought joy to a lot of people over the years," Andrew observed.

"My father believed in it," Brandon said, the words carrying unexpected weight. "Said if you were blessed with land, you shared it. Stewardship meant more than just taking care of something—it meant making it available for others to enjoy too."

"That's a beautiful philosophy. You still believe that?"

Brandon was quiet for a long moment, watching the wind move through the distant corn. "I don't know what I believe anymore, Pastor. I go through all the motions—preparing for visitors, maintaining the tradition, keeping everything running. But I feel..." He struggled for words. "Disconnected. Like I'm watching someone else live my life."

"That sounds lonely."

The simple observation hit harder than any elaborate theological explanation might have. "It is," Brandon admitted. "It's like being surrounded by life but not being able to touch any of it. Everything's at arm's length."

They'd started walking again, moving toward the mum greenhouses. Andrew seemed content to let silence settle between them, not rushing to fill it with platitudes or easy answers.

"Can I share something?" Andrew asked eventually. "Not as your pastor, but just as someone who's wrestled with similar feelings?"

Brandon nodded.

"My grandfather and I had a special bond. We were inseparable. He died when I was sixteen. I remember feeling like I was living behind glass. I could see everyone else continuing with their lives, but I couldn't quite reach them. Even prayer felt like shouting into an empty room." Andrew paused, choosing his words carefully. "I found this verse in Romans that saved me, honestly. Chapter eight, verse twenty-six. 'The Spirit helps us in our weakness. We do not know what we ought to pray for, but the Spirit himself intercedes for us through wordless groans.'"

"Wordless groans," Brandon repeated, something resonating in the phrase.

"Sometimes that's all we've got," Andrew said. "And according to Paul, that's enough. The Spirit translates our inarticulate pain into prayer. We don't have to have words. We don't even have to have faith that feels sturdy. We just have to show up."

They'd reached the greenhouses where Helen's mums created a symphony of color under the translucent roof. The humid air inside wrapped around them, carrying the green scent of growing things and the subtle sweetness of the blooms.

"Your mother's an artist," Andrew said, taking in the rows of carefully tended plants.

"She finds peace here," Brandon said. "Says tending plants is like prayer—constant attention, patience, and trust that growth will happen even when you can't see it."

"Maybe that's what you're doing too," Andrew suggested. "Tending things, maintaining them, even when you can't feel the growth. That's not nothing, Brandon. That's faithfulness."

Brandon touched one of the mum blooms, its petals soft beneath his fingers. "I haven't been to church in months."

"I noticed."

"Doesn't that bother you? As a pastor?"

Andrew considered the question. "What bothers me is that you're hurting alone. Church isn't a building or a service time. It's community. It's people who commit to walking through life together, especially the dark parts. You've removed yourself from that support."

"I didn't want to be the grieving guy everyone feels sorry for."

"So instead you became the absent guy everyone worries about?"

The gentle challenge in Andrew's tone made Brandon look up. The pastor's expression held no judgment, only a kind of rueful understanding.

"I know what it's like to feel like your grief might swallow you whole if you let it out," Andrew continued. "To think that if you start crying, you might never stop. But, Brandon, trying to contain grief is like trying to dam a river with your hands. Eventually, it's going to find a way through."

They walked out of the greenhouse and continued along a path that led toward the back fields. The afternoon sun cast long shadows, and the mountains in the distance were hazed with the blue that gave them their name.

"I'm angry," Brandon said suddenly, the words erupting from somewhere deep. "At God, at Dad for dying, at Samantha for leaving. At myself for not having seen any of it coming. How do I walk into church carrying all that?"

Andrew didn't answer immediately, but when he did, his voice carried conviction. "You know the story of Jacob wrestling with God? Genesis thirty-two. Jacob fought with God all night long. He wouldn't let go until he got a blessing. And you know what he got along with that blessing?"

"A limp."

"A limp," Andrew confirmed. "A permanent reminder of his struggle. But also a new name—Israel. 'He who struggles with God.' Brandon, God's not afraid of your anger. He's not shocked at your doubts. Some of the most faithful people in Scripture were also the ones who argued with God the most. Job, David, Jeremiah—they all had their wrestling matches."

Brandon felt something shift in his chest, like ice beginning to crack under spring warmth. "I don't know how to come back."

"You don't have to know. You just have to be willing to consider it. That's all—just openness to the possibility."

They'd circled back toward the barn, the walk having covered most of the public areas of the farm. Tom's truck was still there, and Brandon could see him through the barn doors, working on fitting platforms to the framework.

"There's this verse in Ecclesiastes," Andrew said as they paused outside the barn. "Chapter three. 'There is a time for everything, and a season for every activity under heaven.' Including mourning. Including grief. But Brandon, seasons change. They're meant to. Staying in perpetual winter isn't natural—it's a choice."

"What if I'm not ready for spring?"

Andrew's expression softened. "Then you're not ready. But could you consider that maybe someday you might want to be ready? Not commitment, not promise. Just... possibility?"

Brandon felt the weight of the question, the way it pressed against all his carefully constructed walls. Everything in him wanted to retreat, to shut down this conversation and return to the safer numbness he'd been cultivating. But something else—small, fragile, persistent—wanted to reach for what Andrew was offering.

"I'll think about it," he managed.

"That's all anyone can ask." Andrew clapped him gently on the shoulder. "And Brandon? You're not alone, whether you come to church or not. This community loves you. We're not going anywhere."

They entered the barn where Tom was making adjustments to the platforms. He looked up with a grin.

"Everything is fitting together as I had hoped," Tom announced. "Amanda's going to be thrilled when she sees this tonight."

Tonight. Brandon had almost forgotten—the volunteers would arrive at six. Amanda would be here, bringing her enthusiasm and energy and that smile that seemed to light up whatever space she occupied.

"We should probably head out," Andrew said. "Let you get ready."

"Amanda's got quite a crew coming," Tom added, loading his tools back into his belt. "Martha alone is bringing half the church auxiliary."

They walked toward Tom's truck, and Brandon helped them secure the toolbox and make sure nothing would shift during the drive back to town.

"Thank you," Andrew said quietly as they prepared to leave. "For the tour, and for talking. I know it wasn't easy."

Brandon nodded, not trusting his voice. The conversation had scraped him raw in places he'd been protecting, and he felt exposed, uncertain.

As the truck pulled away, Brandon stood in the driveway watching the dust settle. His mother appeared from the farmhouse, dishtowel in hand.

"Good talk?" she asked carefully.

"I don't know," Brandon said honestly. "Maybe."

Helen studied his face for a moment, then nodded. "Sometimes maybe is enough to start with."

Chapter 14

Amanda pulled into the gravel parking area beside the Whitaker barn at ten minutes before six, her planning binder on the passenger seat and a fresh travel mug of coffee secured in the cup holder. She'd changed into her work clothes after closing the shop—faded jeans, an old Laurel Ridge High School t-shirt, both of which had seen better days, and her most comfortable sneakers. Her hair was twisted up in a messy bun, ready for an evening of physical work.

The barn doors stood open, afternoon light spilling across the concrete floor where the parade float waited like a skeleton ready to be dressed. Tom's handiwork stood out, and everything so far looked exactly as she'd envisioned. Everything was ready.

Except the barn was empty.

Amanda stood in the doorway for a moment, listening to the quiet. No Brandon. No sound of tools being arranged or last-minute adjustments being made. Just the distant call of birds and the rustling of corn in the nearby fields.

She set her binder on one of the folding tables and walked around the float, running her hand along the cool metal framework and across all the wood additions.

The sound of tires on gravel pulled her from her thoughts. Martha's sedan led a parade of vehicles into the parking area. Car doors opened, voices rose in greeting, and suddenly the barn began filling with the energy of dozens of eager volunteers. Martha carried a box of what appeared to be decorating supplies, several women from the church auxiliary hauled in plastic totes filled with artificial autumn leaves, and Earl arrived with his son and a trunk full of battery-powered lights and various other electrical equipment they would be installing.

"Amanda!" Martha called out, setting her box on a table with satisfaction. "This is so exciting. I'm ready to start making this the best float ever."

Rachel and Helen arrived next, both carrying bags that probably contained snacks and drinks for the volunteers. The evening was shaping up exactly as Amanda had planned—organized chaos with a purpose.

"Hey," Rachel said, giving Amanda a quick hug. "Ready to make magic?"

"Absolutely." Amanda glanced toward the barn door again, then back at Rachel. "Is Brandon coming?"

Rachel's expression shifted slightly, a flicker of something Amanda couldn't quite read. "I'm not sure. Why don't you ask Mom?"

Helen was arranging water bottles on a side table, humming something under her breath. When Amanda approached, the older woman's face carried a carefully neutral expression that suggested she had things on her mind.

"Helen, is Brandon planning to help tonight?"

Helen's hands stilled on the water bottles. "Oh, honey, I don't know. Tom Bradley and Pastor Andrew were here this afternoon to install the platforms. They did beautiful work, as you can see."

"That's great, but—"

"Andrew asked Brandon to give him a tour of the farm. You know, for when his wife's sister visits with her children next week." Helen's voice carried a note of something—concern, maybe, or uncertainty. "They were gone for quite a while. Walking and talking."

Amanda felt her stomach tighten. "And?"

"When they got back, Brandon looked... well, raw is the only word for it. Like someone had scraped him down to the nerve endings." Helen met Amanda's eyes directly. "Andrew's good at that—getting to the heart of things. Sometimes it's exactly what we need, but it's not always easy to receive."

"Where is he now?"

"I don't know. After Tom and Andrew left, he stood in the driveway for the longest time, just staring at nothing. Then he walked toward his cabin. I haven't seen him since." Helen's voice dropped. "I didn't want to push. When Brandon's processing something, he needs space."

Amanda looked around the barn at the growing crowd of volunteers. Mrs. Davenport was already organizing the artificial leaves by color, two high school girls were untangling strings of lights, and Earl's son was studying the framework with the intense focus of someone mentally engineering improvements.

Rachel appeared at her elbow, voice low. "Go to him."

"What? No, I can't. The decorating—"

"Will be fine." Rachel's tone brooked no argument. "Mom and Martha and I have your notes. We know what needs to happen. But

Brandon... he doesn't need his mother or his sister right now. He needs someone who isn't family. Someone who can be objective."

"Rachel, I'm supposed to be leading this."

"Some things are more important than a parade float." Rachel squeezed Amanda's arm. "Go."

Amanda looked between Rachel and Helen, seeing matching expressions of gentle insistence. Around them, the volunteers were already self-organizing, with Martha naturally taking charge of one group and Earl directing another.

"Are you sure?"

"Completely," Rachel said. "Go."

Amanda grabbed her keys before she could second-guess herself, slipping out of the barn and into her car. The drive to Brandon's cabin felt surreal, the familiar farm landscape seeming different in the golden light of early evening. She could still hear voices and laughter from the barn, carried on the breeze through her cracked window.

Brandon's cabin came into view. His truck was parked in its usual spot.

She parked and sat for a moment, suddenly uncertain. What was she doing? Who was she to intrude on whatever he was working through?

But then she remembered Rachel's words: "He needs someone who isn't family."

Amanda got out of the car, closing the door softly. She walked around to the back of the cabin and found him—a still figure on the back porch. He didn't move or turn toward her. As she got closer, she could see a Bible on the small table beside his chair, open to somewhere in the middle—Psalms, maybe. His hands were clasped loosely in his lap, and his gaze was fixed on the distant mountains, but she doubted he was really seeing them.

"Brandon?"

No response. She climbed the first step.

"Brandon?"

He jerked as if she'd shouted, his head whipping around to face her. Confusion clouded his features, followed quickly by something that looked like panic.

"What are you—it's after six. You should be..."

"It's handled," she said. "Rachel and your mom and Martha have everything under control."

"But you're supposed to be supervising."

"I'm exactly where I need to be."

He stared at her for a long moment, and she could see the war playing out across his face—the desire for solitude battling with something else. Maybe loneliness. Maybe need.

"I'm not good company right now," he said finally.

"That's okay. I'm not looking for entertainment."

"You should go back. I'm fine."

"Are you?"

She climbed the steps slowly, giving him time to object, to send her away. He didn't. Instead, he watched her with an expression she couldn't quite read—wariness mixed with something that might have been relief.

Amanda settled on the top step, not taking the empty chair beside him. She wanted to give him space, let him control the distance between them. From here, she could see what he'd been staring at—the mountains painted purple in the evening light, the sense of vastness that made human problems seem both smaller and more significant.

They sat in silence for several minutes. Amanda could feel the tension radiating from Brandon, the way his shoulders held too much tightness, the careful control in his breathing.

"Andrew thinks I'm choosing winter," he blurted, his voice rough like he hadn't used it in a while.

"Okay... the seasons... winter... are you choosing winter?"

The simple question seemed to break something in him. His shoulders sagged, and he rubbed his face with both hands.

"I don't know. Maybe. It's..." He stopped, running a hand through his hair in frustration. "It's safer. Winter. Nothing grows, but nothing dies either. Everything's just dormant... suspended."

"But you're not suspended. You're running the farm, preparing for pumpkin season, helping with the festival. That's not suspended."

"No, that's just motion. Going through the patterns because I know them, not because I feel connected to them." He looked back toward the mountains. "Andrew asked me questions today. About faith. About Dad. About what I believe versus what I'm just maintaining out of habit."

Amanda waited, letting the silence invite more.

"I told him I was angry," Brandon continued, the words coming faster now, like water through a broken dam. "At God for taking Dad. At Dad for leaving. At Samantha for giving up. At myself for not being enough to make any of it work."

"That's a lot of anger to carry."

"Andrew said God's not afraid of my anger. Said some of the most faithful people in scripture were the ones who wrestled with God." Brandon's laugh was bitter. "I told him I didn't know how to come back to church carrying all that. You know what he said?"

"What?"

"That I should come back exactly as I am. That trying to clean myself up first was like trying to dam a river with my hands." Brandon picked up the Bible beside him, not opening it but just holding it. "He talked about Jacob wrestling with God. Getting a blessing but also a limp. A permanent reminder of the struggle."

"That sounds like Andrew," Amanda said softly. "Never one for easy answers."

"He asked if I could consider the possibility of being ready for spring. Not now, not commitment, just... possibility." Brandon set the Bible back down carefully. "I couldn't even answer him."

The pain in his voice made Amanda's chest ache. She shifted slightly, turning more toward him while still maintaining the distance he seemed to need.

"Can I share something?" she asked.

He nodded.

Amanda reached for the Bible, and he handed it to her. Her fingers finding a passage she'd turned to countless times. "Second Corinthians, chapter five, verse seventeen. 'Therefore, if anyone is in Christ, the new creation has come: The old has gone, the new is here.'"

She handed the Bible back to him, open to the passage. "I used to think that meant everything old just disappeared. Like you became a Christian and poof, a new person, no baggage. But that's not what it means."

"What does it mean?"

"I think it means we're constantly being made new. Every day, every choice, every moment we choose to trust instead of fear. The old doesn't disappear—it becomes part of the foundation for what's being built."

Brandon was quiet for a moment.

"What are you thinking about?" Amanda asked.

Brandon stood abruptly, moving to lean against the porch railing. "I knew on my wedding day that it was wrong. Can you believe that? Standing there in that courthouse, saying vows, all I could think was,

'This is a mistake.' But I thought... I thought commitment could create love. That if I just tried hard enough, wanted it enough, it would become right."

"But it didn't."

"No. She needed things I couldn't give her. Adventure, excitement, freedom from the very life I wanted and had built here. And I needed..." He paused, searching for words. "I needed her to be someone she wasn't. Someone who could love this land, this life, the way I do."

"That's not failure, Brandon. That's recognition."

He turned to look at her. "I failed her by marrying her when I couldn't give her what she needed."

Amanda stood now too, moving to lean against the railing a few feet from him. "Or maybe the failure would have been staying in something that was never meant to be. Maybe letting her go was the bravest thing you could have done."

"I wanted marriage to work more than I wanted her specifically," Brandon admitted, his voice barely above a whisper. "What kind of person does that make me?"

"Human. Lonely. Someone who wanted to build a life with another person. There's nothing wrong with wanting that."

Brandon's hands gripped the railing, knuckles white. "But that's just it. I forced something with someone I barely knew, while..."

"While what?" she prompted gently.

He turned to face her, and the look in his eyes made her breath catch.

"You were right there. All those years. Rachel's best friend. At church. Around town. In my mother's kitchen. And I never saw you. Not really."

The words hit her like physical blows, confirming every fear she'd ever had about being forgettable, invisible. She forced herself to keep her voice steady.

"You saw what you were ready to see. We all do."

"No." The word came out harsh. "That's not an excuse. I looked right through you as if you were furniture. What kind of selfish, blind person does that? You were there, Amanda. At every family dinner Rachel dragged you to. Every church event. Every festival. And I never once really looked at you."

Amanda felt heat rising on her face. "I was good at being invisible."

"What?"

The question forced her to meet his eyes. "I said I was good at being invisible. It's safer. If no one really sees you, they can't reject who you really are. They can't find you wanting."

Brandon moved closer, and she could see something like horror in his expression. "Is that what you thought? That you weren't worth seeing?"

The question touched her deepest wound, and her voice came out smaller than she intended. "I wasn't the kind of girl Brandon Whitaker would notice. Star quarterback. Everyone's golden boy. I was just... Amanda. Average Amanda, who helped out at church and ran a gift shop and never did anything remarkable enough to catch anyone's attention."

"Stop. You're not average. You've never been average. I was just too stupid and self-absorbed to see it."

"Brandon—"

"No, let me..." He ran his hands through his hair, clearly struggling for words. "I'm looking at you now, really looking, and I can't understand how I missed everything. The way you see beauty in the smallest things. How you make everyone around you feel valued. Your laugh—Geez, Amanda, your laugh changes the whole temperature of a room. You make ordinary moments feel special, and I was too blind to see any of it."

Amanda's heart was racing, but she forced herself to stay calm. "We're different people now than we were even a year ago."

"Are we? Or am I just finally paying attention?" Brandon turned to look at her directly. "You terrify me, Amanda Baker."

The confession was so unexpected that Amanda actually pulled back slightly. "I terrify you?"

"Yes." He looked away. "Because you matter. Because when you're not here, I notice the empty space. Because you make me want things I thought I was done wanting."

"What things?"

"Connection. Hope. The possibility that maybe spring could come again, even though I'm scared to death of leaving winter." His voice dropped. "I don't trust my judgment anymore. I married the wrong person for the wrong reasons. I missed seeing my father's exhaustion before his heart attack. Everything I thought was solid fell apart. I've made so many mistakes. But somehow, despite all that, I trust... you. And that terrifies me most of all."

Amanda felt tears prick at her eyes, but she blinked them back. This wasn't the moment for her feelings. This was about Brandon finding his way through the darkness.

"I'm not going anywhere," she said carefully. "Whatever this is, whatever we're becoming—friends, or... more—we don't have to figure it out tonight, or tomorrow, or the next day. You're still processing everything Andrew said. You're still grieving. And that's okay."

"What if I'm never ready? What if I'm too broken to offer anyone anything?"

Amanda reached over and rested her hand on his. "You're not as broken as you think. Broken things don't care about fixing themselves. You do."

He stared at their hands. "I don't know how to do this."

"Do what?"

"Feel things again. Want things again. Hope for things again." He met her eyes. "Care about someone again."

The admission hung between them, delicate as spun glass. Amanda knew that one wrong word could shatter whatever was building here, send Brandon retreating back into his safe winter isolation.

"Then don't," she said simply. "Don't try to do anything. Just... be. Let yourself feel whatever you feel without having to name it or fix it or understand it completely. Isn't that what faith is? Trusting even when we can't see the whole picture?"

Brandon was quiet for a long moment. Then, so softly she almost missed it, he said, "My dad really liked you."

"I liked him too. He was always kind to me."

"He saw people," Brandon said. "Really saw them. I used to think I'd inherited that from him, but..." He gestured helplessly.

"Maybe you did. Maybe it just got buried under other things for a while."

From the barn, a burst of laughter rose into the evening air. Amanda became aware of how long she'd been gone, though it couldn't have been more than thirty minutes. Still, she should check on things.

"We should probably head back," she said reluctantly.

Brandon nodded. "Amanda?"

"Yes?"

"Thanks."

"That's what friends are for."

The word "friends" carried weight—both limitation and promise. Brandon heard it too; she could see it in the way his expression shifted, not quite disappointment but acknowledgment.

"I'll follow you back," Brandon said, stepping away.

"You don't have to help tonight."

"I want to. I need to... be around people."

Amanda nodded and walked toward her car, aware of his eyes following her movement. As she reached for her door handle, he called out.

"Amanda?"

She turned.

"The thing about spring," he said slowly, "is that it comes whether you're ready or not. The ice melts, things start growing, and you either embrace it or fight it. But it comes anyway."

She waited, sensing more.

"I think... I think I'm tired of fighting it."

Chapter 15

Brandon stood among his mother's chrysanthemums, surrounded by bronze and gold blooms that seemed to mock his inability to focus on the simple task of checking irrigation lines. For the third time in ten minutes, he'd lost track of which row he'd already inspected, his mind circling back to Monday night like water finding its level.

Amanda's hand on his. Her voice said she wasn't going anywhere. The way her eyes had held his when he'd admitted she terrified him.

The greenhouse door opened, and Helen entered, carrying a pair of pruning shears and a collection basket. She hummed as she moved down the opposite row, dead-heading spent blooms.

"The burgundy ones are looking good this year," she said without looking up. "Pastor Andrew's wife called this morning asking if she could reserve a dozen for the church fellowship hall."

"Mmm-hmm."

Helen continued working, her shears making soft snipping sounds. "And Rusty said the last hay field should be ready to cut by Friday, just in time before we open to the public."

"Good."

"Oh, and the circus elephants we ordered arrived this morning. I had them put it in the corn maze."

Brandon's hand stilled on the irrigation valve. "What?"

His mother's laughter filled the humid air. "There's my son. I was beginning to wonder if you'd left your body here while your mind went wandering."

Heat crept up Brandon's neck. "Sorry. I was... thinking."

"I noticed." Helen moved to the next plant, her movements unhurried. "You've been thinking quite a lot since Monday night. Walking the property at odd hours, starting projects and abandoning them halfway through. This morning I found you standing in my kitchen just holding the coffeepot, not pouring, not moving, just... holding."

Brandon rubbed the back of his neck. "Has it been that obvious?"

"To someone who changed your diapers and taught you to tie your shoes? Yes." Helen set down her basket and turned to face him fully. The morning light through the greenhouse glass caught the silver in her hair, and for a moment Brandon saw his father in her expression—that same patient willingness to wait for truth to surface in its own time.

"Mom, I—" The words tangled in his throat. He turned away, focusing on a particularly full bronze mum whose petals caught the light like burnished copper. "I'm sorry about church."

The words came out rougher than intended, scraped raw by months of absence.

Helen was quiet for a moment. When she spoke, her voice carried no reproach, only gentle curiosity. "Sorry for missing it, or sorry for how it makes me feel?"

Brandon's hands clenched at his sides. Trust his mother to cut straight to the distinction that mattered.

"Both. But mostly..." He forced himself to meet her eyes. "Mostly for disappointing you. For being one more thing you have to worry about when you've already lost—" His voice cracked. "When you've already been through enough."

Helen's expression softened, and she closed the distance between them, resting her hand on his arm. "Oh, sweetheart. You think your absence from church is about disappointing me?"

"Isn't it?"

"No." The word was firm, brooking no argument. "It's about watching my son try to carry burdens alone that were never meant to be carried that way. It's about seeing you cut yourself off from the very community that could help hold you up. Church isn't about perfect attendance, Brandon. It's about belonging to something bigger than our own pain."

"Pastor Andrew said something similar. About the church being a community, not just a building."

"Andrew's a smart man." Helen picked up her shears again but didn't resume cutting. "Is that what you two talked about during your walk? You were gone quite a while."

"Among other things." Brandon moved to check the thermostat, needing something to do with his hands. "Mom, can I ask you something?"

"Always."

Brandon turned from the thermostat, making himself face her directly. "You never said much about my marriage. Even when things were clearly falling apart. Why?"

Helen set down her tools completely and settled onto the wooden bench his father had built years ago for her to rest during long greenhouse sessions. She patted the space beside her, and Brandon sat, his long legs stretched out in front of him.

"What would you have wanted me to say?" she asked quietly.

"The truth. That it was wrong from the beginning. That I was making a mistake." The words rushed out. "You knew, didn't you? You could see what I couldn't."

Helen sighed, the sound carrying the weight of a careful silence maintained too long. "I saw a young woman who loved the idea of what you represented more than who you actually were. And I saw my son trying so hard to make something work that was never meant to be."

"Why didn't you say anything?"

"Because you weren't ready to hear it." Helen's voice was gentle but frank. "You had to learn for yourself that marriage isn't about forcing pieces together that don't fit. It's about finding someone whose edges align with yours naturally, even the broken parts."

Brandon dropped his head into his hands. "I wanted it to work so badly. I thought if I just tried harder, loved more, gave more—"

"You can't love someone into being the right person for you," Helen interrupted. "Love isn't about changing someone or yourself to fit an ideal. It's about seeing someone clearly and choosing them anyway, rough edges and all."

"I never saw Samantha clearly," Brandon admitted to his hands. "I saw what I wanted to see. Someone who would share this life with me, who would want the same things I wanted. I projected a whole person onto her that never really existed."

"And she did the same with you," Helen pointed out. "She saw the former football star, the successful farmer, the small-town golden boy. She never saw the man who finds peace in dawn chores and evening prayers, who wants nothing more than to build something lasting on the land his family has tended for generations."

Brandon lifted his head, staring at the rows of chrysanthemums without really seeing them. "I've been thinking about patterns lately. How I've spent my whole life looking past what's right in front of me."

Helen waited, patient as always.

"Amanda." The name emerged on an exhale, like something that had been held too long. "Mom, how did I never see her? All those years, she was right there. In our house, at church, around town. Rachel's best friend. And I just... looked through her like she was wallpaper."

"Do you want the comfortable answer or the true one?" Helen asked.

"The true one."

"You weren't ready to see her." Helen's voice was matter-of-fact, without judgment. "The Bible talks about having eyes to see and ears to hear. Sometimes God puts people in our path long before we're prepared to recognize their significance. You had to go through what you went through—the marriage, the divorce, losing your father—to become someone who could truly see Amanda Baker."

Brandon's throat felt tight. "That sounds like God has a cruel sense of timing."

"Or perfect timing," Helen countered. "Think about it. If you'd noticed Amanda in high school, what would have happened? You were heading different directions—she went to college, built her business, became the woman she is today. You stayed here, learned the farm, tried to force a marriage that wasn't meant to be. If you'd gotten together then, before either of you became who you were meant to be, it might have ended badly."

"But—"

"And Amanda," Helen continued, warming to her point, "she needed to build her own life first. To prove to herself that she could succeed on her own terms. Can you imagine how different she'd be if she'd just been Brandon Whitaker's girlfriend from the start? Never building her business, never finding her own strength? Never figuring out who she is?"

Brandon thought about Amanda's confidence when she talked about her shop, the way she commanded a room full of volunteers, her vision for the festival that went beyond anything that had been done before. His mother was right—that Amanda couldn't have existed if she'd been defined by being his high school girlfriend.

"She's remarkable," he said quietly. "The way she sees beauty in everything. The way she makes everyone around her feel valued. Her faith that isn't showy but runs deep. And that laugh—" He stopped, aware he was rambling.

Helen's smile was knowing but gentle. "Sounds like your eyes are finally working properly."

"Monday night, I told her she terrified me."

"Good."

Brandon looked at his mother in surprise. "Good?"

"Of course. Real love should terrify you a little. It means you recognize how much power you're giving another person—the power to matter, to affect your happiness, to change your life's direction. If it doesn't scare you at least a little, you're not paying attention to how significant it is."

Brandon stood and paced to the window that looked out over the back fields. The morning sun was climbing higher, burning off the dew that had silvered the grass at dawn. "What if I mess this up too? What if I hurt her? What if—"

"What if you don't?" Helen interrupted. "What if this is exactly what God's been preparing you both for? What if all those years of

Amanda being invisible to you were just God's way of protecting something precious until the right moment?"

"You really believe that?"

Helen rose and moved to stand beside him at the window. "I believe that God's timing is rarely our timing, but it's always perfect. I believe that sometimes we have to break before we can be rebuilt into who we're meant to be. And I believe that Amanda Baker has been waiting for you to really see her for a very long time."

"How do you know that?"

"Moms notice things." Helen's voice carried gentle affection. "The way she looked at you when she thought no one was watching. The way she lit up when you entered a room, even when you barely acknowledged her presence. The way she's thrown herself into this festival with such determination—she's not just organizing an event, Brandon. She's creating reasons to be near you."

The observation hit him with unexpected force. "You think she—even after all these years?"

"I think Amanda has a faithful heart. And I think she's been incredibly patient. The question is, what are you going to do about it?"

Brandon turned from the window to face his mother directly. "I don't know how to do this. Dating, romance, whatever you want to call it. I'm thirty years old, and I feel like I'm starting from scratch."

"Then start from scratch," Helen said simply. "But start. Don't let fear keep you frozen in the winter you've been living in. Spring's trying to come, sweetheart. You just have to let it."

Brandon thought about Amanda's voice on Monday night, steady and sure: "Then don't. Don't try to do anything. Just... be."

"She told me not to try to force anything," he said. "To just feel whatever I feel without having to name it or fix it or understand it completely."

"Smart girl," Helen observed. "Though I'm not surprised. Amanda's always been wise beyond her years."

Helen returned to her pruning, and Brandon found himself actually able to focus on the irrigation system he'd come to check.

As he worked, his hands steady on the valves and gauges, his mind kept circling back to one thought: What was he going to do about Amanda Baker?

The answer, when it came, was so simple he almost laughed.

Something. He was going to do something. Not nothing, not avoidance, not retreat. Something intentional and deliberate and maybe a little terrifying.

"Mom?" he called across the greenhouse.

"Hmm?"

"I'm gonna drive into town."

Helen's smile was audible in her voice. "That sounds like a good idea. Might want to clean up first, though. You've got potting soil in your hair."

Brandon ran his hand through his hair and, sure enough, came away with dirt. "When did that happen?"

"Probably when you were leaning against the potting table earlier, staring into space while I talked about elephants."

Brandon laughed—really laughed. The sound echoed off the greenhouse glass, mixing with his mother's gentle chuckle, and for a moment, the space felt less like a greenhouse and more like a sanctuary.

"Brandon?" Helen called as he headed for the door.

"Yeah?"

"Your father would be proud of you. Not for being perfect, but for being brave enough to try again."

"Love you, Mom."

"Love you too, son."

Chapter 16

"No, Mrs. Peterson, I completely understand your frustration." Amanda kept her voice soothing while internally calculating how quickly she could get the special-order ceramic angel collection shipped from her supplier. "I promise you'll have them by Thursday. Yes, in plenty of time for your daughter's shower on Saturday."

With the phone tucked between her shoulder and ear, Amanda typed rapid notes into her computer while simultaneously gesturing to Whitney to help the customer who'd just entered. The Wednesday afternoon rush was in full swing—tourists browsing for souvenirs, locals picking up gifts, and her phone ringing every few minutes with festival questions she couldn't answer right now.

"I'll call you the moment they arrive," Amanda assured Mrs. Peterson for the third time. "Yes, I'll personally inspect each piece. Of course. Thank you for your patience."

She hung up and immediately turned to April, who was wrestling with the new inventory system at the other computer. "The angels should arrive tomorrow. Can you make sure—"

The bell above the door chimed again. The entire shop seemed to pause, as if someone had lifted a needle from a record as Brandon Whitaker entered.

He wore clean jeans and a white button-down shirt, his hair still damp at the edges like he'd recently showered. His hands were shoved deep in his pockets, and he stood with the uncertain posture of someone who'd entered the wrong classroom and was debating whether to back out quietly or brave it through.

Brandon's eyes found hers across the organized chaos of her shop, past the display of harvest candles and around the table of decorative pumpkins. Something in his expression—determination mixed with nervousness—made her stomach perform a slow flip.

"Brandon." His name came out breathier than she'd intended.

Whitney stood frozen beside the greeting card display, openly staring. April's fingers had stilled on the keyboard. Even Coral, never at a loss for words, seemed struck silent. The only sound was the soft Celtic music playing from the shop's speakers.

Brandon navigated through the displays with the careful movement of someone in a china shop who actually was aware of the bulls inside himself. He stopped at the counter.

"Hi," he said, then cleared his throat. "I was wondering—that is, if you're not too busy—" He glanced around at her obviously busy shop, and color rose in his cheeks. "You're busy. I should have called."

"No," Amanda said quickly. "I mean, yes, we're busy, but—" She stopped, aware of three pairs of eyes ping-ponging between them like spectators at a tennis match.

Brandon shifted his weight, and his elbow bumped a display of small glass pumpkins. He caught one before it could roll off the counter, his hands sure despite his obvious discomfort. "Would you—could we—" He took a breath, seeming to gather himself. "Would you have lunch with me?"

The question hung in the air like a held note, beautiful and precarious.

Amanda felt her mouth open, but no words came out. Brandon Whitaker was standing in her shop, in the middle of a Wednesday afternoon, asking her to lunch. Not discussing festival supplies. Not here because Rachel sent him. Just... asking.

"I haven't eaten," he added, as if that explained everything. "And I thought maybe you hadn't either. And Martha makes that chicken salad on Wednesdays." He stopped, clearly realizing he was rambling. "You don't have to. I just thought—"

"Yes."

The word escaped before Amanda could second-guess it. Brandon's face transformed, tension melting into relief mixed with surprise, as if he hadn't quite expected her to agree.

"Okay," he said. "Good. That's—okay."

Amanda turned to April, who was watching with the intensity of someone memorizing every detail for later recounting. "Can you—"

"Go," April said immediately. "We've got everything covered."

"But the Peterson order—"

"Will be handled." April made a shooing motion with her hands. "Go have lunch."

Coral had recovered enough to add, "Take your time. We'll manage the afternoon rush."

Amanda grabbed her purse from behind the counter, hyperaware of Brandon waiting, of her employees watching, of the way her hands trembled slightly.

"I just need to—" She gestured vaguely toward the back office.

"Sure," Brandon said. "I'll wait outside."

He retreated through the door, and the moment it closed behind him, all three women turned to Amanda with expressions of barely contained excitement.

"Oh. My. Word," Whitney whispered.

"Brandon Whitaker just asked you to lunch," Coral said, as if Amanda might have missed it.

"In public," April added significantly.

Amanda pressed her hands to her cheeks, feeling the heat there. "What am I doing?"

"You're going to lunch," April said firmly. "You're going to walk out that door and have lunch with a man who looks at you like you hung the moon."

"He doesn't—"

"He does," all three women said in unison.

Amanda glanced toward the door, where she could see Brandon through the glass, standing with his hands in his pockets, studying the window display with fierce concentration.

"Go," April said gently. "We've really got this."

Amanda nodded, smoothed her skirt—why had she worn such an old skirt today?—and walked to the door. The bell chimed cheerfully as she stepped out into the September afternoon.

Brandon turned immediately, and something in his expression—relief that she'd actually come out, maybe—made her chest tighten.

"Hi," she said, then felt ridiculous. They'd already done the greeting portion inside.

"Hi," he replied, and the corner of his mouth lifted slightly. "Thanks for saying yes."

"Thanks for asking."

They stood there for a moment, two people who'd known each other for years suddenly unsure how to navigate this new territory.

"Should we—" Brandon gestured toward Martha's.

"Sure."

They began walking down Main Street, the familiar storefronts and brick sidewalks suddenly feeling different with Brandon beside her. Amanda was acutely aware of the space between them—not quite close enough to touch but closer than casual acquaintances. She caught Loretta Dunbar watching from the Book Nook window and felt heat rise in her cheeks.

"Busy day?" Brandon asked, his voice carefully neutral.

"The usual Wednesday craziness. Festival questions, custom orders, inventory issues." She glanced up at him. "You? How's the farm preparation going?"

"Good. We're ready for Friday's opening."

They lapsed into silence, but it wasn't entirely uncomfortable. More like two people feeling their way through unfamiliar steps, trying not to trip.

The familiar red-and-white striped awning of Martha's Diner came into view, and Brandon reached for the door handle, holding it open for her. The gesture was simple, automatic probably, but it made Amanda's pulse quicken anyway.

The diner's interior wrapped around them with its familiar comfort—the scent of coffee and cinnamon and homemade bread, the soft murmur of conversation, the clink of silverware against plates. The lunch crowd had thinned, leaving several empty booths.

Martha appeared immediately, her silver hair neat as always, her smile warm but contained. "Brandon! And Amanda. How nice to see you both."

Her tone was perfectly calibrated—pleased but not overly so, treating this like any other lunch between friends. But Amanda caught the quick assessment in Martha's eyes, the way she took in Brandon's nervous energy and Amanda's careful posture.

"How about that nice corner booth," Martha said, already moving.

She led them to a booth in the back corner, more private than the ones by the windows. The red vinyl seats were worn soft with age, and a small vase of daisies and black-eyed Susans sat on the table.

"Coffee to start?" Martha asked. "Just brewed a fresh pot."

"Please," Amanda said.

"Coffee sounds good," Brandon agreed.

Martha poured, the rich aroma rising with the steam. "I'll give you a few minutes to look at the menu."

She disappeared before either of them could respond that they both knew the menu by heart.

Amanda wrapped her hands around the warm ceramic mug and risked a glance at Brandon across the table.

He was studying his coffee with intense focus, his jaw tight with concentration. Or nerves. When he looked up and caught her watching, they both looked away quickly.

"This is weird," Brandon said suddenly.

Amanda's stomach dropped. "Oh. We can—"

"No, not bad weird." He ran a hand through his hair, messing it slightly. "Just... I realized I've never actually done this. Sat across from you. Just the two of us."

It was true. In all the years, through all the connections—Rachel, church, community events—they'd never just... been. Together. Alone.

"We haven't, have we?"

"I've been thinking," Brandon started, then stopped. He lifted his coffee mug, set it down without drinking. "After Monday night. I've been thinking about what you said. About just being. Not forcing things."

Amanda waited, her heart performing a complicated rhythm against her ribs.

"But I realized something else," he continued. "I can't just be with someone I don't actually know. And I don't—" He met her eyes directly. "I know facts about you. You run a gift shop. You're Rachel's best friend. You volunteer for everything. But I don't know you. Not really."

The honesty in his voice made Amanda's throat tighten.

"So I guess what I'm saying is—" Brandon paused, seeming to search for words. "Would you tell me? About you? Not the facts everyone knows, but... you?"

The question was so earnest, so unexpected, that Amanda felt tears coming. When was the last time someone had asked to know her—really know her—beyond her roles and responsibilities? Never.

"What do you want to know?"

"Everything," he said simply. "But let's start with something easy. What's your favorite time of day?"

The question was so unexpected that Amanda laughed—a real laugh, not the polite one she used for customers. "Early morning. Before the world wakes up. When everything's still quiet and full of possibility."

"Why?"

"I like the potential of it. That clean-slate feeling. Like anything could happen." She paused, then admitted, "I usually spend it on my back porch with coffee, watching the mountains wake up. It's when I do my best thinking. Or my best not-thinking, depending on the day."

Brandon smiled—a genuine smile that reached his eyes. "I wouldn't have guessed morning. You seem like a night person."

"Because of all the evening meetings?"

"Because you light up rooms. Night people are usually the ones who bring energy when everyone else is fading."

The compliment, delivered matter-of-factly, made heat rise in her cheeks.

Martha appeared with perfect timing, just as Amanda was struggling for a response. "Ready to order?"

They hadn't even looked at the menus, but Brandon said, "Chicken salad sandwich?"

"Same," Amanda said, grateful for the reprieve.

"Two Wednesday specials." Martha's smile was small but pleased. "Good choice."

She vanished again, leaving them in their corner of the world.

"Your turn," Amanda said, finding her courage. "What's something about you that would surprise me?"

Brandon considered, his fingers tracing patterns on the condensation from his water glass. "I read poetry."

Amanda blinked. "Poetry?"

Color rose in his cheeks. "Started in high school, actually. English class assigned Robert Frost, and something about it just... stuck. The way poems can say complicated things simply. Or simple things in complicated ways." He shrugged, clearly embarrassed. "Dad found me reading Emily Dickinson once and asked if I was feeling okay."

"What's your favorite?"

"'Hope is the thing with feathers,'" he said without hesitation, then looked surprised at himself. "I haven't thought about that poem in months."

"'That perches in the soul,'" Amanda continued softly. "'And sings the tune without the words, And never stops at all.'"

Brandon stared at her. "You know it."

"I love Emily Dickinson. The way she found the infinite in the ordinary. I wouldn't have guessed poetry for you."

"Because I'm just a farmer?"

"Because you're so self-contained. Poetry requires a certain willingness to be vulnerable, even if just with yourself."

Brandon was quiet for a moment. "Maybe that's why I stopped reading it. Got too good at containing everything."

Martha arrived with their sandwiches, the plates landing gently on the table. The chicken salad was piled high on fresh bread, accompanied by Martha's homemade potato chips and a pickle spear.

"Everything look good?" Martha asked.

"Perfect," Brandon said, and Amanda nodded agreement.

They ate in comfortable quiet for a few minutes, the tension from earlier gradually dissipating like morning mist. Amanda found herself stealing glances at Brandon, noticing things she'd never paid attention to before—the way he automatically moved his pickle to the side of his plate first, how he ate his chips one at a time instead of grabbing handfuls.

"Can I ask you something?" Brandon said suddenly.

"Sure."

"What made you stay in Laurel Ridge? You went to college, you had options. But you came back."

Amanda set down her sandwich, considering. It was a question she'd been asked before, but something in Brandon's tone suggested he really wanted to understand.

"Everyone always asks it like staying was settling," she said carefully. "Like choosing Laurel Ridge meant choosing less. But for me, it was choosing more. More than a career in some city where I didn't know anyone. More than success measured by someone else's standards."

"More how?"

"More connection. More purpose. More... home, I guess." She traced the rim of her water glass with one finger. "I tried the city life during college. Internship at a marketing firm in Charleston. I was good at it, too. They offered me a job after graduation."

"But you didn't take it."

"No. Because I realized I didn't want to spend my life selling things people didn't need to people I'd never see again. I wanted to be part of something. To matter in a way that was tangible, personal." She looked up at him. "Does that make sense?"

"Perfect sense," Brandon said quietly. "It's exactly how I feel about farming. The land, the community, the continuity of it all."

"But people understand that for you. A man choosing to work his family's land—that's noble. A woman choosing to run a gift shop in her hometown—that's quaint."

Brandon frowned. "Who says that?"

"Not directly. But you see it in their eyes sometimes. College friends who visit and can't quite hide their pity. Relatives who ask when I'm going to do something 'bigger.'" She picked up a chip, and set it down again. "As if building a successful business and being part of this community isn't big enough."

"It's more than big enough," Brandon said. "You've created something that matters to people. Your shop isn't just a place to buy things—it's where people go to find the perfect way to show someone they care. That's not quaint. That's essential."

Amanda felt her eyes burn with sudden emotion. "Thank you."

"For what?"

"For seeing it. For seeing—" She stopped, afraid she'd say too much.

"For seeing you?" Brandon finished gently.

Their eyes met and held, something shifting in the air between them.

Martha materialized beside their table, breaking the moment. She set down a single plate with a generous slice of apple pie and two forks.

"On the house," she said simply. "My apple pie's too good not to share."

Before either could respond, she was gone again.

Brandon looked at the pie, then at Amanda. "She's not subtle, is she?"

"Martha? Subtle isn't in her vocabulary." Amanda picked up one of the forks. "But she's right about the pie."

They ate from opposite sides of the plate. The apple filling was perfect—tart and sweet with just enough cinnamon, the crust flaky and buttery.

"Can I tell you something?" Brandon said suddenly.

Amanda nodded, mouth full of pie.

"I thought about coming to your shop probably fifty times over the past year. After Dad, after—" He paused. "After everything changed. I'd drive by and see you through the windows, arranging displays or helping customers, and I'd think about going in."

"Why didn't you?"

"Because I didn't know what to say. 'Hi, I'm falling apart but your windows look nice'? Or 'Hi, I have no idea why I'm here but for some reason, I just wanted to stop by.' I think God had been putting you in my path for awhile now, I just never stopped to pay attention." He gave a self-deprecating laugh. "And then Monday happened, and you showed up at my cabin, and you just... sat with me. Didn't try to fix anything. Didn't need me to be anything other than what I was in that moment."

"Brandon—"

"I'm not good at this," he said quickly. "At talking, at feeling things, at knowing what comes next. But I know that Monday night, after we were done working on the float and I went back home... the cabin felt emptier than it ever has. And I know that I want to know you—really know you. Not because you're Rachel's friend or because we're working on the festival, but because you're you."

Amanda's hands trembled slightly as she set down her fork. "I want that too."

"Yeah?"

"Yeah."

They looked at each other across the remains of the pie, two people who'd orbited each other for years suddenly finding themselves in the same gravitational pull.

"This is a lot to take in. This may sound like an excuse any really it's not but.....I need to pull back and process a little bit. I should probably get back to work too," Amanda said reluctantly, glancing at her watch. "Wednesday afternoons are always busy."

"Right. Of course." Brandon signaled for the check.

"You two take your time," Martha said, setting the check by Brandon's elbow. "No rush."

But they were already sliding out of the booth, the spell of the lunch broken by the return of real-world responsibilities.

Brandon left cash on the table, and they walked toward the door. As they passed the counter, Amanda caught Martha watching them with an expression of such maternal satisfaction that she had to look away.

Outside, they walked back toward Indulgences more slowly than necessary, neither quite ready for this to end.

"Thank you," Amanda said as they reached her shop. "For lunch. For... all of it."

Brandon stopped walking, turning to face her fully. "Can we do this again?"

The question was simple, but his eyes held uncertainty, hope, fear—a whole conversation in a glance.

"I'd like that," Amanda said softly.

"Tomorrow's Thursday."

"Yes, it is."

"Would you—that is, if you're not busy—dinner? Not at Martha's. Somewhere... different?"

Amanda felt a smile bloom across her face. "Are you asking me on a date, Brandon Whitaker?"

Color rose in his cheeks, but he held her gaze. "I'm asking you to have dinner with me. We can figure out what to call it later."

"Yes."

"Yes?"

"Yes."

Brandon's smile was like watching the sun come out—gradual, then all at once. "Okay. Good. I'll... pick you up? Seven?"

"Seven."

They stood there for a moment, neither moving, the space between them charged with possibility.

Through the shop window, Amanda could see all three of her employees clustered near the register, not even pretending not to watch.

"I should go," she said.

"Yeah."

Neither moved.

"Amanda?"

"Hmm?"

"I'm really glad I finally walked into your shop."

Before she could respond, he turned and walked away, his long stride carrying him down Main Street. Amanda stood frozen on the sidewalk, watching until he turned the corner.

The shop door burst open behind her.

"Amanda Baker, get in here immediately and tell us everything," Coral demanded.

Amanda turned, seeing three eager faces waiting. "We just had lunch."

"Just lunch?" April repeated skeptically.

"He asked me to dinner tomorrow."

The squeal that erupted from Whitney could probably be heard at Martha's.

Amanda let them pull her inside, their excitement infectious. But part of her remained on the sidewalk, holding onto the memory of Brandon's smile when she'd said yes. Again.

Chapter 17

Brandon pulled his sweat-stained work shirt over his head, tossing it toward the hamper in the corner of his bedroom. His shoulders ached and dried dirt clung to his forearms despite his earlier attempt to rinse off at the outdoor spigot. The afternoon sun slanted through his bedroom window, reminding him that time was moving whether he was ready or not.

He walked toward the bathroom, mentally planning his shower—hot enough to ease the muscle tension, quick enough to leave plenty of time to get ready. After all, he needed to figure out what time to leave to pick Amanda up by seven.

His hand froze on the bathroom doorknob.

Pick her up.

Pick her up where?

The question hit him like cold water to the face. He stood there, shirtless and dusty, one hand on the doorknob, as the full magnitude of his oversight crashed over him.

"Where does Amanda live?"

He said it out loud, as if hearing the words might somehow produce an answer.

Brandon's mind raced through what he knew about Amanda Baker. She owned Indulgences Gift Shop. She was Rachel's best friend. She loved morning coffee on her porch. She knew Emily Dickinson's poems by heart.

But where did she live?

Somewhere in town. That much he knew. She'd mentioned her porch this afternoon at lunch, something about watching the mountains wake up. But which porch? Which house? Which street?

"Oh, no." The words came out as a groan. Because if he didn't know where she lived, that meant—

The second realization hit even harder.

He'd never told her where they were going.

The Riverside Inn wasn't Martha's Diner. It wasn't casual. It required actual nice clothes, the kind of outfit you planned, not something you threw on assuming you'd be eating burgers somewhere local. Amanda had no idea she needed to dress for an elegant restaurant with white tablecloths and a wine list.

His stomach dropped further as the third, most catastrophic realization dawned.

He didn't have her phone number.

No way to text her the restaurant name. No way to tell her the dress code. No way to even confirm they were still on for seven. She was probably at home right now—wherever home was—trying to figure out what to wear for a date when she had no idea where she was going.

Brandon looked at the clock on his nightstand. 3:32 PM.

Less than four hours until he was supposed to pick up a woman whose address he didn't know, for a date at a restaurant she didn't know about, with no way to contact her.

"Rachel."

His sister would know Amanda's address. She'd have Amanda's number. She'd also never let him live this down.

Brandon grabbed his phone from the dresser, his thumb hesitating over Rachel's contact. He could already hear her laughter. But what choice did he have?

He hit call.

One ring. Two rings. Three—

"What's up, brother?" Rachel cheerfully answered.

"Rachel, I need your help. Right now."

The cheer vanished, replaced by concern. "Brandon? What's wrong?"

"I have a date with Amanda at seven—"

"I know!" The excitement returned to her voice. "She's been texting me all day about what to wear. She's adorable, Brandon. She sent me three different outfit photos asking which—"

"She has?" Brandon interrupted, his panic ratcheting higher. "What did you tell her?"

"Nothing! I said you'd probably keep it casual, nothing too fancy, but honestly I have no idea where you're taking her. Where are you taking her?"

Brandon closed his eyes. "The Riverside Inn."

The silence on the other end stretched for three long seconds.

"THE RIVERSIDE INN?" Rachel's voice shot up an octave. "Brandon, that's fancy! That's like... an actual nice restaurant fancy!"

"I know!"

"Amanda's probably pulling out casual clothes thinking you're going to Martha's or maybe that burger place over in Fayetteville!"

"I KNOW!"

"And you haven't told her?"

"I can't tell her because I don't have her phone number! And even if I did, I couldn't pick her up because I don't know where she lives!"

This time the silence was followed by laughter. Not gentle, sympathetic laughter. Full-bodied, gasping for-air, sister-discovering-her-brother-is-an-idiot laughter.

"Rachel, this isn't funny!"

"Oh, but it is," she managed between gasps. "You asked a woman on a date without getting her phone number or her address?"

"It seemed romantic at the time! We were at Martha's, and the moment was perfect, and—"

"And you're a disaster," Rachel finished, but her tone was fond. "Okay, okay. Stop panicking. What time did you tell her?"

"Seven."

"It's 3:35. We have time. I'm coming over right now."

"You know where she lives, right?"

"Brandon! Get a grip! Of course, I know where she lives. I'm her best friend, not some romantically impaired farmer who asks women out without basic information."

"Rachel—"

"247 Maple Street. Blue Craftsman house with white trim. You've driven past it literally hundreds of times."

"Thank you," Brandon breathed.

"Don't thank me yet. I'm coming over to make sure you don't screw this up further. Do NOT do anything until I get there. Don't get dressed; don't make any decisions. Just... stand there and try not to panic."

"I'm already panicking."

"Then panic quietly. I'll be there in fifteen minutes."

She hung up. Brandon stood in his bedroom, still shirtless, still processing the fact that he'd almost catastrophically ruined the date before it even began.

Fourteen minutes later, his front door burst open without a knock.

"Where are you?" she called out.

"Bedroom."

She appeared in his doorway, taking in his state of half-undress and general dishevelment with the expression of someone discovering their dog had rolled in something unfortunate.

"You haven't even showered yet?"

"Nope."

"Oh my gosh, you're hopeless." But she was already pulling out her phone, typing rapidly. "Okay, first things first. I'm texting Amanda right now."

"What are you saying?"

"That you wanted her to know you're taking her to The Riverside Inn and she should dress nice but not formal."

She hit send, and her phone buzzed with a response in seconds.

"What did she say?"

Rachel's grin was wicked as she read aloud. "OMG, The Riverside Inn?? Thank you for the warning!"

Relief flooded through Brandon so fast it made him dizzy. "She's not upset?"

"Upset? Brandon, I'm sure she's thrilled. She just sent another text—'I need to completely reconsider my outfit. THANK YOU FOR THE HEADS UP.'" Rachel looked up from her phone. "Crisis averted. Now she has time to get ready properly. Speaking of which—you. Shower. Now."

"I can handle—"

"While you're in there," Rachel continued as if he hadn't spoken, "I'll go through your closet and find something appropriate for you to wear."

"I can dress myself, Rachel."

"You were going to wear khakis, weren't you?"

Brandon didn't answer, which was answer enough.

"Shower. Go. Use the good soap Mom gave you for Christmas, not that industrial degreaser you usually use."

"It's not industrial—"

"Brandon."

He went.

The hot water helped clear his head, washing away the dirt and sweat along with some of the panic.

When he emerged, towel wrapped around his waist, she had laid out clothes on his bed with the precision of a surgical nurse preparing instruments.

"The dark blue shirt—it brings out your eyes. The black dress pants—Mom bought you for Christmas that you never wore."

"I don't remember those."

"You're hopeless." She held up a belt. "This one. Real leather, not that fabric thing you usually wear."

"That fabric thing is perfectly—"

"And this cologne." She produced a bottle from his dresser that he'd forgotten existed. "Not too much. Just here and here." She pointed to her wrists and neck. "Women notice smell more than men realize."

Brandon grabbed the clothes, waiting for her to leave. She didn't.

"I'm not getting dressed with you standing there."

"Right. I'll go raid your kitchen while you make yourself presentable. But hurry up. We need to talk."

She left, and Brandon dressed quickly in the clothes she'd selected. He had to admit, looking in the mirror, that Rachel knew what she was doing. The shirt fit well; the dress pants were definitely nicer than jeans, and together they made him look... like someone who'd made an effort. Like someone going on a date.

He found Rachel in his kitchen, eating an apple.

"Better," she pronounced, looking him over. "Much better. Turn around."

"Rachel—"

"Turn."

He turned. She stepped forward and adjusted his collar, smoothing the fabric across his shoulders.

"Are you ready for this?" she asked quietly.

"No."

"Good. That means it matters."

Brandon met his twin's eyes. "What if I'm not ready to...?"

"Then you fake it till you make it."

"That's terrible advice."

"That's the only advice. Brandon, you can't wait to be ready. Readiness doesn't come by waiting. It comes from doing the thing that scares you and discovering you survived it."

"When did you become wise?"

"When my brother needed me to be." She pulled him into a quick, fierce hug. "Dad would want this for you. He'd want you to be happy."

"I know."

"And Mom's probably at home right now praying up a storm for this date to go well."

Despite his nerves, Brandon smiled. "Probably."

Rachel stepped back, studying him with the critical eye of a sister who'd spent years perfecting the art of brotherly assessment. "You'll do. You clean up nicely when you try."

"Thanks. I think."

"I'm gonna go because you need time to clean that disaster you call a truck."

Brandon groaned. "The truck." He hadn't even thought about the state of his vehicle—receipts, empty water bottles, various tools, and who knows what else.

"Go clean it. Like, really clean it. Not just shoving everything under the seats."

"I don't just shove—"

"Brandon."

"Fine."

Rachel headed for the door, then paused. "Hey. You've got this. Just be yourself. Well, maybe the slightly better-groomed version of yourself."

"Very encouraging."

"I try." She grinned. "Oh, and Brandon? The whole town knows about this date. April told Coral, Coral told her sister, her sister told Martha—"

"Of course she did."

"So no pressure, but everyone's going to want details tomorrow."

She left with a laugh, leaving Brandon alone in his cabin. He looked at the clock. 4:52 PM. Just over two hours until the most important date of his... well, possibly his life.

No pressure at all.

He spent the next forty minutes cleaning his truck, discovering receipts from two years ago, three different types of pliers, a coffee mug he'd been looking for the past month, and enough loose change to fund a small vacation. By the time he finished, the vehicle looked almost respectable.

Back in the cabin, he took extra care with the final preparations. His father's watch went on his wrist. A final check in the mirror showed someone he almost didn't recognize—cleaned up, dressed nicely, looking like someone who had his life together.

"Fake it till I make it," he murmured to his reflection.

At 6:35, he climbed into his truck and headed toward town. The drive felt both endless and far too quick.

Maple Street appeared before he was ready for it.

247 Maple Drive. Blue Craftsman house, white trim, perfectly maintained, with fall decorations that looked like something from one of those magazines his mother read. Of course Amanda's house would be perfect. It was so essentially her that it made his chest tight.

He parked at the curb and sat for a moment, watching the minute hand on his father's watch tick toward seven. At 6:58, he got out, walked up the stone path lined with mums in harvest colors, and climbed the three steps to her porch.

Brandon knocked—three solid raps that he hoped sounded confident rather than nervous.

Footsteps approached from inside. The door opened.

And Brandon forgot how to breathe.

Amanda stood in her doorway wearing a deep green dress that made her eyes look impossibly blue, falling just past her knees, with some kind of delicate pattern he couldn't quite make out in the porch light. Her hair was different too, curled in soft waves that framed her face. She'd done something with makeup that made her eyes look bigger, her lips pinker, her whole face somehow more Amanda than ever.

"Wow," he said, because apparently that was the only word his brain could produce.

Color rose in her cheeks, but she smiled. "You look pretty wow yourself."

They stood there for a moment, two people who'd known each other for years trying to navigate this new territory where everything familiar had become thrillingly foreign.

"Should we…" Brandon gestured toward his truck.

"Let me grab my purse." She disappeared briefly, returning with a small clutch that matched her shoes—something else he'd never noticed before, that Amanda paid attention to things like matching shoes and purses.

He offered his arm as they walked toward the truck, a gesture that felt both old-fashioned and exactly right. She took it naturally, her hand light on his forearm, and Brandon was suddenly hyperaware of every point of contact.

At the truck, Brandon opened the passenger door.

"Such a gentleman."

"My mother would disown me if I weren't."

She climbed in, careful with her dress, and Brandon closed the door before walking around to his side.

As he started the engine, Amanda said, "I have a confession."

"Already?"

"Rachel told me about your panic attack this afternoon."

Heat flooded Brandon's face. "She did?"

"She said you realized you didn't know where I lived and had what she called 'a complete meltdown of epic proportions.'"

"It wasn't a complete meltdown. It was more of a… significant moment of concern."

Amanda's laugh filled the cab of the truck, warm and genuine. "It's actually really sweet."

"Sweet is one word for it."

"That you were that nervous about tonight? That you wanted everything to be perfect? Yeah, Brandon. That's sweet."

She reached over and briefly touched his hand where it rested on the gearshift. The contact lasted maybe two seconds, but Brandon felt it like electricity.

"I was nervous too," she admitted, pulling her hand back. "Still am."

"Yeah?"

"I changed my outfit four times. Rachel can confirm because I sent her pictures of each one."

"And this was choice number four?"

"Five, actually." She smoothed the fabric of her dress. "I've wanted to go to the Riverside Inn for years but never had a reason."

"And now you do?"

"Now I do."

They drove through Laurel Ridge as the sun began its descent behind the mountains, painting everything in shades of gold and amber. The familiar streets looked different in this light, or maybe it was just that Brandon was seeing them through different eyes—eyes that kept drifting to the woman beside him, who was looking out the window with a small smile playing at her lips.

"You know what's funny?" Amanda said as they passed the town limits.

"What?"

"We've known each other for most of our lives, but this feels like the first time we're really... meeting each other."

Brandon glanced at her, finding her already looking at him. "Yeah," he agreed. "It does."

The road curved ahead, following the river toward the restaurant.

"I'm glad you panicked today," she said.

"Why?"

"Because it means this matters to you as much as it matters to me."

Brandon held out his hand toward her, and Amanda's fingers interlaced with his.

"It matters," he said simply.

They drove the rest of the way, hands linked across the console, while the sky deepened from gold to pink to the first hints of purple. The Riverside Inn appeared ahead, lights twinkling in the growing dusk.

He squeezed Amanda's hand gently as he turned into the restaurant's parking lot.

She squeezed back.

And for the first time in longer than he could remember, Brandon Whitaker felt like he was exactly where he was supposed to be.

Chapter 18

The hostess led them through the indoor dining area of The Riverside Inn. Amanda followed, hyperaware of Brandon's hand resting lightly at the small of her back.

Crystal glassware caught the candlelight on every table they passed, and the soft murmur of conversation mixed with a soft country song playing in the background. The other diners looked comfortable in their elegance, like they belonged in this world of white tablecloths and multiple forks, and Amanda felt a flutter of uncertainty. She ran a gift shop. She arranged window displays and ordered inventory and helped customers find the perfect thank-you card. What was she doing in a place like this?

"Your table is on the patio," the hostess said, reaching for the French doors that opened onto the back of the restaurant. "Mr. Whitaker requested riverside seating."

The doors opened, and Amanda's breath caught.

String lights created a canopy of stars overhead, their warm glow reflecting off the dark water of the New River below. Their table sat in a corner position, offering both privacy and a perfect view of the water tumbling over rocks, the sound mixing with the soft country music that drifted from hidden speakers. A candle flickered in a hurricane glass at the center of their table, and the place settings included more silverware than Amanda typically used in a week.

Brandon pulled out her chair, and she settled into it, still taking in the romantic atmosphere that seemed almost too perfect to be real.

"This is beautiful," she said. "I can't believe I've lived here my whole life and never been here."

Brandon took his seat across from her. "I wanted tonight to be special."

The simple honesty in his voice made her heart perform a complicated rhythm. "It already is."

A waiter appeared—an older gentleman with silver hair and the kind of dignified bearing that suggested he'd been doing this longer than either of them had been alive.

"Good evening. I'm Charles, and I'll be taking care of you tonight. May I start you with something to drink? We have an excellent selection of wines, or perhaps something else?"

Amanda glanced at Brandon, who seemed to be leaving the decision to her.

"Sweet tea?"

"Two sweet teas," he told Charles, who nodded as if they'd ordered champagne.

"I'll give you a few moments with the menu," Charles said, disappearing as smoothly as he'd arrived.

Amanda opened the leather-bound menu and tried not to react to the prices. Everything was à la carte, with a few words she didn't recognize and descriptions that made simple food sound like poetry.

They studied their menus in comfortable quiet for a moment, the sound of the river and distant conversation creating a peaceful backdrop. Amanda found herself stealing glances at Brandon over the leather-bound folder, noting how the candlelight played across his features.

"Tell me something else I don't know about you," Brandon said suddenly, setting his menu aside.

She looked up from the bewildering array of entrees to find him watching her with those blue eyes that seemed darker in the candlelight.

"I wanted to be a teacher," she said. "When I was little. Elementary school, specifically. I used to line up my stuffed animals and teach them lessons, make little tests for them."

"Do you ever regret not following that path?"

"No. I love what I do. I love being part of people's celebrations and commemorations. I love that they trust me with their special moments."

Charles reappeared with their sweet teas and to take their orders. After a brief discussion about the menu—Brandon admitting he didn't know what half the words meant either—they both ordered the ribeye with roasted vegetables, laughing at their matching choices.

"Your turn," Amanda said when Charles left. "What did you want to be? Before you knew the farm would be your life?"

Brandon was quiet for a long moment, turning his tea glass in slow circles on the tablecloth.

"An architect," he said finally. "I loved the idea of building things that would last. Creating spaces where people would live their lives, make memories. I used to draw house plans in my notebooks during algebra."

"What kind of houses?"

His face relaxed into something almost boyish. "Farmhouses, mostly. Big wraparound porches, kitchens with windows overlooking gardens. Places that felt like they grew out of the land rather than being imposed on it."

"You could still do that," Amanda said carefully. "Design things, I mean."

"Maybe." He looked out toward the river. "The farm is a different kind of building, I guess. Building soil health, building community connections through the harvest season. Still creating things that last. My dad always said that what we build with our hands is temporary, but what we build in community and faith—that's eternal."

The mention of his father and faith felt natural, unforced, and Amanda saw the truth of it in Brandon's eyes.

Their food arrived—beautiful presentations that looked almost too good to disturb. But the first bite proved the appearance wasn't just for show. The meat was perfectly cooked; the vegetables roasted to caramelized perfection.

They ate and talked; the conversation flowed more easily with each passing minute. Amanda learned that Brandon loved reading mystery novels. He'd taught himself to play the guitar but only played when no one was around to hear. He missed his best friend from high school, Caleb, who now lived in Oregon and only communicated through occasional texts about football scores.

"What makes you happiest?" Amanda asked, emboldened by the way he listened to every answer she gave as if it mattered deeply.

Brandon thought about it, cutting a piece of steak. "Sunday mornings when the mist is rising off the fields or the river. That first cup of coffee on my porch when the world's still quiet. The sound of rain on the barn roof. Watching things grow that I planted." He paused, then looked directly at her. "Tonight. This makes me happy."

Amanda felt heat rise in her cheeks, but she didn't look away. "What scared you most about taking over the farm completely?"

"That I'd fail it. Not fail at it—fail it. The land, the legacy, the responsibility of it all. Three generations of Whitakers made that farm what it is. What if I'm the one who loses it?"

The vulnerability in his voice made Amanda reach across the table. Brandon met her halfway, their fingers intertwining next to the candle.

"You won't," she said firmly. "You're too stubborn to fail at anything you care about."

"Is that what you think? That I'm stubborn?"

"I think you're careful. Deliberate. You don't do anything halfway." She ran her thumb across his knuckles, feeling the calluses from years of hard work. "When you commit to something, you're all in."

"Is that good or bad?"

"Both. Neither. It just is."

They'd finished eating without Amanda really noticing, too absorbed in the conversation and the warm weight of Brandon's hand in hers. Charles appeared to clear their plates, offering dessert, which they both declined in favor of coffee.

The night had deepened around them. The other diners on the patio created a soft backdrop of conversation and occasional laughter. The string lights seemed brighter against the darker sky, and the river's sound had become a constant, soothing rhythm.

Then the music changed.

The upbeat country song faded into a slower melody, sweeter and more romantic. Amanda recognized the gentle rhythm of a classic country love ballad immediately, the kind that had been playing at weddings and anniversaries for decades. The melody drifted across the patio, and she saw Brandon go still, his attention shifting to the music.

He was quiet for so long that Amanda wondered if something was wrong. Then, he stood.

"Dance with me?"

Amanda looked around at the other diners, the servers moving between tables. "Here?"

"Right here."

He extended his hand, and without hesitation, she took it.

Brandon led her to the small space between their table and the patio railing, where the sound of the river mixed with the music. Other diners glanced their way, but Amanda found she didn't care. All that mattered was Brandon's hand settling at her waist, her hand finding his shoulder, their free hands clasped together.

"I should warn you," Brandon said as they began to move, "I haven't done this in a very long time."

"You're doing fine," Amanda said, and meant it. He moved with surprising confidence, guiding her in a simple pattern that felt as natural as breathing.

The world shrank to just this—the music, the river, the warmth of Brandon's hand at her waist. Amanda was aware of other things peripherally—someone at a nearby table smiling at them, a server pausing to watch—but none of it seemed important compared to being held like this, moving together like they'd been doing it for years instead of seconds.

"I should have done this years ago," Brandon said, his voice low enough that only she could hear.

"Done what?"

"Seen you. Really seen you." His hand tightened slightly at her waist. "You were right there all those years, and I just... looked past you. I regret that."

"It wasn't meant to be back then," Amanda reminded him. "God's timing, not ours."

"Maybe you're right." The words were thoughtful. "I wasn't ready then. I was blind. Self-absorbed. Stupid."

"Brandon—"

"I'm not anymore," he continued. "Blind, I mean. I see you now, Amanda. I see how you light up when you talk about your shop. I see how you care about everyone around you. I see how you make ordinary moments special just by being in them."

Amanda's throat felt tight. She let her head rest against his chest, feeling the steady thump of his heartbeat through his shirt. His cologne—woody and warm—mixed with the night air and the faint scent of autumn leaves.

"I used to dream about moments like this," she admitted to his shirt.

"Like what?"

"Dating you. Dancing with you. All of it."

His hand moved from her waist to her back, holding her closer. They swayed together as the song reached its bridge, the lyrics about God blessing the broken road that led to love washing over them.

When the music finally faded, they stayed there for a moment, neither ready to let go. Then soft applause broke out from the surrounding tables, and Amanda became aware again of where they were.

She pulled back, her face warm, but Brandon kept hold of her hand as they walked back to their table. Everything felt different now—charged, significant, full of possibility.

"That was beautiful," an older woman at the next table said. "You two make a lovely couple."

Brandon squeezed Amanda's hand, and they sat back down, their hands still linked on the table.

"I haven't felt this way in so long," Brandon said quietly. "Like the future is something to look forward to instead of something to endure."

"What changed?"

"You. You... with your festival plans and your enthusiasm and your way of seeing beauty in everything, and suddenly I remembered what it felt like to want things again."

Charles appeared with the check, and Brandon paid the bill.

They left the restaurant, Brandon's hand at her back again as they walked through the main dining room. Other diners smiled at them with the knowing looks of people who recognized new love when they saw it.

Outside, the night had turned cooler. Stars were visible now, away from the town's lights, scattered across the sky like promises. Brandon opened the truck door for her, and she climbed in, already missing the warmth of his hand.

The drive home was quieter than the drive there, but it was a comfortable quiet filled with possibility. Their hands found each other across the console, fingers intertwining as naturally as breathing. The radio played something soft and instrumental, and the familiar landmarks of Laurel Ridge appeared in the headlights—the church, the town square, Martha's Diner closed for the evening.

"Thank you for tonight," Amanda said as they turned onto Maple Street.

"Thank you for saying yes. Both times—yesterday and today."

Her house appeared too soon, the porch light on just as she'd left it.

Brandon parked and came around to open her door, offering his hand to help her down. They walked to her porch slowly, neither wanting to rush this last part of the evening.

At her door, they stopped, turning to face each other. The porch light cast a warm glow around them, and somewhere in the distance, a dog barked once and fell silent.

"I had a wonderful time," Amanda said, meaning it more than any words could convey.

"So did I." Brandon still held her hand from helping her up the steps. He looked down at their joined fingers, his thumb tracing gentle circles on her palm.

Then, with deliberate slowness, he lifted her hand. Amanda's breath caught as he brought it to his lips, pressing a soft, lingering kiss to her fingers. The gesture was old-fashioned, courtly, and absolutely perfect. She felt warmth spread from her hand all the way to her heart.

"Goodnight, Amanda," he said softly, still holding her hand.

He released her fingers slowly, reluctantly, his own hand dropping to his side as if he didn't quite know what to do with it now. He stepped back, shoving his hands in his pockets. "I'll call you tomorrow. I have your number now."

The callback to his earlier panic made them both smile, easing the intensity of the moment.

Amanda watched him walk to his truck, memorizing the way he moved, the set of his shoulders, and the way he turned back once to look at her before climbing in. She stayed on the porch as he drove away, his taillights disappearing around the corner.

Only then did she lift her hand to look at it, touching the spot where his lips had been. She could still feel the warmth of his kiss, the gentle pressure, and the unspoken promise in the gesture.

Tomorrow, he would call. Tomorrow they would have to figure out what this was becoming.

But tonight—tonight had been perfect.

She went inside, closed the door, and leaned against it, her hand pressed to her heart and a smile she couldn't suppress spreading across her face.

Chapter 19

The autumn candle display had been perfect the first time Amanda arranged it. And the second. But her hands needed something to do with all the energy thrumming through her veins, so she adjusted the placement of a cinnamon-scented pillar for the third time.

Morning light poured through Indulgences' front windows, transforming ordinary glass into panels of liquid gold. The whole shop seemed brighter somehow, as if someone had turned up the saturation on everything. Even the familiar creak of the old wooden floors beneath her feet sounded like music.

Amanda moved through the shop alone, the peaceful morning quiet wrapping around her like a warm hug. But underneath that peace, energy bubbled through her veins like champagne. She straightened the display of harvest-themed tea towels that didn't need straightening and adjusted the angle of the decorative pumpkin that was already perfectly fine as it was.

The sound of the back door opening pulled her from her reverie. April's voice carried from the storage room.

"Morning, Amanda! I brought the new invoice sheets you wanted to review." April pushed through the swinging door and stopped mid-step, the folder in her hands forgotten. Her chestnut brown hair was pulled back in a ponytail, and her professional composure vanished as she stared at Amanda. "Okay, what happened? You're literally glowing."

The back door opened again, and Coral's cheerful voice preceded her entrance.

"Sorry we're a few minutes late! I made April stop so I could grab muffins from—" Coral emerged through the storage room door, her curly brown hair with its honey highlights bouncing as she moved. Her eyes immediately zeroed in on Amanda. "Oh, my goodness. You had your date last night! Come on... tell us!"

The back door opened once more, and Whitney hurried in, her backpack bouncing against her hip.

"Mornin' everyone! Mom dropped me off before—" The seventeen-year-old stopped, her blonde ponytail swinging as she looked between the three women. "What's happening? What did I miss?"

"Amanda had a date with Brandon Whitaker last night," April informed her.

Whitney's backpack hit the floor with a thud. "Brandon Whitaker? The farmer guy? The one with the really nice—"

"Whitney!" Amanda interrupted, her face now definitely resembling one of the crimson maple leaves decorating the shop windows.

"I was going to say truck," Whitney finished with an impish grin. "That blue pickup of his is awesome."

All three employees converged on Amanda, forming a semicircle of eager faces demanding information.

"We open in half an hour," Amanda said.

"Which gives you thirty minutes to tell us everything," Coral said firmly. "Start talking, boss. Where did he take you?"

Amanda glanced at the clock, then at the three expectant faces. Her resistance crumbled. "The Riverside Inn."

The collective gasp could have sucked all the oxygen from the shop.

"The Riverside Inn?" Whitney clutched the counter dramatically. "That's like, anniversary-level fancy. That's where my parents go for special occasions."

"What did you wear?" April demanded.

"What did you eat?" Coral added.

"Did he kiss you?" Whitney asked, then clapped both hands over her mouth as if the words had escaped without permission.

"Whitney!" Amanda's laugh bubbled up, impossible to contain.

"It's a valid question," April defended. "Look at her face! Something definitely happened."

Amanda tried to focus on the morning tasks—straightening the greeting card display.

"I've never seen you like this," Coral said. "Whatever happened, it was good for you."

"It was..." Amanda searched for words. "It was perfect. He was perfect. The whole evening was—"

"Perfect?" April bounced on her toes. "Amanda said perfect three times. This is serious."

The shop opening preparation continued in a distracted fashion, while Amanda told them the condensed version of her unforgettable dinner—her nervousness, the riverside table, the unexpected dance—all while attempting to count the cash drawer and arrange displays. Her hands moved through the familiar tasks, but her mind was entirely focused on the previous evening.

At precisely 10 AM, Amanda flipped the sign to OPEN and un-locked the door.

Mrs. Garrett swept in moments later, her silver hair perfectly coiffed despite the morning breeze, her lavender cardigan buttoned precisely. Her eyes found Amanda immediately.

"Good morning, Amanda dear," she said, her voice carrying a par-ticular tone that meant she knew something. "It was such a lovely evening last night, wasn't it? Perfect weather for dining riverside."

Amanda's stomach dropped. Of course. In Laurel Ridge, privacy was more mythology than reality.

"Yes, it was a beautiful evening," Amanda managed, aiming for casual and missing by approximately a mile.

Mrs. Garrett's smile widened, creating a network of laugh lines around her eyes. "I was there with Harold for our anniversary. Forty-seven years yesterday." She moved closer to the counter, lower-ing her voice to a stage whisper that everyone could still hear perfectly. "Wasn't that you I saw? With the Whitaker boy?"

"We... yes. We had dinner."

"Dinner?" Mrs. Garrett's eyebrows rose. "My dear, what I saw was considerably more than dinner. The way that young man looked at you when you were dancing..." She pressed a hand to her heart. "Re-minded me of my Harold when we were courting. Honey... I enjoyed watching the two of you... made me feel young again."

"Such a lovely young man," she continued, selecting a small au-tumn-scented candle from the display Amanda had been fussing with. "It's about time that boy remembered how to smile. And you, dear..." She patted Amanda's hand as she paid for her purchase. "You were glowing. Still are."

After Mrs. Garrett left. The morning continued with a steady stream of customers. Amanda rang up a five-dollar purchase as fifty dollars, and April had to fix the error in the computer system. She placed the new shipment of harvest-themed tea towels with the Christmas ornaments before Coral redirected her. She stared at the same inventory sheet for ten minutes without seeing a single number.

A little after eleven, the door didn't just open—it practically exploded inward, the bell jangling in protest.

"Amanda Rose Baker!"

Rachel stood in the doorway, hands planted on her hips, trying to look stern but losing the battle against the grin that threatened to split her face in two. Her eyes sparkled with barely contained excitement.

"Don't you dare hold out on me!"

"Rachel—"

"No. No excuses, no deflecting." Rachel marched across the shop with the determination of someone on a critical mission. "I've been waiting all morning to hear from you. I can't take the suspense any longer." She grabbed Amanda's arm. "Office. Now."

"Rachel, I can't just—"

"Coral, April, Whitney, you've got the shop, right?"

"Absolutely," Coral said, making shooing motions with her hands. "Go."

Rachel practically dragged Amanda to her office, closing the door firmly behind them.

"Sit," Rachel commanded, pointing to Amanda's desk chair.

Amanda sat. Rachel perched on the desk itself, her feet swinging like a child's, though her expression was anything but childlike.

"DETAILS," she demanded. "Every single one. Start from the beginning. And I mean the actual beginning—when he picked you up."

Amanda took a breath, trying to organize her thoughts, but they kept scattering like startled butterflies. "He was nervous."

"Brandon was nervous?"

"Adorably nervous. He opened my door. The truck door and the restaurant door. Every door."

Rachel's expression softened.

"The restaurant was beautiful," Amanda continued. "Our table overlooked the river."

"What else?" Rachel leaned forward eagerly.

"We danced."

Rachel's hands flew to her mouth. "He asked you to dance? In public? At the Riverside Inn? Wait... there's no dance floor."

"Nope. No dance floor. We danced on the patio. Right there on the patio. One song," Amanda said softly. "But Rachel, the way he held me, the way he looked at me... It felt like we were the only two people in the world."

"Did he kiss you?"

"My hand. When he was saying goodnight. It was actually more romantic than a regular kiss would have been. The way he did it—so gentle and deliberate—like I was something precious."

Tears suddenly appeared in Rachel's eyes. "Oh, Amanda."

"What's wrong?"

"Nothing's wrong. Everything's right. It's just..." Rachel wiped at her eyes, laughing at herself. "He texted me at midnight last night."

"He did?"

"Just said, 'Thank you for the help with everything.'" Rachel's voice went thick with emotion. "Such a simple text, but Amanda, Brandon doesn't thank people for emotional stuff. He just doesn't. And this morning he joined us for breakfast? He hasn't done that in ages. And he was whistling."

"Whistling?"

"Like an actual human who was happy. Mom nearly dropped her coffee mug. She literally stood there with her mouth open, holding the pot like she'd forgotten what it was for."

"Really?"

"I haven't seen him this happy since before Dad died. Wait... it's been quite a while, actually." Rachel grabbed both of Amanda's hands, squeezing tight. "You're bringing my brother back to life."

"Rachel—"

"No, listen. I've been praying for this for so long."

"I don't know if—"

"Listen to me. None of this 'I don't know' stuff. You deserve someone who sees how amazing you are, Amanda, and I believe my brother has finally opened his eyes."

Amanda felt tears spill over. "I really do like him, Rachel... this is so much more than a crush."

"Brandon needs someone like you," Rachel said softly. "You both deserve each other. Gosh... you and my brother... finally!"

They were both crying now, laughing at themselves while wiping tears.

"This is ridiculous," Amanda said, reaching for the tissues on her desk. "We're crying over a date."

"We're crying over answered prayers," Rachel corrected. Then, more seriously, "I imagine Mom's probably already planning the wedding."

"Rachel!"

"I'm just saying. Helen Whitaker doesn't—"

Coral's voice interrupted, calling through the door with barely contained excitement. "Amanda! You need to come out here. Now!"

Amanda and Rachel exchanged glances.

"What is it?" Amanda called back.

"Just... you need to see this!"

They emerged from the office to find Coral standing behind the counter, holding what had to be the most stunning flower arrangement Amanda had ever seen. April and Whitney flanked her, all three beaming like they'd won the lottery.

"These just arrived for you," Coral said, her voice reverent.

Amanda's legs felt unsteady. The arrangement was gorgeous. Soft pink peonies nestled against pristine white hydrangeas, while lavender roses peeked through like secrets. Sprigs of berries and baby's breath created a delicate cloud around the edges. A burgundy ribbon was tied around the vase.

"Oh my," Amanda breathed.

Rachel was practically vibrating beside her. "There's a card!"

Amanda's hands shook as she reached for the small envelope tucked among the blooms. The surrounding women held their breath as she opened it, her eyes scanning the masculine handwriting while Rachel peeked over her shoulder.

Thank you for saying yes. Three times now. Looking forward to many more. -B

Rachel's squeal could probably be heard in the next county. "THREE TIMES? What three times?"

"When he asked me to lunch at Martha's," Amanda said softly, touching one of the peonies with a reverent finger. "When he asked me to dinner. And when he asked me to dance, I took his hand."

"He counted each one!" Rachel grabbed Amanda in a hug so tight that breathing became optional. "My brother... the romantic. Geez... why can't I find a man like this?"

Whitney already had her phone out, snapping photos from multiple angles. "This is definitely the most romantic thing I've ever seen. Can I post this on Instagram? Not with your name, just the flowers?"

"These are gorgeous," April sighed, leaning in to smell the blooms.

"That boy knows what he's doing," Coral said with satisfaction. "These aren't 'I had a nice time' flowers. These are 'I'm seriously interested' flowers."

A customer approached the counter. "Young love," she sighed, placing her hand over her heart. "There's nothing quite like it. Congratulations, dear, cherish every moment."

"Thank you," Amanda managed, unsure if she was floating or if her feet were still touching the ground.

"I have to go," Rachel announced suddenly. "But lunch. Today. Martha's. I want you to tell me every aspect of your date again. I just cannot believe this. My brother... gosh, he's good!"

She pulled Amanda into one more fierce hug, whispering, "I'm so happy for you both. You have no idea how happy."

And then she was gone in a whirlwind of energy and joy, leaving Amanda standing there with her flowers and her memories and her heart so full she thought it might burst.

The shop gradually settled back into its rhythm, though every new customer who entered immediately noticed and commented on the spectacular arrangement now prominently displayed where Amanda could see it from anywhere in the shop.

She caught herself staring at them between customers and re-reading the card multiple times.

"You haven't stopped smiling for two hours," April observed during a brief lull, hip-checking Amanda gently as she passed.

"I don't think I can stop," Amanda admitted.

"Good," Coral said. "It's about time you had something—someone—to smile about like this."

"This is like a real-life romance movie!" Whitney sighed, straightening a display of bookmarks.

Amanda picked up the card one more time.

Three times now. Looking forward to many more.

She thought about his nervousness picking her up, the way he'd laughed at dinner, and the feeling of being held in his arms while music drifted across the water.

So am I, Brandon, she thought, her heart so full of hope and possibility that she could barely contain it. *So am I.*

Chapter 20

Brandon pulled open the heavy wooden door of Laurel Ridge Community Church, the familiar creak of the hinges mixing with the sound of the congregation settling into their pews. Morning light streamed through the tall stained-glass windows, painting swaths of amber and crimson across the polished wood floors. The sanctuary smelled exactly as he remembered—lemon furniture polish, old hymnals, and the faint sweetness of flowers from the altar arrangement.

He paused just inside the doorway, letting his eyes adjust from the bright October morning to the softer interior light. The church was filled with families greeting each other in the aisles, children being hushed by their parents, and older couples making their way to the pews they'd sat in for years. The pre-service hum of conversation wrapped around him like something half-remembered, half-new.

His white button-down shirt felt stiff against his shoulders. He'd changed three times that morning before settling on the shirt and khakis—church clothes that had hung untouched in his closet.

Brandon moved down the center aisle, nodding to a few people who caught his eye. Mrs. Henderson gave him a warm smile from her usual spot. Tom Bradley raised his hand in a brief wave from where he sat with his wife and sons. No one made a fuss, no one stared, but Brandon felt the subtle shift in awareness as people noticed his presence.

He found them easily—his family always sat in the same general area, about halfway back on the right side, close enough to hear clearly but far enough back to avoid feeling like they were on display. Helen's silver hair caught the light first, then Rachel's animated gesture as she talked with someone in the row in front of them. And there was Amanda, with her blonde hair falling in soft waves past her shoulders, wearing a deep blue dress.

Beside Amanda sat two people he recognized but had never formally met—Amos and Janelle Baker, Amanda's parents. He knew them the way everyone knew everyone in Laurel Ridge, through years of parallel lives in a small town. Amos Baker was built like what he was—a carpenter who'd spent years working with his hands, broad shoulders and weathered face, his gray hair neatly trimmed. Janelle had the same soft features Amanda had inherited, her brown hair touched with silver, wearing a floral dress with a cream cardigan.

Brandon had reached the pew before Rachel noticed him. Her face lit up with surprise and delight, and she immediately tapped Amanda's leg, whispering, "Look."

Amanda turned, and the smile that bloomed across her face made something ease in Brandon's chest. She looked genuinely pleased to see him, not surprised exactly, but pleased in a way that suggested she'd hoped but hadn't expected.

"Move over," Rachel said to Amanda, already scooting toward their mother. "Make room."

A brief shuffle ensued—Rachel sliding closer to Helen, Amanda moving closer to her mom, hymn books being relocated, Janelle's purse being pulled closer to her feet. Within moments, a space had opened between Rachel and Amanda, perfectly Brandon-sized.

"Good morning," Brandon said quietly as he stepped into the pew.

Amos Baker stood and extended his hand. His grip was firm, calloused—a working man's handshake that Brandon recognized and respected. "Brandon. Good to see you."

"Mr. Baker," Brandon acknowledged.

Janelle stood, her smile warm and maternal. "Morning, Brandon."

"Mornin', ma'am."

He settled into the pew, and Helen leaned forward to catch his eye, and the look on her face—relief, joy, and maternal pride mixed together—made his throat tighten slightly. He'd put that worry in her eyes with his absence, and seeing it replaced with happiness was humbling.

The organist began the prelude, and conversations gradually died away as people found their seats. Brandon picked up a hymnal from the rack in front of him, the weight familiar in his hands. How many Sundays had he held this same book, sung these same songs, taken this ritual for granted?

Pastor Andrew entered from the side door near the altar. His eyes swept the congregation, paused briefly on Brandon with the slightest nod of acknowledgment, then continued their pastoral survey.

"Good morning, church family," Pastor Andrew's voice carried easily through the sanctuary. "What a beautiful October morning God has blessed us with. Let's begin our worship with hymn number 347, 'Great Is Thy Faithfulness.'"

The congregation rose as one, the rustle of movement and pages turning filling the space. Brandon stood, sharing his hymnal with Amanda.

The familiar words rose around him, hundreds of Sunday mornings compressed into this one moment of return. His voice was rusty at first, barely above a whisper, but as the hymn progressed, he sang more strongly. Beside him, Amanda's clear soprano blended with Rachel's slightly off-key enthusiasm and Helen's steady alto.

"Morning by morning new mercies I see," the congregation sang, and Brandon felt the truth of it settling into his bones. He was here. He was singing. He was surrounded by family and community, and somehow, that was enough for this moment.

When they sat back down after the hymn, Brandon felt Amanda's hand brush his where it rested on his thigh. A question maybe, or an offer. Without overthinking it, he turned his palm up and let her fingers slip between his. Her hand was small and warm in his, and when he glanced sideways, she was looking straight ahead, but a soft pink had risen in her cheeks.

Pastor Andrew led them through the morning prayer, and Brandon bowed his head, though his mind was more on the gentle pressure of Amanda's fingers than on the words being spoken.

The offering plate passed, and Brandon released Amanda's hand long enough to add his contribution, then found it again as naturally as breathing. He could feel Rachel noticing from his other side, could sense her barely suppressed glee, but he didn't care. Let her be happy. Let the whole town talk if they wanted.

"Turn in your Bibles to Ecclesiastes chapter eleven," Pastor Andrew said, and the sound of pages turning filled the sanctuary. "We're going to talk this morning about sowing in faith, even when we cannot see the harvest."

Brandon reached for the Bible in the pew rack with his free hand, fumbling it open one-handed rather than let go of Amanda. She squeezed his fingers gently.

"'Cast your bread upon the waters,'" Pastor Andrew read, "'for after many days you will find it again. Give portions to seven, yes to eight, for you do not know what disaster may come upon the land.'"

The sermon unfolded with Pastor Andrew's characteristic blend of scholarly insight and practical application. He talked about the ancient practice of sowing grain in flooded fields, how farmers would cast seed onto waters that would eventually recede, leaving fertile ground. The apparent foolishness of throwing grain onto water, the faith required to waste what looked like good seed on what seemed like impossible ground.

"The writer of Ecclesiastes understood something we often forget," Pastor Andrew said, pacing slowly across the platform. "We cannot control outcomes. We can only control our obedience. We sow in faith, not because we're guaranteed a harvest, but because sowing is what we're called to do."

Brandon found his mind wandering to his father, who had understood this principle in his bones. James Whitaker had sown constantly—kindness, generosity, faith, work—without always seeing the harvest. He'd planted trees he'd never see reach maturity, taught lessons that wouldn't bear fruit for years, loved people who didn't always love him back.

"Verse four," Pastor Andrew continued. "'Whoever watches the wind will not plant; whoever looks at the clouds will not reap.' How often do we wait for perfect conditions that never come? How often do we let fear of the unknown keep us from sowing what God has given us to sow?"

Amanda's thumb traced a small circle on Brandon's palm, and he wondered if she was thinking about her festival planning, about the risks of trying something new, about the courage required to step into leadership. Or maybe she was thinking about them, about whatever this was becoming, about the seeds being sown in the space between their joined hands.

"The beautiful promise in verse six," Pastor Andrew said, his voice warming with the joy of the text. "'Sow your seed in the morning, and at evening let your hands not be idle, for you do not know which will succeed, whether this or that, or whether both will do equally well.'"

Brandon thought about the morning he'd spent sowing winter rye in the backfield, the evening he'd spent helping Amanda with the festival float, the seeds of returning faith he was planting by sitting in this pew. Which would succeed? Which would fail? The text suggested it didn't matter—the calling was to sow, not to control the harvest.

The sermon wound toward its conclusion, and Pastor Andrew's voice gentled. "Some of you are in sowing seasons right now. You're casting bread upon waters that look impossible. You're planting in fields that seem barren. Keep sowing. Some of you are waiting to see what will grow from seeds planted long ago. Keep waiting. And some of you have forgotten how to sow at all, have let fear or grief or disappointment keep your hands idle. Today is the day to pick up your seed bag again."

Brandon felt the words settle into his chest like seeds into prepared soil. He'd been the latter—hands idle, seed bag abandoned, fields lying fallow. But here he was, sitting in church, holding Amanda's hand, choosing to re-enter the rhythm of sowing and hoping.

The sermon ended with prayer, and then the congregation rose for the final hymn. "In the Garden" rang out through the sanctuary, and Brandon sang with more conviction than he'd felt in months.

Amanda's voice beside him was sweet and sure, and when she glanced up at him during the chorus, her eyes were bright with joy.

As the service concluded and people began filing out, Janelle Baker leaned around her daughter to speak to Brandon. "We're so glad you could join us this morning," she said, and there was something knowing in her maternal smile, the same look Helen got when she was pleased but trying not to be obvious about it.

"Thank you, Mrs. Baker," Brandon said. "It's good to be here."

They moved with the flow of people toward the back of the church, where Pastor Andrew and his wife, Lily, stood greeting congregants. The morning had warmed considerably, and through the open doors, Brandon could see the sun shining brightly and the mountains beyond painted in autumn colors.

When they reached Pastor Andrew, the minister clasped Brandon's hand firmly. "Good to see you this morning, Brandon."

"Good sermon, Pastor."

"The text preached itself, really. Those agricultural metaphors always resonate at this time of year. Hope we'll see you next week."

"Planning on it," Brandon said, and meant it.

They emerged into the sunshine, the whole group naturally walking to the right of the church. The wooden pavilion sat behind the church on the wide, expansive lawn, past the recreation hall. Its open sides and strings of lights looked welcoming in the morning light. Tables were already set with large coffee urns and platters of cookies that various church members had brought—Brandon recognized his mom's snickerdoodles and Martha's chocolate chip cookies.

The fellowship area was filling with clusters of conversation, children darting between adults' legs, teenagers clustered in their own corner trying to look too cool for church fellowship while secretly enjoying the cookies. It was fellowship, familiar and comforting, the kind of community gathering Brandon hadn't realized he'd missed until he was back in the middle of it.

Amos Baker fell into step beside Brandon as they approached the coffee table. "Heard your having a good harvest season," he said, his tone conversational, man to man.

"Better than expected," Brandon replied. "The wet spring had me worried, but the summer dried out just right."

"Funny how that works sometimes. The seasons we worry about most turn out to be the ones that surprise us." Amos poured a coffee. "Same with wood. Sometimes the lumber I'm sure is going to warp turns out to be the strongest."

Brandon accepted the filled cup, recognizing the parallel being drawn without it being hammered home. "Your renovation work must keep you busy. I heard you're working on the Johnsons' kitchen."

"Almost done with that one. Janelle's already got me lined up for three more projects before Christmas." Amos chuckled. "Forty years of marriage teaches you not to argue with scheduling."

"James always said the same thing," Helen interjected, approaching with her own coffee. "Though he usually added something about how the smartest thing a man could do was marry a woman smarter than himself."

"Wise man," Amos agreed. His eyes drifted to where Amanda stood talking with Rachel and his wife, the three women laughing about something. "Though I suspect wisdom runs in the Whitaker family."

The comment was mild, but the meaning was clear enough. Brandon met the older man's steady gaze and nodded slightly.

Martha Kincaid approached their small group, carrying a plate of cookies. "Brandon. Good to see you this morning."

"Martha," Brandon acknowledged, accepting the cookie she pressed into his hand.

"I was just telling Earl the other day," Martha continued, "that October's always been a month for returning. Geese come back south, leaves come back to earth, and people come back to where they belong."

Before Brandon could formulate a response to that bit of philosophy, Earl himself joined them, moving with the careful dignity of his sixty-some years. "Morning, Brandon. Good to see you, son."

The "son" hit something tender in Brandon's chest. Earl had been his father's friend, had served as a pallbearer at the funeral, had sent a sympathy card with a handwritten note about James's integrity that Brandon still kept in his Bible.

"Morning, Earl."

"Your daddy would be pleased," Earl said simply, and then moved on to refill his coffee, leaving the words to settle however they would.

The conversation shifted and flowed around him—Helen discussing the upcoming harvest Sunday service with Janelle, Amos drawn into a discussion about lumber prices with Tom Bradley, Rachel pulling Amanda away to greet one of their friends. Brandon found himself standing with his coffee, watching the easy rhythm of community fellowship happening around him.

"Overwhelming?" Amanda appeared at his elbow awhile later, having escaped Rachel's social whirlwind.

"No," Brandon said, considering. "Actually, no. It's like... muscle memory. I know how to do this, even if I haven't in a while."

"Like riding a bike?"

"More like..." Brandon searched for the right comparison. "More like coming back to a house you lived in as a kid. Everything's familiar but looks different because you're different."

Amanda slipped her hand into his. "Different how?"

Brandon thought about it, watching his mother laugh at something Janelle had said, seeing Rachel eat another cookie while straightening the platters, noting how the morning light through the pavilion's open sides caught the silver in Amos Baker's hair.

"I think I spent so long trying not to feel the hard things that I forgot how to feel the good things too," he said quietly. "Like I shut down all of it instead of just the pain."

"And now?"

"Now I'm thinking about what Pastor Andrew said. About sowing in the morning and the evening. About not knowing which will grow." He squeezed her hand gently. "About being willing to try, anyway."

Mrs. Henderson approached with a plate of cookies. "Brandon, dear, you're looking too thin. Have another cookie."

"Mrs. Henderson, I've already had two—"

"Nonsense. Growing boys need proper feeding." She pressed two more cookies into his free hand, patted his cheek like he was still twelve, and bustled away before he could protest further.

Amanda laughed, the sound bright in the morning air. "Growing boy?"

"I'm thirty years old," Brandon said with fond exasperation. "I haven't been a growing boy in over a decade."

"You'll always be twelve to Mrs. Henderson. She probably still sees you in your little league uniform."

"Please. I peaked in high school football. Everything since has been downhill."

"I don't know," Amanda said thoughtfully. "I think you might be entering your prime."

Before Brandon could respond to that, Rachel appeared with their mothers in tow. "We're heading out," she announced. "Mom wants to check on the pork roast, and I promised to help with lunch."

"Amanda, dear, you and your parents are welcome to join us," Helen offered. "I made plenty."

Janelle smiled warmly. "That's so kind, Helen, but we have plans with my sister's family today. Perhaps another Sunday?"

"Any time," Helen said, and the way the two mothers looked at each other suggested they were already making silent plans, the kind of maternal coordination that happened below the surface of regular conversation.

The group moved toward the parking lot together, the October sun warm on their faces. The mountains surrounding Laurel Ridge were showing off their autumn colors—scarlet maples, golden birches, orange oaks—like God had taken a paintbrush to the landscape.

At the cars, there was the usual dance of goodbye hugs and see-you-laters. Amos shook Brandon's hand again, his grip firm and approving. Janelle surprised Brandon by giving him a quick hug.

"Lunch with your mom?" Amanda asked as her parents got into their car.

"Wouldn't miss it," Brandon said.

She smiled, that bright smile that had been drawing him in since she'd shown up at his farm weeks ago with her enthusiasm and determination. "Good. I'll see you there."

As the Bakers drove away and Helen, Rachel and Amanda headed to their vehicles, Brandon stood in the church parking lot, not quite ready for the morning to end. The church bells began to ring the hour, and the sound carried across the valley like it had every Sunday for longer than anyone could remember.

"Brandon?" Amanda had paused by her car. "Thank you for being here today. I'm proud of you."

"You made it easier," he said.

She tilted her head slightly. "I didn't do anything."

"You held my hand."

"That's nothing."

"No," Brandon said firmly. "It's not nothing. It's..."

He searched for the right words, standing there in the October sunshine with the church bells still echoing and the mountains watching and this woman waiting patiently for him to figure out what he was trying to say.

"It's sowing seeds," he said finally. "Even when we don't know what will grow."

Amanda's expression softened into something so tender it made his chest ache. "Then let's keep sowing," she said simply.

She got into her car and drove away, leaving Brandon standing in the parking lot. But he didn't feel left behind. Instead, he felt like someone who had finally remembered what it was like to plant things, to hope for growth, to trust that some seeds—maybe the ones that mattered most—would find good soil.

Helen honked the horn of her car gently. "You coming to lunch, or are you going to stand there all day looking moonstruck?"

Rachel's laughter carried through the open car window. "Leave him alone, Mom. He's processing. Brandon processes externally by staring into space. It's his spiritual gift."

Brandon walked to his truck, shaking his head but unable to suppress his smile. "I'll meet you at the house," he called to them.

As he drove home, following the familiar roads that wound through Laurel Ridge toward the farm, Brandon thought about sowing and reaping, about bread cast on waters, about the mysterious ways that faith and hope and love could take root even in soil that seemed too damaged to produce anything worth harvesting.

The church bells had long since stopped ringing, but their echo seemed to follow him home, a benediction over this ordinary Sunday that had somehow become a marker of something new beginning. Or maybe something old beginning again. Or maybe it was both at once, the past and future meeting in this present moment of choosing to show up, to hold on, to sow seeds even when the harvest remained beautifully uncertain.

Chapter 21

Amanda stretched from the ladder, her fingertips barely grazing the lamppost as she tried to loop the harvest garland at just the right angle. The morning sun caught the copper and gold leaves woven through the greenery, making them shimmer like nature's own jewelry. If she could just reach another inch—

"Careful there."

Brandon's hands steadied her waist from below, warm and solid through her flannel shirt.

"I've got it," she said. The garland cooperated on her next attempt, wrapping perfectly around the black iron of the vintage lamppost.

"I know you do. But I'd rather not explain to Rachel how I let her best friend fall off a ladder on my watch."

Amanda secured the garland with the spool of wire she'd tucked into her pocket and made her way down, Brandon hovering near until her boots were firmly on the sidewalk.

"Thank you."

"Anytime." He held her gaze for a moment before turning back to his truck. "Where do you want the big pumpkin display? Mom's asking."

Amanda consulted her mental map of Main Street's transformation. All week she'd been dreaming about this morning, when her vision would finally become reality. "The intersection at Cedar and Main. Those hay bales Earl set up need something spectacular as a centerpiece."

"On it." Brandon headed back to the flatbed trailer that held a beautiful collection of pumpkins. Each one had been selected carefully—no blemishes, no flat sides, just pure autumn perfection in shades ranging from deep orange to cream to that dusty green that only heirloom varieties achieved.

Main Street hummed with activity; several volunteers had shown up to help. Rachel stood on a ladder of her own outside the Sweet Shoppe, directing teenage volunteers hanging a massive "Fall Festival" banner between buildings. The letters cut from burlap and outlined in burgundy ribbon caught the breeze and danced against the clear October sky.

"A little higher on the left," Rachel called out. "No, your other left, Marcus!"

Martha and Helen had commandeered the planters that lined the sidewalk, filling them with chrysanthemums in shades of rust and gold. The two women worked with the efficiency of long practice, their conversation a steady stream that jumped from topic to topic without apparent logic but perfect understanding.

"These burgundy ones are gorgeous, Helen," Martha said, nestling another pot into place. "You've outdone yourself this year."

"The secret is bone meal in August," Helen replied, then raised her voice slightly. "Amanda, dear, should we cluster these tighter or leave room for the gourds?"

"Leave about six inches," Amanda called back, already moving to help Coral and April with the window displays. "We'll tuck the small white pumpkins between them."

Every storefront on Main Street had agreed to participate this year. Even the new insurance office that had just opened up had requested decorations, though Amanda suspected that had more to do with peer pressure than genuine enthusiasm.

She grabbed an armload of fodder shocks from Brandon's truck bed, the dried corn stalks rustling like whispers. Their sweet, earthy smell always brought her back to her childhood, when she'd helped her parents set up their own front porch display.

"Those go to the corner by the bank," Brandon said, appearing beside her with his own armload. "I'll help—these are heavier than they look."

They walked together, finding an easy rhythm that had developed over weeks of working on the festival. Amanda had discovered that Brandon was a man of few words but decisive action. He didn't need constant direction or validation—he saw what needed doing and did it.

"I can't believe it's almost time for the festival," she said as they positioned the fodder shocks against the bank's brick facade.

Brandon's hands stilled on the raffia he was using to secure the stalks. "Time flies when you're having fun, right?" He said with a wink.

Before Amanda could respond, a voice called out from across the street.

"Oh my stars, Amanda Baker, this is absolutely stunning!"

Dorothy Garrison approached with the determined stride of a woman who'd been walking these streets for all of her seventy-three years. Her silver hair was set in perfect waves, and she wore a quilted vest covered in appliquéd fall leaves that had probably been in her closet since 1985.

"Mrs. Garrison, thank you. We're trying to make it special."

"Special? Honey, this puts every other year to shame. Especially last year…" Dorothy paused, her eyes sliding to Brandon. "Last year, my goodness… remember Brandon? Your Samantha had all those modern ideas from Charleston. What did she call it? Minimalist harvest?"

Amanda felt Brandon tense beside her.

Dorothy chuckled. "Of course, by festival time she was already complaining about the early mornings. I remember her telling me she didn't understand why everything in Laurel Ridge had to start before sunrise. 'Dorothy,' she said, 'in Charleston, civilized people don't begin working until after nine.' Can you imagine? My goodness, Brandon… all that poor girl did was complain about this and complain about that. Good riddance."

The older woman shook her head, still smiling at the memory.

"Poor dear just wasn't cut out for small-town life, was she? These girls with their big-city ideas don't always understand what it really means to be part of a place like this." Dorothy patted Amanda's arm with affection. "Not like you, dear. You're one of us. Although with how successful that shop of yours has become, I sometimes wonder if Laurel Ridge will be enough to keep you here. My niece in Beckley says stores like yours could thrive anywhere. You could open locations all over the state!"

Amanda's smile felt frozen on her face. "Laurel Ridge is my home, Mrs. Garrison. I'm not going anywhere."

"Of course it is, dear." Dorothy's attention shifted to the window display April was arranging. "Oh, would you look at that! Precious!"

She wandered off, leaving Amanda and Brandon standing by the fodder shocks in silence that felt heavier than the morning fog that was just starting to burn off the mountains.

"I should check on the banner," Brandon said finally, not meeting her eyes.

Amanda watched him walk away, his shoulders rigid with a tension that hadn't been there five minutes ago.

The morning pressed on, a steady rhythm of decisions and directions. Amanda threw herself into the work, but Dorothy's words kept echoing.

She positioned pumpkins with mathematical precision, each one exactly where her sketches had indicated. But now she second-guessed every choice. Was the asymmetrical grouping near the gazebo too modern? Did the color gradation from orange to white seem pretentious?

"You're overthinking," Rachel said, appearing at her elbow with two cups of coffee from Martha's. "I can see it on your face."

"Just want it to be perfect."

"It is already perfect." Rachel handed her a cup—exactly how she liked it. "Stop worrying about what everyone thinks."

Amanda took a sip, the warmth spreading through her chest, but it didn't ease the knot that had formed there. She glanced around to make sure they were relatively alone, then pulled Rachel a few steps away from the main activity.

"Dorothy Garrison just compared me to Samantha."

Rachel's eyebrows shot up. "What? Why would she—"

"Not directly. She was talking about last year's festival, how Samantha had all these 'modern ideas' and was complaining about early mornings." Amanda wrapped both hands around the coffee cup. "Then she said something about how girls with big-city ideas don't understand small-town life."

"But you're from here."

"I know. That's what makes it worse. She patted my arm and said, 'Not like you, dear, you're one of us,' but then in the next breath wondered if Laurel Ridge would be enough to hold me since my shop is doing so well."

"Dorothy Garrison needs to mind her own business." Rachel's face shifted from confusion to understanding to irritation in the span of three seconds. "This is really bothering you, isn't it? What's going on with you?"

Amanda set her coffee on the nearest hay bale and picked up a small pumpkin, turning it in her hands just to have something to do. "This whole thing with Brandon has happened so fast. We went from nothing... to whatever this is... in just a few weeks."

"So?"

"So maybe I'm letting myself get carried away by the romance of it all. The festival, the autumn colors, working together. What if I'm just this year's enthusiasm that fades by winter?"

Rachel grabbed the pumpkin from Amanda's hands and set it aside. "Okay, stop. First of all, you've had feelings for my brother since high school. This isn't some random festival fling."

"I hope not."

"Amanda, my brother adores you... I can tell by the way he looks at you. He's here, helping with decorations when he could be doing a hundred other things on the farm."

"He helped last year too. With Samantha."

Rachel's expression softened. "You're not her."

"How do you know? How does he know? What if—"

"Amanda, I need those gourds!" Coral called as she was working on a display near the gift shop.

"Be right there!" Amanda called back, then lowered her voice. "What if I'm too much? I have all these ideas for the festival. I'm always planning something bigger and better. I'm wanting to expand my shop and make it bigger. What if Brandon wants someone who's content with exactly what is, not always looking at what could be?"

Rachel grabbed Amanda's shoulders. "Listen to me. Samantha wanted to change everything about this place, including Brandon, because she wasn't happy. You want to celebrate what's already here and make it shine. There's a huge difference."

"Ladies, where do you want these signs?" Brandon's voice made them both turn. He stood a few feet away with a stack of painted wooden signs, his expression neutral. Amanda wondered how long he'd been there, if he'd heard any of their conversation.

"Um, those go in the town square," Amanda said. "One at each end of the square."

"Got it." He started to turn away, then paused. "Everything is looking great, by the way."

Then he was gone, heading toward the square with long strides.

Amanda watched Brandon position the first sign, taking care to make sure it was straight. "I should help him."

"You should. But Amanda?" Rachel waited until she had her full attention. "Stop comparing yourself to someone who was never right for this place or for him. You've been part of Laurel Ridge's story your whole life. One thoughtless comment from Dorothy Garrison doesn't change that."

Amanda nodded, trying to let Rachel's words sink in. She picked up her coffee and headed across the street to the town square, where Brandon was working on the second sign.

"Need help?" she offered.

"I could use someone to hold it steady while I secure the base."

She knelt beside the sign, holding it in place while he worked. The morning sun had climbed higher, warming her back through her flannel shirt. Around them, Main Street continued its transformation—Martha calling out instructions about ribbon placement, teenagers laughing as they tangled themselves in garland, and the gentle buzz of community coming together.

"Dorothy Garrison mentioned Samantha," Amanda said quietly, keeping her eyes on the sign.

Brandon's hands stilled on the sign. "She did."

"Her comment really bothered me."

He was quiet for a moment, then resumed working, each movement deliberate and careful. "People don't mean any harm when they bring her up. It just happens. This town has a long memory."

"Must be hard on you, hearing it all the time."

Brandon sat back on his heels and finally met her eyes. "It is. But you know what's harder? Watching it bother you." He set down his tools and gave her his full attention. "Amanda, Dorothy Garrison has opinions about everyone and everything. Last month she told Martha her pie crust was getting tough. Can you imagine?"

Despite herself, Amanda felt her lips twitch toward a smile. "She didn't."

"She did. Martha nearly banned her from the diner." His expression grew more serious. "My point is, people are going to talk. They're going to compare. But Dorothy doesn't know what she's talking about. She sees the surface of things, not what's real."

"What's real?"

Brandon reached over and brushed a piece of dried corn silk from her sleeve, the gesture so gentle it made her throat tight. "This is real.

You and I working together. Not because we have to, but because we want to. That's completely different from last year."

Is it though? The thought whispered through her mind before she could push it away.

"Maybe I'm overthinking this," she said.

"Maybe." He stood, offering her his hand to help her up. "Or maybe overthinking is better than not thinking at all, which is what I did with Samantha."

Tom Bradley's truck pulled up at the curb.

"Brandon! Need your help to unload these props over on Oak Street. Those hay bale arrangements are heavier than they look!"

Brandon squeezed Amanda's hand once, his thumb brushing across her knuckles. "We'll finish this conversation later. When there aren't fifty people around and we can actually talk." He paused, studying her face. "Don't let Dorothy Garrison get in your head, okay?"

Amanda nodded, watching him walk toward Tom's truck.

Chapter 22

Brandon hefted the massive pumpkin, his muscles straining against its weight as he positioned it in the center of the float platform. The Harvest of Blessings display was coming together exactly as Amanda had envisioned—layers of autumn abundance arranged with an eye for color and proportion.

"A little to the left," Tom Bradley called from the ground level, squinting up at the arrangement. "That's it. Perfect."

The barn buzzed with activity. Pastor Andrew and Earl worked on securing the corner blessing stations while Martha directed a group of church ladies arranging dried wheat sheaves. The float had transformed over the past weeks from a bare framework to something that told the story of Laurel Ridge's gratitude and grace.

Brandon climbed down from the platform, brushing his hands on his jeans. The festival started Friday—just two days away—and this was their final run-through before the parade. Everything needed to be tested, adjusted, and secured.

"Brandon, can you help me with these?" His mother stood near the Heritage Family's station, holding a collection of framed photographs she'd gathered from various households. "I want to make sure they're anchored properly."

He joined her near the corner platform, taking the frames as she handed them up. Each photo captured a piece of Laurel Ridge history—the Talbot family at their general store's grand opening, the Henderson clan at a church groundbreaking, and then Helen held up the last frame.

"This one goes in the center," she said softly.

Brandon's hands stilled as he took the photograph. Last year's festival, captured in the golden light of an October afternoon. His father stood in front of the farm's pumpkin display, one arm around Helen, the other around Rachel. Brandon stood slightly apart with Samantha, both of them smiling at the camera. But now, knowing how that story ended, he could see what he'd missed then—the distance in Samantha's eyes, the way she stood just far enough away that they weren't quite touching.

"Your father was so proud that day," Pastor Andrew said, appearing beside the platform. "I remember him pulling me aside, talking about traditions continuing through generations. New branches on the old tree, he called it."

The words settled in Brandon's chest like stones. New branches. His father had been talking about Samantha then, about the family Brandon would build without having a clue about how his marriage to her really was behind closed doors.

"It's a beautiful photo," Brandon managed, securing it carefully among the others.

"Brandon, can you check these mums?" Amanda's voice pulled him from his thoughts. She stood by the main display, surrounded by burgundy and gold chrysanthemums, her hair pulled back in a messy bun that had wisps escaping to frame her face. "I think we might have too many on the left side."

He moved to help her, grateful for the distraction. Together, they adjusted the arrangement. Amanda had a smudge of dirt on her cheek, and Brandon reached over and wiped it away with a grin.

"You're beautiful," he said.

Amanda smiled.

"Looking good up there!" Rachel called out, walking through the barn doors with a tray of cookies. "I brought snacks for everyone."

The volunteers gradually gathered around Rachel's offering, the conversation flowing easily among people who'd known each other for years. Brandon found himself standing slightly apart, watching Amanda laugh at something Martha said, her head thrown back in genuine amusement.

He already imagined next year's festival with her. Already seeing her directing volunteers, her vision coming to life, her joy in bringing the community together.

"What's going on in that head of yours?" Tom asked quietly, appearing at his elbow. "I can practically hear the gears grinding."

"Wouldn't you like to know?"

Tom's weathered face creased in a knowing smile. "Well, there's plenty of time for thinking later. Come on, let's hook this thing up and take it for a test drive. See how she handles."

Brandon backed his truck up to the float trailer. He and Tom hooked the trailer onto the hitch, checked the connections and safety chains. As he started the engine, the other volunteers stepped back, ready to watch the parade float take its maiden voyage.

"I'm riding along," Amanda announced, climbing onto the platform. "Someone needs to watch how everything holds while it's moving."

"Me too," Rachel added, hopping up beside her friend.

Brandon eased the float out of the barn and into the afternoon sunlight. The driveway stretched ahead, long enough to get a feel for how the display would handle the trip to town and the parade route. He kept the speed slow and steady, watching in his mirrors as the float tracked behind.

They'd made it halfway down the drive when he heard Amanda call out, "Hold up! Something shifted."

He stopped gradually, avoiding any sudden movements that might topple the carefully arranged display. By the time he reached the float, Amanda and Rachel were already examining one of the corner blessing stations.

"The Heritage Families platform moved," Amanda said, kneeling beside the wooden base. "Not much, but enough that the photos could fall during the parade."

Brandon grabbed his toolbox from the truck bed. "The weight distribution must be off. We'll need to add some additional bracing."

Rachel wandered off to update the others while Brandon and Amanda worked together to steady the platform. They knelt side by side, Brandon holding the frame steady while Amanda repositioned the support brackets.

"That photo of my family has got me thinking," he said quietly.

"About?"

"About how I convinced myself Samantha belonged in those family photos. About how I convinced myself I could make that marriage work even though when that photo was taken, our marriage was in a terrible state. I was so sure I knew what I was doing." He adjusted his grip on the platform, the wood rough beneath his palms. "Amanda, I need you to know something. What I feel for you—it's different. Deeper. Real in a way that honestly terrifies me."

Amanda's hands stilled on the bracket. "Terrifies you?"

Brandon set down his wrench, finally meeting her eyes. "Because I don't trust my judgment anymore. I look at you and I see my future, but I saw that before too, and I was completely wrong. What if I'm wrong again? What if I'm just really good at convincing myself of things that aren't true?"

Amanda sat back on her heels, dirt smudging the knees of her jeans. "You want to know what scares me? Dorothy Garrison's comment from the other day... her comment about whether Laurel Ridge would be enough to hold me. And for a second, I wondered too. Not because I want to leave, but because I keep thinking maybe I want too much. Maybe I am too much. My shop, the festival, always planning something bigger. Her comment really got into my head, and I'm questioning and overthinking everything I do." She looked down at her hands. "What if you wake up one day and realize I'm exhausting?"

"You're not—"

"But Samantha probably wasn't either, at first. Things change. People disappoint each other." Amanda picked up a stray piece of raffia, twisting it between her fingers. "I watched my parents work through hard seasons in their marriage. It's not always about the big betrayals. Sometimes it's the slow realization that you want different things."

Brandon reached over and stilled her restless hands with his own. "So what do we do? How do we know if this is real or if we're both just lonely and it's October and everything feels more romantic than it actually is?"

"I don't know. Maybe we can't know. Maybe all we can do is be honest with each other about what we want and see if those wants line up."

"What do you want?"

Amanda turned her hands palm up, lacing her fingers through his. "A partner. Someone who sees my ambition as a strength, not a threat. Someone who understands that I can love this place and still want to help it grow. Someone who won't run when things get complicated. Someone who makes me stop and get a grip when I'm overthinking or complicating things." She squeezed his hands gently. "What do you want?"

"Someone who chooses this life, not just tolerates it. Someone who understands that the farm isn't just my job, it's who I am. Someone brave enough to build something that lasts, even knowing it might not. And most importantly... someone who's honest."

They stayed there for a moment, kneeling in the gravel beside a parade float, holding hands like teenagers and talking like adults.

"Those sound compatible to me," Amanda said.

"Yeah, but wanting and doing are different things. I wanted forever before—"

"Brandon, you're allowed to be scared. I'm scared too. But being scared and being wrong aren't the same thing." She pulled one hand free to tuck a strand of hair behind her ear. "Maybe the fact that we're both questioning everything is exactly why this might work."

"Or maybe it means we both know deep down it won't."

Amanda stood, pulling him up with her. "Maybe. But I'd rather find out than wonder."

Before Brandon could respond, Rachel's voice carried across the yard. "Everything okay over there? The natives are getting restless!"

"Just making adjustments," Amanda called back, then dropped her voice. "We should probably finish the test drive."

Brandon nodded, but he didn't move immediately. "Amanda, I want this to work. I want us to work. I just—"

"Need to be sure. I know. So do I." She brushed the dirt off her jeans with quick, efficient movements. "But Brandon, at some point we have to decide if we're going to let fear of what might go wrong keep us from what could go right."

She walked back toward the float, leaving Brandon standing by his truck. He watched her climb back onto the platform, checking the other blessing stations with the same careful attention she brought to everything.

Brandon got back in the truck and completed the test drive, the float tracking smoothly behind. When they returned to the barn, the volunteers cheered and applauded. The float was ready. The festival would begin in two days. Everything was proceeding exactly as planned.

So why did he feel like he was standing on the edge of something that could either complete him or shatter him all over again?

"Brandon!" Tom called out. "Help me load these tools."

He threw himself into the familiar rhythm of work, but his eyes kept finding Amanda across the barn. She was demonstrating something to Martha, her hands moving expressively as she talked. When she caught him looking, she smiled.

Chapter 23

The truck lurched forward, and Amanda grabbed the door handle to steady herself as Brandon navigated the corner onto Main Street. Behind them, the Harvest of Blessings float rolled along, and ahead, the Laurel Ridge High School marching band struck up "Country Roads" with gusto.

The parade moved at a leisurely pace, stopping and starting as the various entries spread out to maintain proper spacing. Amanda had watched plenty of fall festival parades from the sidewalk over the years, but the view from inside Brandon's truck offered a new perspective. She could see the faces of all the children lined up along the route, their cheeks painted with pumpkins and scarecrows. Teenagers clustered together, pretending they were too cool for parades while snapping photos on their phones. And everywhere, the familiar faces of Laurel Ridge residents who'd known her since she was a pigtailed little girl.

"Judges' stand coming up," Brandon said, easing the truck to a stop in front of the reviewing platform.

Mayor Thompson stood with his clipboard, flanked by three other judges, including Loretta Dunbar from the Book Nook and Sam Cooper from the veterinary clinic. They circled the float with serious expressions of people who took their parade-judging duties as solemnly as Supreme Court justices.

"Looking mighty fine up there!" Earl Smith's voice boomed from somewhere near Brandon's window. The hardware store owner materialized beside the truck, his John Deere cap pushed back on his head and his weathered face split in a wide grin. "That float sure turned out to be a real beauty. Best one I've seen in all my years. Glad I got to be a part of it."

"It was all Amanda's doing," Brandon said, and the pride in his voice made a blush rise in her cheeks.

Earl's eyes twinkled as he glanced between them. "So, are you two officially an item now, or what?"

Brandon's hand moved across the seat and found hers, his fingers intertwining with hers in a gesture that was both tender and purposeful.

"Yes. We are."

Earl slapped the side of the truck with satisfaction. "Well, it's about time! I've got twenty bucks riding on y'all being engaged by Christmas. Don't let me down now!"

"Earl!" Amanda protested, but she was laughing, and Brandon's thumb was tracing gentle circles on her palm, and the whole world felt lighter than air.

The parade resumed its progress, winding down Main Street past familiar storefronts decorated with the cornstalks and pumpkins she'd helped arrange only days before. Brandon kept her hand securely in his as he drove.

"You alright with that?" he asked. "What I told Earl?"

"More than alright." She gave his hand a squeeze. "Though apparently there's a betting pool we need to know about."

"Martha's probably running it. She's known for things like that."

They passed by Indulgences, and Amanda saw April and Whitney standing outside, both of them bouncing and waving with exaggerated enthusiasm. Coral stood beside them with her hands clasped over her heart in a melodramatic swoon that made Amanda roll her eyes even as a smile tugged at her lips.

"Real subtle bunch you've got working for you," Brandon observed wryly.

Amanda chuckled softly as memories washed over her—all the years of carrying a quiet torch for Brandon, of watching him from afar, of believing that someone like him would never truly see or pay attention to someone like her.

In a gesture that made her heart flutter, Brandon brought their joined hands to his lips and pressed a gentle kiss to her knuckles, right there in the middle of the parade route with half the town looking on.

The parade concluded at the edge of town. Brandon parked the truck in the designated area, and they climbed out to inspect the float's condition after its journey. Everything had held together perfectly, and the central harvest display looked even more stunning in the warm afternoon sunlight than it had back in the barn.

"Amanda! Brandon!" Rachel's elated voice preceded her arrival by mere seconds. She flung her arms around Amanda in an exuberant embrace that nearly knocked them both off balance. "Did you see that crowd? Did you hear them cheering when our float passed by? Mrs. Abernathy was actually crying!"

"Mrs. Abernathy cries at dog food commercials," Brandon pointed out.

"Oh hush, this is different, and you know it." Rachel punched his arm playfully. "Mom's over by the festival entrance, says you two need to come see—Oh no…"

Her sudden change in tone was due to a forceful gust of wind that swept across the town, sending vendor tent flaps snapping and paper plates cartwheeling. Amanda turned just in time to see the massive welcome arch—twenty feet of meticulously arranged corn stalks, vibrant autumn leaves, and painted wooden letters spelling out "Laurel Ridge Fall Festival"—sway precariously.

"Watch out!" someone shouted from the crowd.

With an ominous groan and a resounding crash that could be heard over the festive music, the arch toppled backward. Startled yelps erupted from the crowd of onlookers nearby.

Amanda and Brandon took off at a run toward the commotion, with Rachel following close behind. The once impressive arch now lay in a dejected heap, a mess of scattered decor. Visitors milled around in confusion, some snapping pictures of the disaster on their phones, while the festival volunteers wrung their hands helplessly.

"Anyone hurt?" Amanda called out as she pushed her way through the crowd.

"Looks like no injuries, thank the Lord," Tom Bradley reported, who stood beside the collapsed structure with obvious relief. "Gave some folks quite a scare though."

Brandon was already kneeling beside the ruined arch, assessing the extent of the damage with a focused frown. "Base wasn't weighted properly for that kind of wind."

"Think you can fix it?" Diane Morrison asked.

"Yep, we can get this put to rights," Brandon declared confidently as he stood and rolled up his sleeves. "Tom, grab those concrete blocks from my truck bed, if you don't mind. Rachel, my toolbox should be behind the seat. And Amanda—"

"I'm on crowd control and rounding up some extra hands to help," she finished for him, already moving to take charge of the situation.

While Brandon set to work troubleshooting the arch's structural issues, Amanda took on the task of redirecting foot traffic away from the area. She quickly assembled a team of volunteers, assigning some to gather up the scattered decorations while others were put to work holding pieces steady as Brandon worked.

"Alright, lift on three," Brandon instructed, and six burly men heaved the main crossbeam back into position while Amanda kept the support post from wobbling. Brandon secured the joints with swift, practiced movements, his hands sure and steady despite the sweat dampening his brow and the wayward breeze tousling his dark hair.

In less than half an hour, the welcome arch stood tall once more, sturdier than before thanks to the concrete reinforcements and Brandon's know-how. The watching crowd burst into spontaneous applause as the final piece was secured into place. Brandon stepped back, swiping his sleeve across his forehead, and turned to find Amanda at his side.

"Nice work," she said softly, her voice rich with warm admiration.

"We do make quite a team."

Hand in hand, they took a moment to survey the bustling festival sprawled out before them. Hundreds of smiling faces roamed between the colorful craft booths and tempting food stalls, laughter and chatter mingling with the lively music floating on the crisp autumn air.

"Amanda, dear, might I have a quick word with you and Brandon?" The hesitant question came from Dorothy Garrison as she approached the couple, her weathered hands fidgeting with the clasp of her sensible purse.

"Of course, Mrs. Garrison. Is everything alright?" Amanda's brow creased with concern at the older woman's uncharacteristic nervousness.

Dorothy inhaled deeply, as if gathering her resolve. "I owe you both an apology, I'm afraid. The things I said the other day about...well, about Brandon's former wife...it was thoughtless and hurtful of me. I've been absolutely eaten up with shame ever since."

Amanda felt Brandon tense beside her at the mention of Samantha.

"I have a terrible habit of speaking without thinking sometimes," Dorothy continued, her voice thick with remorse. "It's a shortcoming I've been working on, truly I have. But seeing the two of you together today, seeing you looking so happy again, Brandon...it made me realize just how wrong I was to dredge up painful memories that way. That girl was never right for you, and I had no business bringing up—"

"It's okay, Mrs. Garrison," Brandon gently cut her off, his tone soothing and sure. "We all say things we regret now and then."

"You're far kinder than I deserve." Dorothy dabbed at her misty eyes with the handkerchief she tugged from her purse. "Your daddy would be so proud of the fine man you've become, Brandon. And Amanda, you've brought the light back to this boy's eyes in a way I haven't seen in far too long. That's a blessing worth more than all the fall decorations in the world, and it's an answer to prayer for certain."

She patted Amanda's arm with a trembling hand before hurrying away, overcome with emotion.

"Well now, that was... unexpected," Brandon said after a moment of thoughtful silence.

"Just goes to show that people can always surprise you." Amanda laced her fingers more securely through his. "You okay?"

"More than okay, darlin'."

The remainder of the afternoon passed in a whirlwind of activity and laughter. They judged the fiercely competitive pie contest (with Martha taking the coveted blue ribbon for her famous caramel apple crumble, to no one's surprise), cheered on the youth group's energetic dance performance that featured an impressive amount of break dancing prowess, and helped referee the highly anticipated Great Gourd Race, where pint-sized competitors determinedly propelled pumpkins across the grass with long-handled wooden spoons.

As the shadows began to lengthen and the air turned pleasantly cool, Brandon and Amanda found themselves meandering hand-in-hand through the rows of artisan booths, admiring the lovingly crafted wares and sampling tempting homemade treats. At Mr. Henley's woodworking display, Brandon paused, his attention snagged by an array of delicate pendant necklaces.

"Cardinals," the elderly craftsman said with a twinkle in his eye, noting Brandon's interest. "West Virginia's state bird, ya know. Each one's carved from a different piece of local wood, so no two are exactly alike."

Brandon lifted one fashioned from richly hued cherry, turning it to admire how the intricate details made the tiny bird look poised for flight. The pendant hung from a simple strip of soft leather, rustic yet undeniably lovely.

"They say cardinals are messengers from heaven," Mr. Henley added, his gnarled hands carefully straightening the velvet cloth beneath his display. "If one catches your eye, it means someone who loves you is watching over you from the other side."

Brandon's fingers stilled on the necklace, and Amanda saw a flicker of wistful emotion dance across his handsome face—there one moment and gone the next, like the shadow of a passing cloud.

"We'll take this one," he decided, fishing his wallet from his back pocket to pay the smiling artisan.

"It's beautiful, Brandon," Amanda breathed as he turned to her with the necklace dangling from his outstretched hand.

"Turn around for me."

She swept her hair to the side, and Brandon's work-roughened fingers brushed the sensitive skin at her nape as he fastened the slender cord. The cardinal pendant settled just below the hollow of her throat.

"I want you to have something to remember today by," he murmured near her ear, his words meant for her alone. "The parade, the festival, all of it."

Amanda turned back to face him, one hand lifting to touch the carved bird that now rested close to her heart. All around them, the festival carried on in a riot of music and motion—children shrieking with carefree glee on the hayrides, friends calling out greetings as they huddled together with cups of spiced cider, and everywhere the smiling faces of a community knitted together by love and history. But in that moment, basking in the light of Brandon's intense blue gaze, Amanda wasn't the small-town girl watching wistfully from the margins, longing to be noticed. She was seen, truly seen, by the man she'd loved from a distance for so many years. More than that, she was valued and cherished.

The lively strains of bluegrass music from the stage drifted to their ears, and Brandon caught her hand in his, tugging her gently toward the wooden dance floor where couples were already beginning to gather.

"Dance with me, Amanda?" His voice was a low rumble in his chest.

"Always," she said, her heart so full she thought it might burst from happiness as she let him lead her around the dance floor, content to twirl the evening away in the arms of the man she loved beneath the rising harvest moon.

Chapter 24

The church grounds vibrated with the joyful sounds of the community potluck. Brandon's hand enveloped Amanda's as he guided her through the lively crowd gathered to celebrate the final night of the Fall Festival. Picnic tables draped in red checkered cloths dotted the lawn, each adorned with a glowing candle lantern and a mason jar filled with autumn leaves and flickering battery-operated tea lights. The scent of Martha's famous fried chicken mingled with the smoky aroma wafting from Earl's barbecue setup, creating a mouth-watering tapestry of smells that made Brandon's stomach rumble despite the festival food they'd sampled throughout the afternoon.

Laughter echoed across the grounds as children chased fireflies that danced in the dusky evening air. Nearby, teenagers clustered around the dessert table, their studied casualness a thin veil for the age-old desire to evade adult supervision. The long serving tables groaned under the weight of casserole dishes, slow cookers, and pie tins—a testament to the culinary prowess of Laurel Ridge's most talented cooks.

"I can't believe it's almost over," Amanda said wistfully as they navigated around families carrying covered dishes and folding chairs. "The festival flew by so quickly."

Brandon squeezed her hand reassuringly. "It was a huge success. You should be proud of everything you accomplished."

"We should be proud," Amanda corrected, nudging him playfully with her shoulder. "I couldn't have done any of it without you."

"Brandon! Amanda!" Pastor Andrew called out, waving them over to where he and his wife Lily stood beside one of the larger picnic tables, their plates piled high with potluck offerings. "Come join us!"

After filling their own plates at the serving tables, Brandon and Amanda made their way over and settled in across from the pastor and his wife. The flickering candle lantern cast dancing shadows across the checkered tablecloth, its warm light catching in Lily's blond hair as she leaned forward, her green eyes sparkling with the enthusiasm that had endeared her to the congregation. "I'm so glad you two are joining us for dinner."

"Before we dig in," Pastor Andrew said, "would you lead us in prayer, Brandon?"

They joined hands around the table—Brandon grasping Amanda's smaller hand in his right and Lily's in his left, the circle complete as Amanda reached across to take Andrew's other hand.

"Heavenly Father," Brandon began, his voice rough with emotion, "we thank You for this day. For the joy of community, the success of the festival, and the abundance before us. Thank You for the hands that prepared this meal, the hearts that serve this town, and the love that binds us all together."

His thumb traced across Amanda's knuckles, drawing strength from her comforting touch.

"Thank You for bringing love and joy back into my life through Amanda," he continued, " and help us to be good stewards of all You've given us. Amen."

A chorus of "Amens" followed, but Brandon felt Amanda's hand tighten around his, her thumb caressing his knuckles in a gesture so tender it made his chest ache with unspoken emotion.

"That was beautiful, Brandon," Lily said softly. "Thank you."

Pastor Andrew nodded in agreement, giving Brandon's shoulder an affirming squeeze. "Amen to that, son."

As they began to eat, the conversation flowed as smoothly as sweet tea on a sun-dappled porch. They talked of festival triumphs, church happenings, and the changing seasons. Somehow, the discussion turned to relationships, prompting Lily to share the story of how she and Andrew had fallen in love.

"We were friends first," she reminisced, her eyes soft with cherished memories. "I think that's why it felt so natural when we finally realized there was something more between us. The best foundations are built on friendship and patience—rushing God's timing never improves the end result."

Brandon found himself nodding in agreement. His own marriage to Samantha had been built on superficial attraction and misguided assumptions—a far cry from the deep connection he now shared with Amanda.

"How did you know?" Amanda asked quietly. "When friendship turned into something more?"

Lily and Andrew exchanged meaningful glances that spoke volumes.

"For me," Lily explained, "it was when I realized Andrew was the first person I wanted to tell when something good happened, and the only one I wanted around when things went wrong. That's when I knew our friendship had grown into love."

Andrew smiled at his wife adoringly. "And I knew when my prayers shifted—when I found myself asking God to bless Lily's life even more than my own."

The poignant words settled into the space between Brandon and Amanda like seeds taking root in fertile soil. Brandon reflected on the past few weeks, marveling at how Amanda's joy had become more important to him than protecting his own heart from potential pain. Her presence in his life had taught him the profound difference between merely existing and truly living.

"Relationships are a bit like tending a garden," Pastor Andrew mused, spearing a piece of watermelon with his fork. "It's the daily attention to small things that nurtures growth, not the occasional grand gesture."

The wisdom of the pastor's words resonated deeply with Brandon. Grand gestures, like their dinner at the Riverside Inn, certainly had their place, but it was the accumulation of countless small moments spent together that had brought him and Amanda to this beautiful point in their relationship.

As if on cue, Helen's warm voice interrupted his thoughts. "Brandon, dear, there you are."

Brandon looked up to see his mother approaching their table, carrying her own plate and searching for a place to sit.

"Mom, join us," he invited, scooting over to make room for her. Helen settled in beside him with a contented sigh, and soon she was regaling the table with heartwarming tales of festivals past, her eyes bright with laughter and cherished memories.

But as the conversation lulled, Helen turned to Brandon with a knowing look—the same one she always wore when she had something important to share.

"What a wonderful evening," she said, her voice filled with wistful joy. "Your father would have loved this—the whole community coming together to celebrate another bountiful harvest season."

At the mention of his father, Brandon felt the familiar pang of loss, but it was softer now, tempered by gratitude rather than sharpened by raw grief.

"He would have been so proud of this festival," Helen continued, her gaze shifting meaningfully between Brandon and Amanda. "And he would have been overjoyed to see you finding happiness again, Brandon."

Brandon's fork stilled on his plate as he absorbed his mother's words. Helen had never been one for subtle hints, and there was a deliberate weight to her statement that went beyond simple encouragement.

"Your father always said the hardest thing about farming was knowing when to let a field lie fallow and when to plant anew," Helen said, her voice gentle but firm. "You can't grow anything in soil that's not ready, but you also can't wait forever for perfect conditions. There comes a time when you have to trust in the earth and sow the seeds of what you hope to harvest."

She reached over and patted Brandon's hand, her touch brimming with maternal understanding.

"It seems to me," she added, casting a meaningful glance at Amanda, "that you've found your planting season, son."

Amanda ducked her head, but not before Brandon caught the smile tugging at the corners of her lips. Around them, the potluck continued its joyful rhythm—families finishing their meals, children growing bolder in their games as darkness descended, and the comforting buzz of community fellowship that had marked countless Saturday evenings at Laurel Ridge Community Church.

"Helen's right," Pastor Andrew chimed in, pushing back his empty plate. "There's a time for everything under heaven—a time to grieve and a time to dance, a time to hold back and a time to embrace what God places in front of us."

As if on cue, the piercing whistle of a firework cut through the evening air, followed by a dazzling burst of gold and silver that painted the sky in temporary brilliance. The crowd around the picnic tables turned their faces heavenward as the Fall Festival's grand finale began.

"The fireworks," Amanda said, her eyes reflecting the shimmering display above. "I completely lost track of time."

Brandon stood and extended his hand to her. "Want to get a better view?"

Hand in hand, they bid goodnight to Pastor Andrew, Lily, and Helen, who shooed them away with knowing smiles and promises to see them at church the following morning.

Brandon led Amanda past the pavilion to the edge of the church property, where a small rise offered an unobstructed view of the sky, free from the chatter of families and the cries of tired babies. As they crested the gentle slope, Brandon turned to face the fireworks, drawing Amanda back against his chest and encircling her waist with his arms.

She melted into his embrace, her head finding the perfect spot on his shoulder, her hands coming to rest over his where they lay on her stomach. Another firework exploded overhead, a cascade of blue and white stars mirrored in the tranquil river below.

"It's perfect," Amanda whispered, her voice barely audible over the distant crowd and the rhythmic booms of the pyrotechnics.

Brandon rested his chin on top of her head, breathing in the comforting scent of her shampoo mingled with the crisp autumn air. "I had an interesting conversation with Earl over breakfast at the diner this morning."

"What did he say?" Amanda asked, curiosity coloring her tone.

"He told me I looked like myself again for the first time since Dad passed," Brandon shared. "When I asked what he meant, he said I'd been walking around like a ghost of my former self, but lately, he could see me coming back to life."

Amanda's hands tightened over his. "Do you feel like yourself again?"

Brandon pondered the question as another series of fireworks set the sky ablaze in a vibrant tapestry of gold and red. Three months ago, he would have said he'd never feel like himself again, that losing his father and his marriage had fundamentally altered the fabric of his being. But standing here with Amanda in his arms, surrounded by the community that had shaped him, watching fireworks celebrate another successful harvest season, he realized the profound truth in Earl's words.

"I feel like a better version of myself," he admitted, his voice thick with emotion. "Not because the grief has disappeared—it hasn't. I still miss Dad every single day. But my heart isn't just holding grief anymore."

A spectacular burst of silver and gold illuminated Amanda's profile as Brandon's thoughts turned to his father's wisdom, to the countless conversations they'd shared during long days working side by side, and to the man who had raised him to understand that life was meant to be embraced fully, not rationed cautiously.

"Dad used to say the heart isn't meant to hold just one feeling at a time," Brandon said, his voice rough with emotion. "He believed it's meant to be full—grief and joy, fear and hope, loss and love all woven together. That's what makes us human."

Amanda turned in his arms to face him, her hands coming to rest on his chest, directly over his heart.

"And what is your heart holding now?" She asked, her blue eyes reflecting the shimmering lights above.

Brandon gazed down at her—Amanda Baker, the woman who had loved him quietly for so long while he searched for love in all the wrong places, who had appeared in his life during his darkest hour with unwavering grace and patience, who had reignited the spark of hope within him and shown him that life held so much more than mere survival.

"You," he said simply, his voice filled with absolute certainty. "It's holding you, Amanda."

The grand finale of the fireworks show began—a rapid succession of explosions that transformed the entire sky into a breathtaking canvas of color and light. But Brandon barely registered the display, too lost in the depths of Amanda's eyes as his heartfelt declaration hung between them.

She rose up on her toes, her hands sliding up to cradle his face, and for a heart-stopping moment, he thought she might kiss him. Instead, she pressed her forehead against his, her eyes fluttering closed as the final firework faded into a sky full of twinkling stars.

"I love you," she breathed, her whispered confession nearly lost amidst the applause drifting up from the crowd below.

But Brandon heard her—heard every word as clearly as if she had shouted them from the rooftops. Her declaration settled into his heart like seeds finding the perfect depth of soil in which to take root and flourish. He ached to say it back, to give voice to the feelings that had blossomed within him, but he wanted to do it right—not as a mere echo of her sentiment, but as a profound proclamation of his own love for her.

So instead, Brandon pressed a soft, lingering kiss to her temple, pouring every ounce of his love and devotion into the simple gesture. He breathed in the moment, the woman in his arms, and the knowledge that some things in life were worth waiting for—worth doing right.

And as they stood there, wrapped in each other's embrace, the last traces of smoke from the fireworks drifting lazily through the star-studded sky, Brandon knew that this was just the beginning of a love story that would rival even the most beautiful of Laurel Ridge's legendary autumn harvests.

Chapter 25

The worn steps of Laurel Ridge Community Church felt solid beneath Amanda's feet as she and Brandon climbed toward the entrance. His fingers wove through hers with the same natural fit as roots finding water in soil.

Inside, the sanctuary hummed with pre-service energy. Children darted between pews while their parents issued half-hearted warnings. The organist ran through scales, preparing for the opening hymn. Sunlight filtered through stained glass, casting patches of ruby and sapphire across the polished floors.

"There's Mom," Brandon said.

In the Whitaker family pew, Rachel scooted over with exaggerated movements. "Finally! I was about to send out a search party."

"The service doesn't start for five minutes," Amanda pointed out, settling between Brandon and her parents.

"Five minutes is practically late by Laurel Ridge standards." Rachel leaned forward to address Amos and Janelle Baker. "Don't you agree, Mr. B?"

Amos chuckled, his weathered carpenter's hands folded over his Bible. "I learned long ago not to get between Rachel Whitaker and her opinions."

"Smart man," Janelle murmured, patting her husband's arm.

The organ swelled into the opening notes of "Great Is Thy Faithfulness," and the congregation rose as one. Brandon and Amanda's voices found harmony without effort. She caught Helen watching them with an expression that reminded Amanda of her own mother's face when she'd successfully matched the right pattern pieces for a complicated quilt.

Pastor Andrew took the pulpit as the hymn concluded, his young face bright with the particular joy he carried after special events. His wife Lily sat in the front row, her hand resting on the gentle swell beneath her church dress—their first child due before Christmas.

"Good morning, church family!" Andrew's voice carried to the back rows without strain. "What a week we've had! I trust everyone's recovered from Friday and Saturday's festivities?"

Gentle laughter rippled through the sanctuary.

"You know," Andrew continued, his hands resting on either side of the pulpit, "I've been thinking about timing this week. God's timing, specifically. We just celebrated our Fall Festival—a time when we gather the harvest, when we see the fruit of seeds planted months ago. But I wonder how many of us really stop to consider the profound theological truth in that simple agricultural rhythm."

He paused, letting the words settle.

"Turn with me, if you will, to Jeremiah chapter twenty-nine, verse eleven. Many of you know this one by heart."

Pages rustled throughout the sanctuary. Brandon's Bible remained closed on his lap, but his attention fixed on Andrew with an intensity Amanda hadn't seen in him before.

"'For I know the plans I have for you,' declares the Lord, 'plans to prosper you and not to harm you, plans to give you hope and a future.'" Andrew looked up from his Bible. "Now, we love this verse. We put it on graduation cards and coffee mugs. But do you know the context? These words were written to exiles. To the people whose lives had been completely upended, who found themselves in a place they never expected to be."

Amanda felt Brandon's shoulder tense slightly against hers.

"God wasn't promising them immediate rescue," Andrew continued. "He was telling them to plant gardens in Babylon. To build houses. To seek the welfare of the foreign city where He'd placed them. Because sometimes—" Andrew's voice gentled, "—sometimes God's plans require us to bloom where we're planted, even when that ground feels foreign. Even when we'd rather be anywhere else."

Mrs. Patterson dabbed at her eyes with a handkerchief. She'd lost her husband just three months before, and everyone knew she'd been considering moving to Richmond to live with her daughter.

"Ecclesiastes chapter three tells us there's a time for everything, a season for every activity under heaven. A time to plant and a time to uproot. A time to weep and a time to laugh. A time to mourn and a time to dance."

Andrew stepped away from the pulpit, moving closer to the congregation.

"Some of you are in your planting season right now. Some are in harvest. Some are watching winter turn to spring and wondering if it's safe to trust the warmth again."

"Isaiah forty-three, verse nineteen, says, 'See, I am doing a new thing! Now it springs up; do you not perceive it? I am making a way in the wilderness and streams in the wasteland.'"

Andrew's voice rose with conviction. "Notice God doesn't say He'll transport us out of the wilderness. He says He'll make a way through it. He'll bring water to the desert places of our lives. Sometimes the miracle isn't the removal of the hard thing—it's the provision within it."

Brandon's hand found Amanda's, their fingers interlocking.

"This weekend," Andrew continued, returning to the pulpit, "I watched our community come together for the Fall Festival. I saw Brandon Whitaker driving the parade float he helped build, even though it was hard because this was the first festival without his father."

Amanda felt rather than heard Brandon's sharp intake of breath.

"I saw Amanda Baker orchestrate decorations that turned our whole town into a celebration of God's abundance, bringing fresh vision to traditions we've held for generations. I saw Rachel and Helen working side by side to bring joy to children at the candy booth. I saw Tom Bradley and Earl Smith—who've been arguing about the proper way to build anything since 1987—work together on that parade float without a single disagreement."

Laughter rose from Tom's direction, along with Earl's distinctive snort.

"And in all of that," Andrew said, his voice dropping to draw the congregation in, "I saw Proverbs three, verses five and six, lived out in real time. 'Trust in the Lord with all your heart and lean not on your own understanding; in all your ways submit to him, and he will make your paths straight.'"

He paused, scanning the faces before him.

"You see, not one person who worked on this festival knew exactly how it would turn out. Amanda didn't know whether her new ideas would be accepted. Brandon didn't know if he could face the memories. Rachel didn't know if the candy would last through both days—"

"Barely made it!" Rachel stage-whispered, earning scattered chuckles.

"But each person trusted," Andrew continued. "They leaned not on their own understanding but on faith—faith in God, faith in each other, faith that somehow, all the pieces would come together. And they did, didn't they? They always do when we stop trying to control every outcome and start trusting the One who sees the whole picture."

Amanda glanced at Brandon's profile, saw the muscle working in his jaw as he wrestled with something internal.

"Which brings me to Romans eight, verse twenty-eight." Andrew's voice took on a particular tone that meant he was building to his conclusion. "'And we know that in all things God works for the good of those who love him, who have been called according to his purpose.'"

He closed his Bible, leaning forward slightly.

"All things. Not just the easy things. Not just the victories. All things. The losses that break us open. The changes we didn't choose. The endings that force new beginnings. The loneliness that makes us reach for connection. The grief that teaches us the true weight of love."

"I want you to hear this today," Andrew said, his voice thick with emotion. "Whatever season you're in—planting, harvesting, or waiting through winter—God is working. He's not absent in your pain. He's not surprised by your doubts. He's not disappointed with your struggles. He's working all things together for good."

Andrew stepped back, his hands spread wide.

"The Fall Festival showed us what that looks like in practice. Different people, different gifts, different seasons of life, all working together to create something beautiful. That's what God does with our lives when we trust Him. He takes our scattered pieces—our joys and sorrows, our victories and failures—and He weaves them into something that glorifies Him and blesses others."

He returned to the pulpit, voice steady and sure.

"So whatever you're facing today, whatever tomorrow holds, remember this: The God who brings harvest from seeds, who turns seasons in perfect time, who makes streams in the wasteland—that God is working in your life right now. Trust His timing. Trust His plan. Trust that He who began a good work in you will carry it on to completion."

Andrew bowed his head. "Let us pray."

As the congregation lowered their heads, Amanda felt Brandon's hand tighten around hers. She squeezed back, offering silent support.

"Heavenly Father," Andrew prayed, "we thank You for Your perfect timing. For plans we can't see but can trust. For new things springing up even when we're looking at dead ground. Give us courage to trust You with our whole hearts. Give us faith to believe You're working even when we can't perceive it. And give us grace to extend to ourselves and others as we navigate the changing seasons of life. In Jesus' name, Amen."

"Amen," the congregation echoed.

The closing hymn was "Blessed Assurance," and Amanda noticed Brandon's lips moving with the words this time, though no sound emerged. As the final notes faded and people began gathering their things, the usual after-service bustle commenced—children released from their best behavior, adults making lunch plans, teenagers checking phones they'd been forced to silence.

"Y'all coming to the fellowship?" Rachel asked, already standing and straightening her skirt.

"Of course," Helen answered. "I brought my apple cake."

"The one with the brown sugar topping?" Amos perked up.

"Is there any other kind?" Helen smiled.

As they filed out of the pew, Brandon remained still for a moment, his eyes fixed on something Amanda couldn't see. Then, with the sudden decisiveness of someone who'd reached a crucial decision, he turned to her.

His hands came up to cup her face, his palms warm against her cheeks. The tenderness in his expression made her breath catch. Around them, the congregation continued their cheerful exit, but Amanda felt suspended in this moment, caught in the intensity of Brandon's gaze.

He leaned forward, pressing his lips to her forehead in a kiss so gentle it felt like a blessing. His breath stirred her hair as he whispered, "I need to be alone for a little while."

Her heart stuttered, but before anxiety could take root, he continued, his thumbs stroking her cheekbones.

"You haven't done anything. Don't question whether something is wrong. Everything is just fine." His eyes searched hers, willing her to understand. "I just need a little time to myself."

And she did understand. How many times had she retreated to her own space to process, to think, to pray through something too large for words?

"Okay," she whispered back.

He kissed her forehead once more, then stepped back, his hands sliding away with obvious reluctance. With a nod to his mother and sister, he made his way down the main aisle, heading for the parking lot.

"Hey." Rachel's hand landed on Amanda's elbow as soon as Brandon disappeared. "He's not running from you, Amanda—he's running to something. I've seen that look before. So don't you go worrying; give him time. Brandon's always been like that... he processes big things better when he's alone."

Helen joined them, her expression knowing. "James used to do the same thing. Several times during our marriage, he would take time alone and go fishing, or hiking, or wander the fields lost in his thoughts, working things out in his mind. He always came back with clarity. Brandon's the same way—he processes best in solitude."

"I understand," Amanda said. "I do the same thing."

Helen's smile was warm with approval. "Then you understand him better than most ever could."

They made their way outside, where the fellowship was already in full swing. Tables had been set up under the pavilion behind the church, laden with coffee urns, Helen's apple cake, Martha's brownies, and dozens of other contributions. Children ran between the adults' legs, their church clothes already showing signs of grass stains.

"Amanda!" Lily Andrews approached, one hand supporting her back. "I forgot to tell you... the parade float was absolutely stunning. Andrew and I were talking about it over breakfast. We've never seen anything like it."

"It was a team effort," Amanda deflected, accepting a cup of coffee from Rachel.

"But it was your vision," Coral interjected, appearing with April and Whitney in tow. "Don't sell yourself short, boss."

For the next hour, Amanda moved through the familiar rhythms of church fellowship. She helped pour coffee when Martha got sidetracked talking. She listened to Earl's detailed analysis of the float's engineering, nodding at appropriate intervals. She admired baby photos on Mrs. Fleming's phone and promised to special-order the candle Mrs. Davies had been wanting.

But through it all, her awareness remained split. Part of her engaged fully with the community she loved, while another part tracked the passage of time, wondering where Brandon had gone, what he was thinking, what decision he was wrestling toward.

"Stop looking at your watch," Rachel murmured, appearing at her elbow with a brownie. "You're being obvious."

"I'm not—"

"You've checked it four times in the past ten minutes."

Amanda accepted the brownie without taking a bite. "It's been more than an hour."

"So go." Rachel's expression softened. "He's probably at his home."

"What if he wants to be alone?"

"Then he'll tell you." Rachel squeezed her shoulder.

Amanda looked across the fellowship gathering—at Helen laughing with a group of women, at her parents deep in conversation with the Hendersons, at the community that had embraced her vision for the festival and celebrated its success. This was her place; these were her people. But somehow, her heart had already left, following a path toward a cabin in the woods and a man wrestling with something.

"Go," Rachel repeated, giving her a gentle push. "We'll make your excuses."

Amanda hugged her friend quickly, then made her way to her car, forcing herself not to run. The drive to Brandon's cabin took fifteen minutes on a normal day, but she made it in ten, her hands gripping the steering wheel as her mind replayed the morning.

The intensity in Brandon's eyes during Andrew's sermon. The way his hand had tightened around hers at every mention of new beginnings. The tender desperation in his kiss to her forehead, as if he was both holding on and letting go at the same time.

A month ago, she would have panicked at his need for space. Would have interpreted it as rejection, as a confirmation of her deepest fear that she wasn't enough to hold someone's attention. Would have convinced herself that he was pulling away, that she'd somehow failed some invisible test.

But that was before. Before she'd learned his patterns and rhythms. Before she'd recognized that his retreats weren't escapes from her but journeys toward something—toward clarity, toward decision, toward the kind of intentional choice that Brandon never made lightly.

She understood because she was the same way. How many times had she closed her office door at the shop, needing silence to work through a problem? How many evening walks had she taken alone, letting her feet find their rhythm while her mind untangled complicated emotions?

They were alike in this, she and Brandon. Both needing solitude to process. Both required quiet to hear what their hearts were really saying.

The road to Whitaker Farms curved through stands of oak and maple, their leaves at peak color—scarlet and gold and orange so bright it almost hurt to look at. Sunlight slanted through the canopy, creating patches of light and shadow on the gravel road. She passed the farmhouse, continuing deeper into the Whitaker property toward Brandon's home.

His truck came into view first, parked at its usual angle beside the cabin. So he was here. She pulled in beside it, turning off her engine but not immediately getting out.

The cabin looked peaceful in the afternoon light.

Taking a deep breath, Amanda opened her car door and stepped out into the October afternoon.

Chapter 26

Amanda found him on the back porch of his cabin. Brandon sat in one of the weathered rocking chairs, his father's Bible open across his lap, autumn light filtering through the trees to paint everything in shades of copper and gold. Beside him on the small wooden table sat the framed photograph from the parade float—the one from last year's festival with his parents, Rachel, himself, and Samantha, all frozen in a moment before everything changed.

He looked up at her approach, and what she saw in his eyes made her breath catch. Not turmoil, not confusion, but something clear and purposeful, like still water that runs deep.

"Amanda."

"Hi," she said softly, pausing at the bottom of the porch steps, unsure whether to climb them.

"Please," he gestured to the empty chair beside him, "come sit with me."

She climbed the steps slowly, noticing as she drew closer that his Bible was open to the book of Ruth. Her eyes caught the familiar words of chapter one, verse sixteen, that were highlighted in yellow: "Where you go I will go, and where you stay I will stay. Your people will be my people and your God my God."

Brandon followed her gaze and gave a rueful smile. "I'm sorry for leaving like that. For missing fellowship. I just—"

"You don't need to apologize," Amanda interrupted gently, settling into the chair beside him. "Taking time to think and pray isn't something to be sorry for. It's wisdom."

He closed the Bible carefully, his father's name embossed on the worn leather cover catching the light. "Pastor Andrew's sermon... it hit me with such force I could barely breathe. All those verses about God's timing, about trusting His plan even when we can't see it." He picked up the photograph, studying it with an expression Amanda couldn't quite read. "I've been thinking about this picture."

Amanda looked at the photo—Helen's radiant smile, James's strong presence, Rachel's characteristic sparkle, Brandon looking confident and whole, and Samantha.

"This was taken maybe two hours before Samantha told me she didn't love me," Brandon said quietly. "Dad had less than three months left. Rachel didn't know she'd soon be holding our family together while I fell apart. Mom had no idea she was about to lose the love of her life." He set the photo down carefully. "Looking at it used to feel like staring at the last moment before everything broke."

Brandon turned to face her fully, his brown eyes holding hers with an intensity that made her pulse quicken. "Now I see it differently. I see God's hand even in the breaking. I've been so focused on the doors that closed—Dad's death, the divorce—that I couldn't see the window God was opening."

He reached for her hands, enveloping them in his larger ones, his thumbs tracing gentle circles on her palms.

"Even my marriage to Samantha," he continued, his voice gaining strength, "as much as it hurt when it ended, I think it was part of God's plan. Not the pain, but the preparation. It taught me what love isn't, so I could recognize what love is when it finally stood in front of me with festival plans and unstoppable enthusiasm."

Amanda's eyes filled with tears, but she didn't pull her hands away to wipe them.

"I left church because I needed to be sure," Brandon said, his grip on her hands tightening slightly. "Sure that I could say what I'm about to say with the gravity it deserves. Not casually tossed out in a crowd or whispered in passing, but given its full weight."

He drew in a deep breath, and Amanda felt the world narrow to just this moment, this porch, this man gathering his courage.

"Amanda Baker," he began, his voice steady but thick with emotion, "I love you."

The words hung in the air between them, precious and profound.

"Not because you helped me begin to heal, though you did. Not because you fit perfectly into my life, though you do." His voice broke slightly, but he pressed on. "I love you because somewhere between the moment you showed up at the farm with all that enthusiasm about the festival and when I finally really saw you—truly saw you—you became my life. When I think about tomorrow, next month, next year, I can't imagine any of it without you."

Tears streamed down Amanda's face now, but she was smiling through them, her heart so full she thought it might burst.

"Brandon," she managed, her voice trembling, "I've loved you since I was eighteen years old."

"Amanda—"

"Let me finish," she said, squeezing his hands. "That eighteen-year-old girl loved an idea, a golden boy who seemed to have it all together. But the woman I am now? She loves the man you are now. Broken pieces, rebuilt faith, and all. Watching you find yourself again, watching you become someone even stronger than before—it's been like watching the sunrise after the longest night."

She freed one hand to touch his face, her fingers gentle against his jaw.

"I thank God every day for His timing," she continued. "For not letting us find each other until now, when we were both ready. When I could see past my insecurities and you could see past your grief. When we could build something real instead of something rushed."

Brandon turned his face to kiss her palm, the gesture so tender it made fresh tears spill down her cheeks.

"Will you pray with me?" he asked suddenly.

"Always."

He took both her hands again, bowing his head. Amanda closed her eyes, feeling the warmth of his hands, the solid presence of him beside her, the rightness of this moment.

"Heavenly Father," Brandon began, his voice rough with emotion, "thank You. Thank You for Your perfect timing, even when we couldn't see it. Thank You for taking our broken seasons and turning them into this harvest of love. Thank You for Amanda—for her patience, her faith, her heart that somehow found room for me even when I couldn't find room for myself."

"Lord, help me love her the way Christ loves the church—faithfully, sacrificially, and joyfully. Give me wisdom to build a life with her that honors You. Help me be the man she deserves, the man You're calling me to be. Guide our steps, Father. Bless the path ahead. Help us trust You with our future the way You've taught us to trust You with our past."

He paused.

"And Lord, if it's Your will—and I believe it is—help me build a life with Amanda that reflects Your love to this community. A life built on the foundation of faith, rooted in Your word, and blessed by Your grace. In Jesus' name, Amen."

"Amen," Amanda whispered, her voice breaking on the word.

When she opened her eyes, Brandon was looking at her with such love, such certainty, that her breath caught all over again. He released her hands only to lean forward and cup her face, his thumbs gently wiping away her tears.

"Amanda," he said softly, and she could feel his breath on her lips, could see the flecks of gold in his brown eyes, could feel the slight tremor in his hands.

Then he kissed her.

A kiss that started tender and careful, as if he was afraid she might disappear. Amanda's hands came up to rest against his chest, feeling his heartbeat racing beneath her palms. The kiss deepened as years of waiting, weeks of growing love, and a lifetime of promise poured into this single perfect moment.

When they parted, Brandon rested his forehead against hers. His hands still cradled her face, and she could feel him smiling even with her eyes closed.

"Amanda Baker," he said, his voice low and serious despite the joy threading through it, "will you build a life with me?"

Her eyes flew open.

"Not just date," he continued quickly, "not just see where this goes, but intentionally build something lasting? I'm not proposing—not yet—I want to do that right when the time comes, and I want it to be special and a surprise out of the blue. But I need you to know that's where I'm headed. You're it for me. The beginning and end of every plan I want to make."

"Yes," Amanda said immediately, her answer coming from the deepest, truest part of her heart. "Yes, to all of it. To building, to growing, to whatever comes next. Yes, Brandon."

He kissed her again, briefer this time but no less meaningful, sealing her promise with his own.

When they separated, Brandon stood and pulled her to her feet, then settled back into his rocking chair and drew her down beside him. It was a tight fit, but Amanda curled into his side perfectly, her head finding that spot on his shoulder that seemed designed just for her.

His arm came around her, holding her close.

"Your mom is going to be insufferable," Amanda said after a moment, feeling his chest rumble with quiet laughter.

"Rachel's going to be worse."

"The whole town will know by tomorrow."

"Good," Brandon said, pressing a kiss to the top of her head. "I want everyone to know. I want to stand in Martha's Diner and tell Earl and Tom and anyone else who'll listen that Amanda Baker loves me. That she's choosing to build a life with me."

Amanda tilted her face up to look at him. "And I want everyone to know that Brandon Whitaker—the boy I loved from afar, the man who found his way through the valley of shadows—chose me. Ordinary Amanda, who runs a gift shop and dreams too big and loves with her whole heart."

"There's nothing ordinary about you," Brandon said firmly. "There never was. I was just too blind to see it."

They fell quiet again, watching as the sun painted the sky in shades of rose and gold.

"I love you," Brandon said.

"I love you too."

The photograph still sat on the table beside them—that frozen moment before everything changed. But now it didn't represent an ending. Now it was simply prologue to a better story, one written by the Author who knew the ending from the beginning, who took their broken pieces and made something beautiful, who turned their winter into spring and their sorrow into joy.

This was their harvest, and it was only just beginning.

Epilogue

The John Deere's engine rumbled as Amanda's hands gripped the steering wheel with the determination of someone who'd conquered many challenges but recognized this particular one might require divine intervention. Through the cab's window, the April morning spread across Whitaker Farm in shades of fresh green and rich brown. The fields stretched before her like blank pages waiting for their story.

"Okay, now ease off the clutch while giving it a little gas," Brandon called from beside the massive tractor, his voice carrying that particular mix of patience and barely suppressed amusement that meant he was enjoying this far too much.

Amanda's engagement ring—a vintage setting with a center diamond surrounded by tiny sapphires that Brandon had chosen because it reminded him of her eyes—caught the morning light as she reached for the gearshift. Three months since he'd proposed on Christmas Eve in front of both their families, and she still wasn't used to how the weight of it on her finger made her heart skip.

"Like this?" She moved the lever with confidence.

The tractor lurched backward with alarming enthusiasm.

"Wrong way! WRONG WAY!" Brandon shouted, but he was laughing—that full, unburdened laugh that had become as natural to him now as breathing.

Amanda slammed on the brake, her heart racing as the fence post behind them stood barely a foot from destruction. "Oh, my goodness! I nearly took out the fence!"

Brandon climbed up into the cab beside her, still chuckling. "Maybe we should start you on something smaller. Like a riding mower. Or a bicycle. Or maybe just walking behind me while I drive."

She swatted his arm. "You said I was ready for the big tractor!"

"I said you were ready to learn about the big tractor. There's a difference." He slid behind her on the seat, his arms coming around her to reach the controls. "Here, let me show you again."

The past six months had been filled with moments like this—Brandon teaching her the rhythms of farm life during her weekends and evenings here, while she taught him that vulnerability wasn't weakness and joy wasn't betrayal of grief. She'd learned to read the weather in cloud formations and the health of plants and crops in the color of their leaves. He'd learned to share his fears instead of shouldering them alone and to accept help without seeing it as failure.

"First," he said, his breath warm against her ear, "remember that forward is actually forward on this model, not backward like apparently you thought."

"How was I supposed to know that?" she protested, but she was smiling.

"Basic physics? Common sense? The fact that I literally just told you?"

"Details," she muttered, making him laugh again.

Under his guidance, she successfully drove the tractor forward this time, making one slow pass along the field's edge. The earth turned beneath the plow attachment, dark and rich, ready for planting. Amanda had come to love this part of farming—the promise inherent in prepared soil, the faith required to trust that seeds would grow.

When they finally stopped for a break, Brandon grabbed the lunch his mother had packed from behind the seat. They settled on the tailgate of his truck, which he'd parked at the field's edge, their legs swinging like children's as they shared sandwiches and sweet tea.

"October fifteenth," Brandon said suddenly, taking her hand. "Are you sure about the date?"

"The Saturday before the Fall Festival begins? Absolutely." Amanda squeezed his fingers. "It's perfect. The church will be decorated for fall, and the weather should be beautiful."

"Rachel's driving you crazy about the dress, isn't she?"

"She's threatened to take me to every bridal shop across the state if necessary." Amanda leaned against his shoulder. "But I already found the one I want. Simple, elegant, with just enough lace to make it special. Your mom cried when she saw it."

"Mom cries at tissue commercials lately," Brandon said, but his voice was fond. "She's just happy."

They'd weathered their share of disagreements over the wedding planning. Amanda wanted simple and intimate; Brandon wanted to give her what he called "everything you dreamed of as a girl." She'd had to convince him that what she'd dreamed of was him, not an elaborate production. They'd compromised: a simple ceremony at the church, but the reception in the barn where they'd built the parade float, transformed with lights and flowers and all the love their community could pour into it.

"Caleb's still good for best man?" Amanda asked.

"He threatened to disown me if I asked anyone else." Brandon smiled at the mention of his childhood friend, who'd moved back to Laurel Ridge in January and now worked full time at the farm. "He says it's about time I made an honest woman out of you."

"And Rachel's already planned her maid of honor speech. She's been writing it since the day after you proposed."

"Should I be worried?"

"Terrified," Amanda confirmed. "She has photos from high school."

Brandon groaned, but pulled her closer. "Pastor Andrew wants to meet with us next week to go over a few things."

"And for our last premarital counseling session." They'd been meeting with Andrew and Lily twice a month, working through a study on building a marriage rooted in faith. Some sessions had been harder than others—especially the one about handling conflict, where they'd had to practice arguing productively about their actual disagreements. But each session had strengthened their foundation.

They spent the rest of the afternoon planting—Brandon driving the tractor with the seed attachment while Amanda stayed nearby in the truck with supplies. She'd learned to read his signals, to anticipate what he'd need before he asked. Partnership, she'd discovered, was less about doing everything together and more about knowing when to lead, when to follow, and when to stand side by side.

By mid-afternoon, they'd finished the east field. Brandon stopped the tractor at the gate, and Amanda met him there. His face was streaked with dirt, his clothes dusty, but his eyes were bright with satisfaction.

"Good day's work," he said, pulling her into his arms despite her half-hearted protest about the dirt.

"Brandon! I have to run to the shop for a few minutes!"

"So you'll be dusty. Your customers already know you're marrying a farmer."

She gave up protesting and wrapped her arms around his neck. "They keep asking if I'm going to close the shop after the wedding."

"And?"

"And I tell them Indulgences isn't going anywhere. I might adjust my hours eventually, especially when..." she trailed off, suddenly shy.

"When?" Brandon prompted, though his knowing smile suggested he could guess.

"When we have children," she finished softly. "Someday."

They'd talked about it, of course. Wanting a family, wanting to raise children on the farm the way Brandon had been raised, with faith and love and roots deep in the mountain soil.

"Someday," Brandon agreed, kissing her forehead. "First, we get married. Then kids right away."

"One hundred and sixty-eight days," Amanda said promptly.

"You're counting?"

"Rachel made me a countdown calendar. It's hanging in the shop."

As they stood at the edge of the freshly planted field. Brandon moved behind her, wrapping his arms around her waist, his chin resting on her shoulder. The view stretched endlessly—their planted fields, the distant mountains, the farmhouse where Helen was probably starting dinner, expecting them both.

"Dad always said love was like farming," Brandon murmured. "Requires faith to put seeds in dark ground, patience to wait through seasons of growth, and wisdom to know that the harvest always comes to those who tend their fields faithfully."

Amanda leaned back into his warmth, thinking of the journey that had brought them here. Eight months ago, she'd been the girl who felt invisible, who'd loved from afar without hope of return. He'd been trapped in winter, frozen in grief, unable to see spring's possibility.

Now, she was seen, known, cherished. He was healing, growing, embracing life with the same wholehearted commitment he brought to everything. They'd found each other not in spite of their broken places but because of them—two people who understood that the deepest love grew from the richest soil, even when that soil had been turned by loss.

"I loved your dad... I sure do miss him," she said softly.

"He loved you," Brandon replied. "He would have loved seeing us together, building this life."

"He knows," Amanda said with quiet certainty. "Somehow, I believe he knows."

They stood there, watching the sky paint itself in brilliant shades of gold. Tomorrow would bring its own work—Amanda had inventory arriving at the shop, Brandon had equipment to service, and they had their first meeting with the wedding coordinator. Next week would bring premarital counseling, cake tasting, and Rachel's insistence on reviewing bridesmaid dress options one more time.

But for now, they stood together at the edge of their planted field, seeing not just the bare earth but the harvest to come. Some harvests took years of patient tending, seasons of faith when nothing seemed to grow, times of pruning that felt like loss but led to fuller bloom. The sweetest fruits were always worth the wait.

Amanda thought of Galatians 6:9, the verse she'd had framed that would hang in the cabin after they were married: "Let us not become weary in doing good, for at the proper time we will reap a harvest if we do not give up."

They hadn't given up. Not on love, not on faith, not on the promise that God could bring beauty from ashes and joy from mourning. And now, standing with Brandon's arms around her and their whole future spreading before them like these planted fields, Amanda understood that every moment of waiting, every season of longing, every prayer that seemed to go unanswered had led to this:

A love worth waiting for. A harvest worth tending. A future worth building.

Together.

Leave A Review

If you enjoyed this book, please consider leaving an honest review on Amazon

Visit Our Website:

www.tarabaisden.com

Visit Our Amazon Author Page HERE

Find Us On Social Media:

Facebook

Facebook Author Page

Instagram

Also by Tara Baisden

<u>Laurel Ridge Series</u>

#1. Season of Hope

#2. Finding Grace

#3. His Perfect Plan

#4. Love Redeemed

#5 Snowbound Blessings

#6 Sheltered Hearts

#7 Restoring Faith

#8 Love Rekindled

#9 Where She Belongs

#10 Shelter in His Arms

#11 Where Love Stands

#12 The Pieces We Mend

#13 Where Love Grows

#14 Where Hearts Heal

#15 Harvest of the Heart

#16 Heart of the Season

#17 Season of Forgiveness

#18 Threads of Grace

<u>Riverbend Valley Series</u>

#1 A Cowboy's Second Chance

#2 Wanderlust & Wild Horses

#3 Heartstrings on the Horizon

#4 Runaway in Riverbend Valley

#5 Mended Hearts

#6 Healing Hearts

#7 Home to Lost Creek

<u>Mistletoe Falls Series</u>

#1 Whisk Me Under the Mistletoe

#2 Once Upon a Christmas

#3 The Mistletoe Express

#4 Candy Canes & Sweet Dreams

#5 Wrapped Up in Christmas

#6 Jingle All the Way Home

About The Author

Tara Baisden is a Contemporary Christian Inspirational Romance author who proudly calls the beautiful state of West Virginia her home. Nestled on a sprawling mountainous property, she is surrounded by the peace and serenity of nature. Her days are happily spent in the quiet of country life, writing heartwarming stories of love, faith, and second chances. Tara also enjoys quilting, working in her garden, tending to her beloved pets, and soaking in the beauty of her surroundings.

With deep roots in West Virginia, family is everything to Tara. One of her favorite pastimes is gathering on the front porch with loved ones, sharing stories, laughter, and enjoying the simple, meaningful moments that life offers. When she's not crafting her novels, Tara can often be found exploring the rich history of her home state, visiting local historical sites, and, of course, stopping by every bookstore she passes! Her passion for reading and discovery always fuels her next adventure.

Tara is the author of the Laurel Ridges series of novels, as well as the Riverbend Valley series of novels, of which have been beloved by fans of inspirational romance. Her novels reflect her love for faith, family, and the timeless beauty of the world we live in.

Known for her sweet and clean romances, she creates characters that feel like family and settings that make readers want to visit again and again.

You can find out more about Tara and her latest releases at www .tarabaisden.com or follow her on social media for updates and behind-the-scenes glimpses of her writing process. Stay connected—you won't want to miss the heartfelt stories of love and family she has in store!

About Laurel Ridge

Welcome to the fictional town of Laurel Ridge, West Virginia!

Nestled deep in the heart of the Appalachian Mountains, Laurel Ridge is a place where time slows down, allowing visitors and residents alike to enjoy life's simple pleasures. With its quaint, brick-paved streets, historic storefronts, and the ever-present backdrop of rolling hills and dense forests, Laurel Ridge is a hidden gem that attracts tourists looking for both serenity and adventure.

<u>A Rich History</u>

The town was founded in the early 1800s by pioneering settlers who were drawn to the fertile land and abundant natural resources of the region. Laurel Ridge began as a small logging community, relying on the towering forests that covered the surrounding mountains. The New River, one of the oldest rivers in the world, provided an essential transportation route for lumber, as well as a lifeline for the early settlers.

As the years passed, the town evolved from a logging outpost into a thriving hub for craftspeople and artisans. By the late 19th century, it had developed a reputation for its hand-crafted furniture, textiles, and pottery, all made by skilled locals. The town's proximity to the New River also made it a destination for adventurous souls seeking to kayak, fish, or hike along the riverbanks.

A Place of Renewal

Though the logging industry faded by the early 20th century, Laurel Ridge adapted to the changing times. Its natural beauty and deep connection to West Virginia's mountain heritage drew travelers from near and far, transforming it into a beloved tourist destination. Local shops, run by generations of the same families, line the town square, offering handmade goods, locally sourced foods, and, most of all, warm hospitality.

The town's signature event, the Harvest Festival, began in the 1930s, celebrating the craftsmanship, music, and traditions passed down through the generations. Each year, visitors flock to enjoy live Appalachian music, taste locally grown produce, and witness demonstrations of old-world techniques like blacksmithing and weaving.

A Town of Faith and Community

At the heart of the town stands Laurel Ridge Community Church, a small, white clapboard building with a steeple that reaches toward the sky. Built in 1876, the church has been a pillar of faith and strength for the community for over a century. Its bell, crafted by the town's original blacksmith, has been ringing on Sunday mornings ever since, calling townsfolk to worship and reminding everyone of the enduring values of faith, hope, and love.

The church's history is intertwined with the town's, serving as a refuge in difficult times and a gathering place in moments of joy. Over the years, the church has grown to include an outreach center that supports local families and tourists in need, providing everything from free meals to spiritual counseling. The church's welcoming atmosphere reflects the town's deep sense of unity and service.

A Growing Tourist Haven

Today, Laurel Ridge has grown to a population of around five thousand people, yet it has managed to retain its small-town charm. Its thriving tourist industry draws visitors year-round. Tourists can stroll through mom-and-pop shops, and dine at the beloved Martha's Diner, famous for its homemade pies and retro charm. The town square, with its white gazebo surrounded by flowering bushes, is often the site of outdoor concerts and farmers' markets, creating a sense of nostalgia and small-town pride.

For nature lovers, the New River offers breathtaking views and the thrill of adventure, whether it's fishing in its crystal blue waters or hiking along the rugged trails that weave through the wilderness. Tourists and locals alike cherish the scenic beauty, often finding peace in the simple pleasures of watching the river flow or taking in the panoramic vistas of the Appalachian Mountains.

Laurel Ridge, with its rich history, strong community spirit, and natural beauty, is more than just a tourist destination—it's a place where past and present blend seamlessly, offering everyone who visits a chance to experience the best of West Virginia's mountain heritage. You'll find that Laurel Ridge is a town that captures the heart.

Welcome to Laurel Ridge. I hope you fall in love with this charming small town and its residents.